Lost SOULS

CHELSEA MUELLER

Lost Souls

©2018 Chelsea Mueller

Cover Design by Picky Me Artist

Formatting by Uplifting Designs

Printed in the United States of America.

First printing, 2018

PRAISE FOR THE SOUL CHARMER SERIES

"Do not miss, fantastic urban fantasy"
— Lauren Dane, *New York Times* & *USA Today* Bestselling Author

"Fantastic … I was really reminded of the early Kate Daniels books by Ilona Andrews"
— *Red Hot Books*

"Chelsea Mueller brings a new and exciting voice to the UF genre."
— Kelly Meding, acclaimed author of *Stray Magic* and the Dreg City series

"Mueller explores an intriguing concept in a seedy, visceral setting that pops to life on the page."
— *Publishers Weekly*

"A terrific world with an unlikely heroine, quiet and determined, with a pure heart and fiery will to protect her family … Definitely recommend!"
— Jeffe Kennedy, author of *The Twelve Kingdoms* and *The Uncharted Realms*

"Gritty realism, pitch perfect characters and a heavy dose of red hot sex. What more could you ask for?"
— Shannon Mayer, author of the national bestselling *Rylee Adamson Series*

BOOKS BY CHELSEA MUELLER

Borrowed Souls

Rogue Souls

Lost Souls

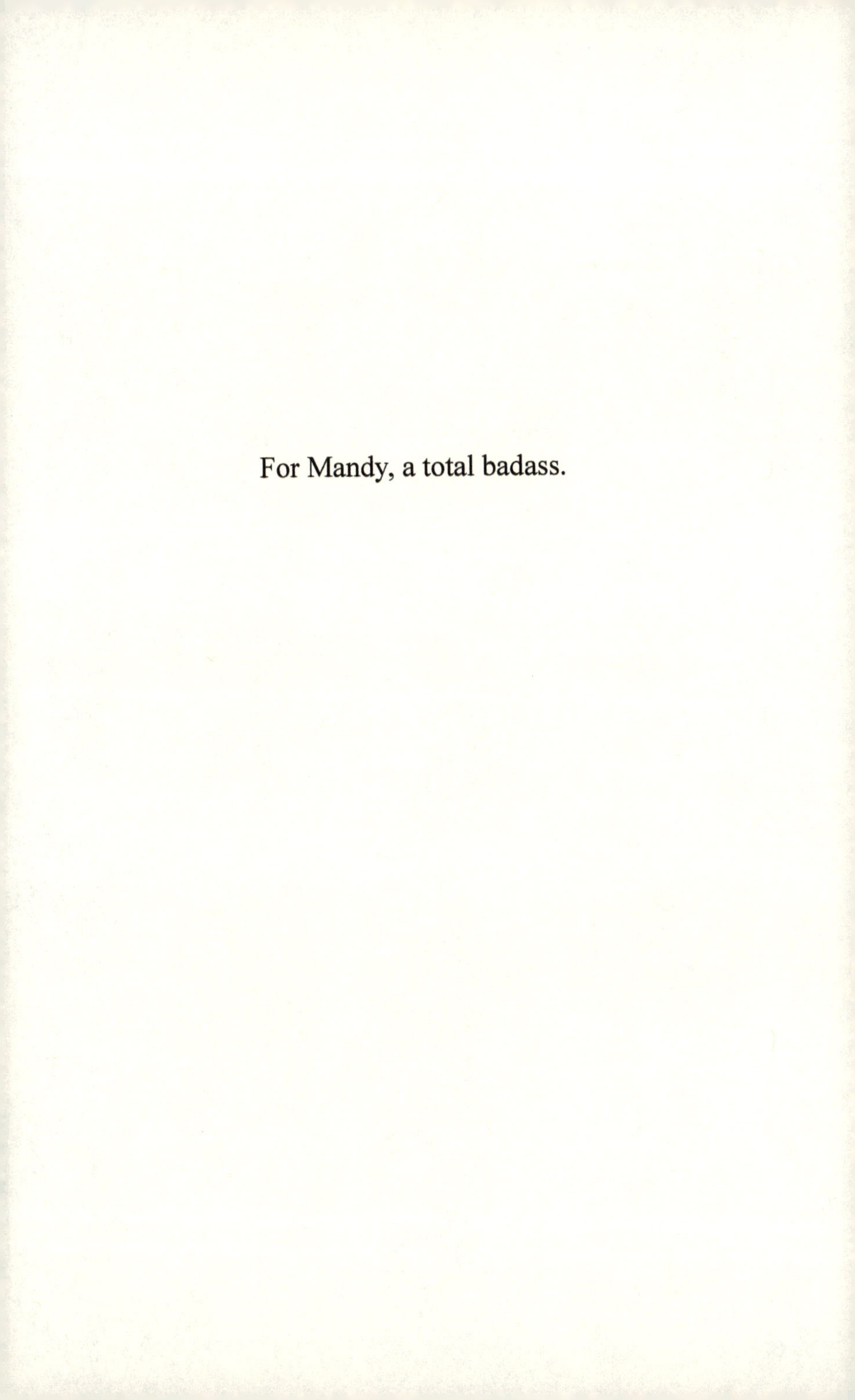

For Mandy, a total badass.

CHAPTER ONE

Callie Delgado needed to find her mom. She also needed to keep her brother sober. And learn everything she could from the Soul Charmer so she and her boyfriend could put Gem City behind them. But before she could do any of that, she needed to find Benton Dally.

The Fall was the type of bar that reminded Callie of the person she never wanted to be. It was too small, too seedy, too familiar. The kind of joint where her shoes clung to the beer- and blood-battered floor.

Outside the dive bar, Gem City shook with sharp storms cutting through the streets with icy winds and dry snowflakes. She took the three deep steps down and opened the door into The Fall. The sticky humidity of other people's sweat slapped her. The crossfit gym down the street at least had the courtesy of propping open a door. These patrons didn't want their activities monitored by anyone—in or out of the bar. Callie was banking on that bad attitude to make this trip quick.

Benton Dally had rented a soul twelve days ago. He'd paid for seven days, the Soul Charmer's max. Callie hadn't pushed the extra soul into the man's body, and she didn't particularly care about his reasons for bulking up on souls. Lying to his boss, cheating on his wife, stealing cash from convenience stores, talking shit at the bar, whatever. As long as he paid the Soul Charmer for the wares and stuck to a single extra soul at a time, she gave no fucks. She had her own problems, and they wouldn't be solved by some carte blanche sinning or blurred fingerprints compliments of a rented soul. Unfortunately, Benton bailed on the return process, and now Callie had to take it back. It was one of the less glamorous parts of her apprenticeship with the Soul Charmer. She was part repowoman, part stock assistant, and part backup magician. None of it was resumé filler, but at least she had a wad of twenties in her pocket now.

A steady itch skewered deep between her shoulder blades. Eyes were on her. Digging, begging, assessing. Did they see the Charmer's apprentice, the woman who had burned the competition, or a twenty-four year old woman with curves and a bad attitude? She hadn't eaten anything solid in four days. Her head throbbed, her fingers ached, and her stomach continued to grind beneath the puddle of ginger ale she'd tossed back earlier.

She spotted Benton at the bar. He wasn't much older than Callie, but he wore his years. His cheekbones jutted out over hollowed apples. His blue plaid button-down was rumpled, untucked, and open over a stained white tee. Callie wouldn't ask if the soul renting or the heroin habit came first, but even from a half dozen paces away she could tell he'd dabbled in both.

Benton was the kind of asshole Callie had grown up with. He might not have gone to high school with her, but she knew the look. He hit the pharmacy at lunch break to buy booze. He talked to too many people. He'd be in a fight by the end of the night if he didn't pass out inside this desolate bar. A knuckle dug in between her ribs. She could have been Benton if she hadn't focused on school. If she hadn't called CPS on her mom. If she'd let her shitty situation drown her. Her Chucks stuck to the floor. The mumbling music from the cheap overhead speakers was loud enough she couldn't hear the crinkle of each step.

Benton couldn't hear it either.

"You know what's fucked, man?" Benton cradled a short glass of whiskey in one hand, but flung the other wide. The seats on either side of him at the bar were empty. She shot a knowing look at Johnny T. The bartender had been serving Callie booze since long before she had ID. She hadn't done a soul collection in his bar before, but the nod he offered was passed with grim knowledge.

Benton hadn't noticed the bartender walking to the far end of the well. He hadn't noticed Callie edging up behind him. Heat suffused her skin. She'd been collecting and renting souls for the Soul Charmer long enough to be familiar with the way her body warmed near people with a bonus soul wedged in their chest. Better than the people who'd rented and were flying solo these days. At least warm fingers didn't stick to everything.

"I've worked security at four other buildings." Benton held up as many fingers. His nails were short and black. Whether from blood or dirt, Callie didn't care to guess.

She stood behind him and leaned forward to speak into his ear. Stale cigar stench clogged her nose. "You've worked jobs, but haven't paid the Soul Charmer."

Benton surged closer to the bar. His whiskey sloshed over the lip of the glass and onto his fingers. He slammed his shoulder backward and shifted to face Callie. The wide, milky eyes and taut tendons in his neck eased. Idiot. He licked the spilled liquor from his fingers. "I have experience, but they still won't even let me take their exam."

She gave two fucks about his ability to get a job. "That must suck. You owe the Charmer."

"What do you mean?"

That's not how this worked, and he knew it. "Cash or souls."

"I ain't got anything on me."

"How are you paying for that Wild Turkey?"

Benton shot scattered looks in either direction. "It just you?"

It was, and normally she hated that. Her boyfriend

Derek typically made these collection calls. He looked the part. Hulking and covered in leather and scars. She hid her wounds on the inside, and wielded dark eyeliner as war paint. Not exactly scary mofo material. Callie needed more from Benton than a simple rented soul, though, and that information need to be acquired alone.

Callie sat on the barstool next to Benton. It sagged to the right, but she managed to keep her spine straight. When you're five foot nothing keeping your head up counted for something. "Did you want to return the soul now or give me what's in your wallet?"

His huff of laughter carried derision she was too well acquainted with. She knew it better than he knew that whiskey. The flask in her back pocket thrummed against her hip. It was a way to hold souls, but it also spoke to the magic running through her veins. It was ready. Was she? Callie grabbed Benton's wrist. Skin to skin. A single bonus soul wouldn't make Callie go *en fuego*, but she was quickly learning how to turn up the heat.

"Please, little girl." Benton said derisively. He tried to yank his arm back.

He couldn't escape her grip, though, not with magic on her side.

She focused on the flutter in her chest and the responding call within his. Callie pooled the magic in her palm. The heat, the energy. She let it coalesce between her palm and his wrist until he began to squirm. Expletives began to bubble from his lips. She let go.

Benton cradled his reddened wrist to his chest.

"What the—"

"No. I ask the questions."

"You can take the soul," he practically shouted. Johnny T shot her a look, and she shrugged back.

"I was going to take it anyway." How was this idiot her source of information? Dark times. "Have you seen Nate?"

There. The reason she'd taken this retrieval instead of sending someone else for this delinquent renter. "Nate?"

"Yes, lanky motherfucker. Talks a lot of shit. Slings narcotic treats. Nate."

"Ford's dead." Benton's voice shook, and Callie understood.

"I know that. I didn't ask about Ford. I asked about his former number two guy. Nate. Have. You. Seen. Him?" She was running out of time. Both in this bar and for answers. Finding Nate was top priority right now, and each day he dodged her calls, the worse her world got.

Benton scratched a phantom itch behind his ear.

She wriggled her fingers close to his face. "Focus."

"No one's seen Nate." Benton paused and licked his cracked lips. "Corner guy near the cathedral on El Paseo got his stuff from him, though."

Callie leaned in. Before she could say anything, Benton added, "That's really all I know. All the dealers are working directly for Nate right now, but word is no one has seen him. That's all I know. Honest."

She believed him. Damn it. "Don't tell anyone I asked, okay?"

"Sure. What about the Charmer?"

She'd almost forgotten about the late dues on the soul. Heat still tingled through her fingers and forearms, but she'd almost associated the discomfort with the heavy energy in the bar and the shimmering fear filling her core. For once, the Soul Charmer wasn't the greatest of Callie's worries.

The missing henchman of a dead man prodded greater terror into her bones. Callie took the highball glass from Nate, and downed its remaining contents into two hard gulps.

He opened his mouth to complain. Callie yanked the flask from her back pocket with smooth familiarity, popped the cap, and slapped it against Benton's chest. A couple soft words of beckoning and the second soul slipped inside.

A neon beer sign lit Benton's face in unnatural orange, but the color was cooler now. The extraction hadn't hurt—though she got the impression she could make it hurt if she better understood what she was do-ing. The guy leaned away from her anyway.

This was the part she wasn't so good at. She could handle collecting the soul. Flask, chest, boom, done. She could even now beckon the soul, and push one back into someone's body. Collecting cash? There she was on less stable footing. She bit the inside of her cheek. What would Derek do?

Demand the money. She was a third of his size, running on fumes, and worried about her own problems, but she had to get this done. She thrust an open hand toward Benton. "Wallet. Now." Her cool tone sounded vicious. She was simply goddamn tired.

It worked, though. He dropped his wallet into her waiting palm. She pulled out a trio of twenties. "Thought you were broke. Couldn't get a job," she muttered.

"Pawned stuff," was all he said, but she didn't want the particulars anyway. Her brother had hawked their mom's good china, her television, and a host of other possessions to enable his meth habit. A pang rose sharp up her sternum. *Mom. Zara.* No. She couldn't think about her now.

Callie caught Johnny T's gaze, and dropped one of the twenties into his tip jar. She shoved the other two in her pocket. Forty bucks wasn't exactly good money for collecting souls, but bringing something back to the Soul Charmer was always better than nothing.

She hurried out of the bar before her bravado evaporated. She hopped over the ice collected in the center of the sidewalk outside. The uneven concrete had made a perfect pool to ruin her day. Inside her car, she cranked the engine and then the heater. Her phone buzzed in her pocket. *Please be Nate. Please be Nate,* she thought. As much as she hated the guy, she needed him to call her back.

It was Derek, though, which was infinitely better. She answered.

"Hey," the chill in her voice melted for him.

"Hey, doll. What's your ETA?"

Callie glanced at the clock on the dash. It was already after eight, which meant sliding into peak time for the Soul Charmer's emporium. By nine o'clock customers would be bustling in every few minutes to get their taste of *carte blanche* sinning and the freedom it afforded. "I got Benton's soul back, but I wanted to make another stop."

She couldn't say she'd gotten a lead on Nate. Not on the phone, but Derek could read her voice well. "I wish I could say that was a good idea. He's upping wards for the back room here. If you aren't back in ten, I expect he's going to be a hot one."

Hot one. That was a nice way of saying she was going to have a ton of souls thrown her direction, and her arms were going to char like a winter log in a chiminea. She swore.

"I'll find us a way to get out to your next stop later tonight. I'd rather go with you."

She'd rather he went with her, too. "I'll be there in ten."

"Thank you." The affection and promise in those two words had Callie putting the car into Drive. He was worried about her. It was still weird to be okay with that, but for now she could let it ride.

First she'd deal with the Soul Charmer, and then she'd work on finding Nate. Both would help her find her mom. The question was who could get her to Zara first.

Whatever it took, she'd do it. Family came first.

It always came first.

CHAPTER TWO

The dilapidated door at the Soul Charmer's front entrance was recessed between the brick-and-adobe mishmash of the alleyway. Customers never complained about the jaunt from the street or the three burned-out light bulbs making the entrance dim. Maybe they were ashamed to be renting a soul. It's not like they didn't know what kind of morally corrupt thing they were going to do once another's soul was popped into their body. You didn't get to this place on accident.

Callie certainly hadn't. Mobster Ford had forced her into this very shop by taking her brother. Blackmail was bullshit. Callie shook off the memory, and entered the shop.

A heavy shoulder crashed into Callie's. She reeled to the right. Her knee met the corner of a table. She hissed, but before she could complain ice shot frigid and fast up her forearm. Her fingers froze in a wide "fuck, my knee" pain pose, but it was the biting beneath her skin that had her staggering back a few extra steps and not the inevitable bruise on her leg.

"Sorry. Forgot about..." said Beck, another of the Soul Charmer's collections guys. He backed up. The icy charge up her arm retreated with each retreating step Beck took. He continued, "Well, I forgot about that."

She wriggled feeling back into her fingers. "You drop off?"

"Brought back the cash, and Genna." He wasn't meeting her gaze. She used to avoid his. He knew she could work soul magic now, and he didn't bother hiding his fear. Score one for being scary.

Callie nodded. She mentally flipped through the regular customers she'd met. Genna wasn't tripping any memories for her. She hadn't been at this long enough to be jaded about the clientele, but she had experienced enough frozen fingers to be irritated every time she discovered a person nearby had bartered with her boss in the past. Ripping that rented soul back out? No one mentioned it came with a smidge of the renter's soul, too. Just her luck, her magic wanted her to feel it. Too little soul, and she was cold. Three or more souls, and flame on. She was the Goldilocks of souls, and fucking nothing was just right.

"Callie?" a deep, familiar voice pulled her back into the moment.

She turned toward the counter at the rear of the storefront. Derek filled the doorway to the back office. His head almost touched the top of the frame.

"Present," she said, and started toward him. Beck booked it out the door.

Derek closed his eyes for a moment, and then offered a small smile. He grunted a thank you, low and steady. Callie had been dating him long enough to know that tone meant more than appreciation. He was tired, too, and worried, and he wouldn't have called her here if it weren't necessary. She took his hand in hers and squeezed. *I know.*

"You got a lead?" Derek asked under his breath. He couldn't dare say Nate's name here.

She wouldn't risk saying anything. "Later."

His stiff nod was solid agreement. "Charmer's in a mood."

Join the club, man. Callie squeezed his hand again. "Might as well get it over with."

She'd been saying that a lot since she started working full-time, on the books for the Soul Charmer. It paid stupidly better than her old job cooking at a retirement home, but the asks there never made your skin pinch and twist. Her days at the home never scared her. She could not say the same about working here.

The Soul Charmer of Gem City's standard mode was 'creepy dude.' He moved too fast. He was too flexible. There was the whole 'could steal your soul' thing. He shouldn't have been able to get any more terrifying.

Shouldn't was a word Callie needed to drop from her vocabulary.

The seventy-something year-old man scuttled out from behind his desk. His wisps of white hair swirled in a flurry to rival the snow outside. His fingers—normally weighed down with garish gold rings—were bare except for a lone signet ring on his index finger. He'd been wearing the same burgundy pajama set the last four times she's been in the shop. At least three days in a row. Pungent sweat slithered beneath the sharp astringent of the soul storage space and workroom.

"Calliope. Finally." The Soul Charmer's tone was as cutting as ever.

She pulled the flask from her pocket and placed it on the oak desk. "Benton's soul, as promised. What was the rush?"

"Every soul that belongs to me is essential."

"Since when," she muttered.

The Charmer stepped close. She hated when he did this. His nose was inches from hers. Backing away wasn't an option. Not with the man who imbued her with the soul magic ability. Not with the man who was supposed to be teaching her to harness the magic. Not with the man who always had plans A, B, and C, and most of them involved fire. Up close, though, Callie could see the changes. The sharpening of his cheeks. The darkening of the delicate skin beneath his eyes. She'd been tormented over her missing mother and Nate's disappearance with her for days now. The Soul Charmer wasn't suffering over Zara, but Callie recognized the look. Desperation was the one look that could make the Soul Charmer downright horrifying.

Callie dug an incisor into her cheek. *Steady. Focus. Appease him. Don't burn. Get out. Find Nate. Get Mom.* She repeated the mantra to herself over and over.

The Charmer remained too close. He didn't speak, but Callie could swear he was digging those beady eyes into her brain or her soul or something. Whatever he was doing, it was unnerving as hell. Callie peeked over his shoulder. Derek fidgeted in the corner. The strain of letting her fight her own battles pulled his jaw tight.

"Where did you put that 1420 jar?" The accusation was almost worse than his breath.

"On the far case." She pointed to the corner of the room.

The Charmer didn't so much step back as pop a few feet away. She had no idea how the old man was so nimble. Magic, probably. He went to the bookshelf in question and began pushing jars left and right. Each jar was crafted from smoky black glass, and was only three inches in diameter. If she had never heard of soul renting, she might be able to pretend they were tins of artisanal tea.

"I can't find it," he huffed.

Derek stepped forward ready to run interference for her. She barely shook her head no, but he got the message. She stepped next to the Soul Charmer. A jar with 1420/2000 written in tiny, perfect script on the front was just to the right of his hand. Callie didn't bother telling him, and simply reached over his hand to pick it up. She was mindful to keep her fingers away from the chalk marking the contents. The last thing she needed was to have to try to prove the soul was the one he was looking for.

"Here."

"Oh. Why did you put it here? The upper-middle range should go on that shelf." He screwed off the lid and peered inside at the gossamer tendrils swirling inside.

Callie bit back the urge to tell him she'd done as he asked. He was too mercurial for that to matter, though.

"Can you explain the measurement system again?" Might as well try to extract a little helpful information while he was in this addled state.

"Purity scores. If you don't already know that, I don't know why I waste time with you." He tilted the jar to let the overhead florescent lights hit the contents fully. The white-silver strands maintained their natural glow. Must be nice.

"Of course. The closer to two thousand, the more pure the soul. I remember." She repeated his words from weeks ago. She could have guessed as much. This apprentice thing worked so much better with a mentor who wanted to teach. That was not the Soul Charmer.

"Then don't ask stupid questions."

A sharp, clean bell rang through the room. The Charmer's gaze fixed on Callie, and the hardened black in his eyes held her in place.

Derek cleared his throat a couple times. The heavy grit of his deep rumble scraped through the room. "I'll see what they want," he said, and then disappeared past the curtain.

The Charmer cupped the 1420 jar in his hand, and closed his eyes. The soul didn't leap from its container, and Callie was far enough away to avoid the sizzling effects of the open lid, but the needling sense that *something* was happening pushed against her chest.

"How do you know what the score should be?" Her voice was barely a whisper, but the sterile room laid everything bare, even her need for any kind of win today.

The Charmer was eerily still. His chest barely flexing with his slow inhalations. But he answered her. "The taste. The scent. The way it feels against you when it begs."

To an outsider that had to sound batshit, but Callie understood. She'd heard the souls beg for a host, for a home. Her boss had let an oddly sexual undertone float beneath the description, but Callie didn't take any pleasure from the souls' needs.

She'd only experienced this a few times. The first couple times were accidents. The others were deep beneath the Cortean Catholic cathedral. Calling souls from a well owned by priests had felt eight kinds of wrong, but it also didn't give her enough experience to follow his words. "Are the pleas different for purer souls?"

His fingertips skimmed against the lip of the jar. His eyes were still closed, and from the deep noise in the back of his throat, she was thankful he wasn't looking at her. Moments passed. Finally, he said, "The darker ones cling to your tongue. The bitter burn of bad decisions coating them. The purer ones light your sinuses with that perfect pepper prickle."

Callie struggled to remember a time when the Soul Charmer had shared so much or been so direct. Maybe sleep deprivation was good for their master-apprentice relationship.

Callie struggled to remember any taste or smell to the souls she'd encountered. The aching fire and the subtle pleas were all she could recall. "Can you taste them only in the jar?"

The clean chime of the storefront's bell charged through the conversation. The Charmer's eyes shot open, and his surly tone returned. "I wouldn't be very good at my job if that were the case. Now get out there and help the customer. I need to handle this."

He still cradled the 1420 jar, but Callie wasn't going to bother asking what he needed that specific soul for. The Soul Charmer wasn't much for sharing plans, and whatever he was getting up to wasn't going to be a good time. It never was.

She edged through the passage to the front. A clump of ashes filled the incense trays on the counter. She was probably supposed to swap them out, but her nasal cavities could use a break from the potent patchouli. Derek's hands were at his side, but his fingers twitched like they wanted to go for the folded knife in his right pocket. He wasn't looking at her, which meant she was going to have to actually deal with a customer. Was it wrong to hope Derek had sent them away?

A stocky woman stood on the other side of the counter. Her eyes were too close together, but shot daggers all the same. "Where's the Soul Charmer?"

"He's busy." Derek injected peak menace into the words, his body, everything. If Callie hadn't known him, she'd have hauled ass out of the room.

She did, though, and she also was obligated to talk to the woman. Because magic and money. "I can help you."

"You?" the woman sneered. A white crust caked the corners of the woman's mouth, and her pupils had absorbed a milky white film. Double junkie: drugs and souls.

Callie put on her best customer service voice. It sounded like the end of her shift, but still minimally bitchy. "What do you need?"

"Soul Charmer knows me."

So much for hospitality. "That's nice."

After half a minute of hard stares from both Callie and Derek, the woman said, "Fine. I'm here to pawn. Need some cash for the weekend." She brushed a scab off her forearm.

"Okay. How much do you need?" Callie had listened to the Charmer do this negotiation a few times, and could at least get things going.

The Charmer didn't do too much pawn business. Technically, people could choose to pawn their soul to him for cash. The catch of course was he would rent their soul out until they returned for it. So you'd probably get back a soul more saturated with sin upon pick up. The kind of person who was okay with pawning their souls tended to be more concerned with their next high than any celestial repercussions. Who cared about rising to Heaven when you could get high now?

"A grand."

Callie almost laughed in the woman's face. She

couldn't feel souls the way the Charmer did, but it didn't take any magical ability to know this lady's soul was bargain-basement quality. "Are you willing to part with it for three months?"

"What? The Soul Charmer doesn't ask that. Get him out here."

Derek's hand found Callie's behind the counter. It was warm and soft, and the squeeze he gave her told her good things lay ahead. "Donna. We both know the Charmer isn't going to give you more than five hundred bucks."

"She don't know that," the woman—Donna's—conspiratorial whisper was loud enough the Charmer had probably heard it.

"She does," Callie deadpanned.

Donna's lips pulled into such a tight pout they were liable to crack. "Fine. What'll you give me?"

Callie stepped around the counter, and discovered the real reason the Charmer kept the incense burning. Whatever was beneath this woman's jacket may have died. Callie stepped backward for the air space, and then folded her arms across her chest. She pretended to appraise the woman. She could hear the woman's soul asking for help—though she suspected it'd be happy for the reprieve—and all she could see was the smudge of blood at the collar of the woman's shirt and a darker substance smeared across the green cargo pants she wore. Neither told her shit about the woman's soul or its value. Normally this would be the time to call the Soul Charmer up front, but he'd just flap his hands at her and tell her to do it anyway. Might as well avoid it.

"I can do $300 for seven days or $400 for ten." That sounded realistic, especially given that the woman had clearly done this before.

Derek gave her the most infinitesimal nod. A tiny tangle of worry in her belly eased. She hadn't completely borked it yet.

Donna huffed, but it was all for show. "Ten days for $400?"

"Yep. Pawning isn't a way to make a living."

"I didn't come here for your judgment."

Callie almost laughed. Literally everyone came here to escape judgment. Escaping judgment is what kept the Soul Charmer in business. "That's nice. You taking the deal?"

Callie flexed her arms. When Derek did it, he looked bigger and more menacing. She probably looked like she was hugging herself.

"Fine. Give me the money."

Callie resisted the urge to tell the lady to fork over the soul first. The Soul Charmer would have done this with style, but she wasn't a real soul magician. The magic simmering inside her wasn't wholly hers, and she barely knew the basics of how to manage it. The latter was what made her incline her head toward the back office. "Do you mind getting him for the extraction?" she asked Derek.

He made a dark sound deep in his throat. Donna jumped. Callie said, "Thank you."

A moment later he returned. "Boss says you can

handle it."

If she could have swallowed her own tongue, she might have. "Are you sure?" she asked for the sake of the customer. She let her fear flush her cheeks.

Derek nodded. It was a somber motion. Slow and understanding.

While Callie had a couple months of practice taking rented souls out of hosts, she'd only ripped the real soul out of a person once. Nate. He'd tried to kill her, he'd tried to kill Derek, he'd angered the Soul Charmer, and the threats that trickled from his bloodied mouth had forced her hand. Or maybe she'd just been too fucking angry. She'd thought about that night in the old airplane hangar a hundred times in the days since, and she still couldn't say what made her take his soul. She had taken it, though, and now it rested in a tiny jar in the back corner of the Soul Charmer's storage shelves. Her fingers began to quake and chill, but she had enough distance from Donna to know it wasn't the woman's soul-renting past that was freezing her. It was worry. It was regret. It was being a goddamn asshole to her mom.

Zara.

Callie had taken Nate's soul, and he'd taken her mother. Now the bastard was missing, and Callie was supposed to just—what—rip another person's soul out like it was nothing? Like the last time hadn't cost her mother fingers? Like it wasn't still costing her? Unshed tears welled at her eyelids. She gritted her teeth and forced them to hold the tight line.

Callie fought to keep her tone even, to hold back

the guilt grinding against the back of her throat. "Now's not a great time."

An icy storm raged in Derek's eyes. His ire at the Charmer was her beacon. It was her redemption. It was all she had right now. He lifted a hand to proffer an empty jar. She took it, and managed not to swear. The glass warmed her palm. The smoky black finish beckoned her attention. It was just a container in the same way a gas station was just a small grocery store. This jar was made to hold those souls detached from a body. Other objects worked, too, but her flask and these jars were some of the best. If you trusted the Soul Charmer, which she did when it came to magic shit.

The Charmer put on a show when delivering souls to renters. He faked like he could anoint them. He spoke words of power that had nothing to do with the soul's movement and everything to do with making his client feel like they were partaking in something powerful. They were, Callie supposed, but not in the way they imagined. She blinked, and the image of souls vying for escape from the Cortean well flashed behind her lids. *Not now*. Callie knocked her chin a little higher, and then stepped toward Donna. A chill bit at her fingertips. She touched the jar's glass, and it muted the frigid effect on one hand. Callie shoved her other hand in her pocket. The fleece inside her pocket clung to her skin. Donna's soul was missing enough pieces to kick her magic into gear. What was going to happen when she was full-on soulless?

Callie bit the inside of her cheek. Might as well find out.

She rolled the jar in her palm until it had Donna's full attention. The woman strove to stand still. Her need for a fix made her forearms and cheek twitch. Her feet stayed glued to the borderline gooey carpeting.

"Are you ready?" Callie asked loud enough to pretend she was asking Donna and not herself.

Donna closed her eyes, and flung her arms wide. The Soul Charmer wasn't the only one for dramatics, apparently. "Just take it."

At least Derek was the only person who would witness this. Callie's heart pounded loud enough to thrum in her temples. She looked to Derek. Could he read the panic in her eyes?. He held Callie's gaze for a moment, and everything slowed. Her breathing, her heart, her fear, her guilt. It's funny how that tiny quirk of his lips, and the softening scar on the bridge of his nose, and the kindness in those grey eyes could offer respite, but they did. *He* did. He nodded once more.

You can do this, she reminded herself. It sounded like a lie even in her head, but the fact was she was going to do this. Fake it till you make it or some shit.

She pressed the open mouth of the jar to Donna's chest. Callie locked her elbow in close to her ribs before her arm could start shaking from the cold. She stared at the other woman's sternum like the soul would give her a little wave. It did not. Donna started to lower her arms. Callie needed to think. This wasn't about Donna. This was about magic. About souls. About homes. She focused on the warmth in her belly, on the cold creeping over her arm. She focused on the magic reacting to Donna and marshaled it toward the jar. The jar appeared to soften to a cloudy grey. Callie pushed the magic further until it touched Donna. It stung, but Callie kept pushing, ignoring the bite. *Come to me*, she called to Donna's soul. When it didn't budge she tried again. This was about home. *Couldn't you use a break from the battering she's given you? Let me give you a safe home. A breath away.* That did it. Only it was too quick, too much.

Donna's soul leapt from its safe body into the jar, and Callie rocked back on her heels from the force. Heat flashed against her palm. No, her hand was burning. The jar slipped from her grip. Flames danced along her fingers. *No, no, no.* She yelled for the soul to return to the jar, to the vessel, but it clung to her skin. It begged for a home within her body, and she denied it. The ache of its exposure pressed against her, and she could relate to the blatant need, but she wasn't taking this junkie's soul into her body. Pepper burned her nostrils. She squeezed her hand closed into a fist. She ordered the soul away. It began to edge toward the discarded jar.

"Calliope, what are you doing?" The Charmer's voice sounded meters away.

A moment later the fire was gone and the Soul Charmer of Gem City was glaring at her. He held the lidded jar. "Next time, maybe cap the jar if you can't control it," he snapped.

She took the jar from him, and backed away without another word. Derek handed over the woman's money. No one else needed her in this room. Fine with her. She needed out. She needed to get a lead on Nate. She needed to save her mother.

CHAPTER THREE

"Everyone out here." Callie didn't recognize the dark baritone voice, but the volume suggested whoever it was knew there were people in the back of the Soul Charmer's store. Damn it. She hadn't left fast enough. The urge to book it out the back bit her jaw. The tang of tinfoil touched her tongue. She couldn't taste Donna's soul for shit, but apparently the air of authority could fill her mouth.

Instead of running, however, Callie held steady in the back. No one was peeking past the curtains yet, and as long as her shoes stayed put on the tile floor she could remain fairly silent.

"Calliope, join us." The Soul Charmer sounded exhausted. At least they had that in common.

She returned to the storefront. Derek was just inside the door. Arms locked tight across his chest. His chin was high enough to enforce his height on others and make every glance a dismissal downward. If he was in fuck-you-up stance, this was not going to be fun.

Two Gem City police officers stood in the center of the room. "Anyone else back there?" the taller one asked. His badge read Grady and his lips flattened into a hard line when he saw Callie. She hadn't done anything to warrant that scowl. Maybe she just had one of those faces. Pickpocket skills were not a recessive gene, and neither were her brown eyes.

"No," she said. She was going to keep it to single-word answers. It worked for Derek. Why not for her? Oh, except that she wasn't six foot plus of badass muscle.

Officer Grady settled his hands on his duty belt. It'd be casual if his fingers weren't touching his firearm. Callie's mother hadn't imparted much wisdom when she was growing up; *Don't hit on seventeen* did not count. She had, however, been firm about cops. Avoid them. If that doesn't work, be polite. If they touch their gun, you best make yourself small and helpless. Zara milked that damsel-in-distress move to pick pockets and to garner favors and cash from tourist business-men in bars. Callie wasn't much for the act usually. Right now, though? Callie hoped she looked like an exhausted college kid and not a mid-twenties apprentice soul magician.

"Ortega." Grady pointed the other cop to the back office. When Officer Ortega didn't move, he added, "Confirm we have everyone."

The other officer watched his feet as he walked

toward the back. He didn't see the Charmer's finger flourish. The soft simmer of magic at her back vanished. Wards down. Odd. It was almost like the Charmer didn't want the police to know how powerful he was. Her boss hadn't been bashful about his skills before. This concealment was for Derek. The Charmer's relationship with her boyfriend was complicated, but at least the magician wasn't trying to put her man in the line of fire. Well, not with the cops anyway.

The room was quiet while everyone waited for the policeman to return. Derek's chest barely moved. The Charmer's lips flattened into a hard line. Everyone waited in silence for the policeman to return, and it for once none of the attention was on her. Grady glowered at the Soul Charmer, and the reprieve allowed Callie to exhale.

Officer Ortega popped his head through the velvet curtain, and confirmed, "It's empty." He skimmed his fingers over the curtain, and then ambled back into the room.

The lead officer harrumphed with a heavy enough rumble to rival one of Derek's grumbles. Callie did a double take. The officer didn't notice. Grady wasn't hot enough to pull off the gruff, sour thing.

Grady narrowed his eyes at the Soul Charmer. "Do you know why we are here?" he asked, his voice loud enough to reach the rooftop..

"I would guess you don't wish to rent a soul." A blasé Soul Charmer would have been a hilarious thing, if it weren't for the cops. The man couldn't help himself. "My patrons do not typically demand to see the back office."

The Charmer tucked his hands in his pockets. A warm static filled Callie's sinuses, and she doubted it was a coincidence. What did he have in there?

"No." Officer Grady's tone was hard.

"I do offer a discount for law enforcement and military members." Only the Soul Charmer would have the balls to taunt cops when he knew full well he'd been involved in crimes. Her boss's needling tone was paired with a silver-toothed smile.

Officer Ortega stood behind his partner, and was pointedly not looking at anyone. Callie thought she heard him snicker. Was he a renter? Callie didn't recognize him, but the customers were already beginning to blur for her.

Officer Grady scowled. "Are you aware of the attacks on the Ford family holdings?"

"The slaughterhouse magnate?" The Charmer had gone monotone. All revelry disappeared from his voice, and the sharp shift snapped a belt of fear around Callie's belly.

Officer Grady's heavy voice hardened. "The councilman, the largest landowner in Gem City, yes."

"He is not a customer."

"Is his son?"

"His son?"

It was Officer Grady's turn to slather on the derision. It wasn't funny when he did it. "Surely you've seen the news. The younger Ford was murdered in his home."

"I heard there was a rash of fires, but I must admit the news doesn't captivate me the way it does others." The Charmer tried to brush it off, to evoke the same casual tone again. He faltered, and the words came a half beat too quickly. "I'd much prefer to talk to clients and focus on aiding our community in the goal of rising to Heaven. Much more noble effort, don't you think?"

Callie sent Derek a what-the-fuck-is-happening look. His wide-eyed response told her he hadn't seen the Soul Charmer this blatant or this rushed before. Sure, the man liked theatrics. He'd make the sign of the cross like what he was doing was holy, but his link with the Cortean Church was secret. He wasn't actually ordained. Why was he risking being exposed? He'd branded her wrist as part of an oath to keep the secret of the soul well and its magic. She rubbed her thumb against the raised ridges in her skin, against her nighthawk mark.

"Mister…" the older cop, Grady, let the opening resonate throughout the space. Heavy tapestries covered the walls in the front of the soul emporium. Hidden by shadow and tarnished by age, they held secrets, but even they refused to muffle the officer's request.

Callie began to edge closer to Derek, and the silent officer shot her a warning glance. She stopped. No one was laughing anymore.

"Charmer will do," Callie's boss said.

The police officers shared a look. Whatever they knew about the Soul Charmer, it wasn't good. "Fine. *Charmer*. We need to know where you were last Saturday night."

The Soul Charmer raised his right hand and held it out to his side. "I am here for my customers when they need me."

The words were placid, but the sense of scraping steel skittered over Callie's skin. The men in the room weren't unnerved, but she fought the urge to rake her fingernails across her chest. The other hand. The Charmer still had a hand buried in his pocket. His knuckles were tenting the satin fabric of his robe with increasing speed. He couldn't have a soul hidden in there. The fire of an unleashed one would have bit at her consciousness by now. Her cheeks burned with the sizzle of magic. Callie might be able to pull a soul from someone's body, and she might be able push one inside, but she was miles from understanding the Soul Charmer's power. He was barely moving, but invisible electricity snapped beneath the soggy carpet. Whatever he was up to, those cops should be running.

Both officers held their place, but Officer Ortega shot a quick look the Charmer's way. He returned his attention to an empty countertop before he said, "Sir, we need a firm answer. Are you saying you were in this building all day on Saturday?"

The scraping sensation sharpened. Her skin was too tight. She needed to get out of this room, and fast. "He was," Callie said. "That was a Saturday after a payday, and we're always slammed hard then."

The muscle in Derek's jaw ticked. Callie refocused her attention on the cops.

"You were here, too?" Officer Grady asked.

"She's my apprentice." The Charmer couldn't keep the grin off his face. That reaction was earnest, which only made it worse. Would a punch to his liver shudder his smile?

Grady produced a small notebook from his pocket, and flipped a few pages in. "What was your name again, miss?"

She might vomit, and it had little to do with whatever magic the Charmer was cultivating in his pocket. She was not supposed to be on the police radar. She wasn't supposed to be interacting with them at all. She should have been living a life free of crime and questions and ripping souls out of people's bodies. *Should have* wasn't getting her far, though.

"Callie Delgado." She didn't bother keeping her voice low or avoiding eye contact. Criminals were uncomfortable around the cops. They were shifty. She could not allow herself to be memorable, to be seen. She had a lot to hide, and didn't need them knowing so.

The cop wrote down her name, and then asked a few basic identifying questions. Nothing concerning. Nothing about a break-in at the police substation, nothing about her use of magic, nothing about Nate.

Officer Grady turned toward Derek, notebook still at the ready. The already grating sensation dug deeper into her chest. Derek had bombed those buildings. He'd done so at the Soul Charmer's behest, but her worry for him wouldn't wound her. She most certainly wouldn't let her concern tip his hand to the police. Whatever their boss was wielding in his pocket was forcing the cop's hesitation, and for once Callie was grateful to the

Soul Charmer.

Instead of asking Derek for his whereabouts, Officer Grady paused. He scrubbed his wrist across his forehead, and then stuttered an apology. "That's it for now, but we do have potential witnesses. If we come back, it will be with a warrant."

The Charmer gestured to front door. "There's nothing to hide here. I merely offer citizens a respite from the burden of sin. I don't have a thing to do with the Ford family or their affairs."

It all sounded like bullshit. Even in the Charmer's standard skeezy tone, but he wasn't lying. The whole reason Ford fired shots in the Soul Charmer's direction was because the Charmer wouldn't rent him souls at a bulk rate. Her boss charged the drug cartel and mobsters more for his services. It didn't have a thing to do with a moral quandary. Charmer gave two fucks about what you did with the soul. It was about volume and inventory. There were plenty of souls vying for a fresh home, but the act of retrieving them wasn't a desirable one.

The officers left, but Callie didn't miss the dark sneer on Officer Grady's face when he closed the door.

"Pests," The Charmer muttered. He turned toward the back room so quickly his robe fluttered behind him.

Callie grabbed his elbow. It was thin and frail beneath her hand. He hissed, and she let go. "What was that?"

Disgust warped his face. Tight lips, flaring nostrils, the whole predatory lizard look. "A threat."

"What? No, those were cops, which it probably isn't safe to discuss. I meant *that*." She pointed at his pocket.

"You're becoming quite observant." It wasn't clear if that was a compliment. After a brief pause, he continued, "I was merely keeping their attention away from him."

Derek.

Sweat dappled his temples. "That's a first," Derek said on a reedy breath. Whatever the Charmer had done, it wasn't only the cops affected.

"We do not need anyone focused on you, especially not those with badges." The Charmer shooed dismissively to where the police had stood moments earlier. "Your work was exemplary and they will not bother you."

Callie didn't quite believe that. Yes, Derek was great at his job, but you don't bomb the house and work places of a mobster without consequences. The cops may not actually miss Ford, and they may not have a lead, but the rest of Ford's colleagues knew.

Nate knew. Is that why he was missing?

"Wait. How did you do that? Did you do something to those cops?" The moral grey area was Callie's favorite, but some shit was too much even for her.

"You're a novice. You couldn't handle it yet. I simply distracted their souls with a tug here and there."

There was an oversimplification if she ever heard one. He'd done *something*, and whatever it was had been big. The burn in her nose was gone, but an echo of pain lingered in her chest.

She shouldn't ask more, but she had to know. "Why did it hurt?"

The Charmer watched her silently for a moment. His black pupils widened until they were deep pools demanding Callie's attention. "The pull and claim of temporary ownership is not a natural process. Do not mention it to the priests."

She hadn't intended to return to the soul well. She wasn't hitting up confession. Why'd he have to bring the men of God into this?

He turned and left the room. Great. More cryptic shit and an order to keep secrets from priests. What was one more bad act when you'd gotten your mother kidnapped?

Derek didn't ask if she was okay. He didn't say anything. He opened his arms wide enough that his leather jacket parted, and Callie stepped forward. She pressed her cheek against his black tee shirt. He enveloped her in a protective hug. He didn't need words. He had actions. The Charmer didn't doubt his loyalty; he'd burned down buildings to protect him. *To protect her.* Callie didn't doubt his love for her either. She didn't understand it—she'd only been his girlfriend for a short time, but she'd already fucked up enough to get a boot out the door. Right now, though? She wasn't going to question it. The subtle spring soap he used in the shower tangled with the clean comfort of her laundry detergent, and that made him smell like home. Like safety. Like hers.

Too soon he pulled back. "You steady?"

If she let loose how she close she was to total exhaustion, her resolve might evaporate, and she simply would not crumple on the Charmer's crusty carpet, and so she simply nodded.

Derek scowled toward the curtain doorway to the soul storage room, and then inclined his head toward the back exit. It was a question.

"Blue's probably still out front." She didn't want another go with the police.

"We'll move fast," he said.

He let her walk through the hallway first. The magic didn't squeeze him the same way it did her. He'd told her it made him want to turn and run, but the magic coated Callie, thick and viscous. The Soul Charmer's back was to them. Normally he'd jump on the chance to needle her again or demand more from Derek. Though he could sense the shift in the wards, he ignored their entrance. Callie didn't linger, moving quickly to the exit. She went through the first door into the short, narrow hallway to the back alley, and stopped short. Derek bumped into her back, and she threw out a hand to brace herself on the wall. Her wrist hummed. Not a racing pulse. Not the thrum of fear or the sizzle of soul magic. Just like her flask. Callie slapped a hand to her pocket, and the container was still there. Hidden, empty, and ready to contain the repossessed souls. Magic was at work here. This wasn't the heady buzz she typically got from the flask when it begged to be filled. This was new, *different*.

"Doll?" Worry seeped into Derek's standard stoic tone.

Callie had been in this hallway more times than she cared to, because the back entrance meant dealing with less of the clientele. The wood-paneled walls didn't match the rest of the interior, and picture frames were squeezed into all of the available space like she was inside the home of someone with the money to support a dozen kids. The glass inside each frame had always been foggy and discolored. The metal around each picture still bore the rust marks and gouges of a long life, but the interiors were no longer empty. Each frame now displayed faces and dates.

Benton's meth-pocked face cast a sidelong stare from an oval silver frame to her right. Were these mug shots? Today's date was scrawled on the bottom of the image in lieu of a booking number. Callie reeled back from Benton's image. If it bore today's date, how did the Charmer get it up? These weren't digital frames. The electricity in the building was shoddy, the WiFi nonexistent, and, honestly, what would be the point. She turned to Derek. His eyes were wide, but completely fixed on her.

"What's wrong?" was all he said, but he'd stitched apprehension into the words.

"You don't see that?" She jutted a shaking finger to the right of his shoulder.

Derek turned toward the wall. "The frames? Sure, doll."

"That—that—that Donna who we just jacked a soul from is here." The squat woman who had pawned her soul not twenty minutes ago glared out from within the black frame.

He looked around the hallway. It was tight with even the two of them in here. "Doll, it's just us."

The gaunt faces watched her from the walls. A miniature funhouse mirror debacle tuned to her own frequency. Her lungs squeezed hard enough she gasped. Was the Soul Charmer collecting scraps of souls from the rented returns? Was she helping him stockpile parts of these people's souls?

Callie ran a thumb over the nighthawk on her wrist again. She didn't think hawks could coo, but this one sure was pleased. The magic in this room wasn't trying to bite or burn her, but it wanted something. Too bad she didn't have anything else to give.

CHAPTER FOUR

The vinyl booth seat in Dott's diner didn't warm beneath Callie. Sleet streaked past the window in shimmering chunks. It was cold and slushy outside, but even in her favorite restaurant Callie couldn't get warm. It wasn't her magic. She'd had surges of icy chills as they'd passed other booths, other people. No one was within a dozen feet of her now. If she focused, she could sense the draw of the ragged edges of the souls inside former clients. She closed her eyes for a moment, and willed her mind to ignore them.

The more she learned about how this magic worked, the more it called her. The more it needed. She'd thought the apprentice gig would earn her control over the power raging beneath her skin. Now it was hers and she didn't want to let it go. Maybe that was sleep deprivation talking.

Callie scowled at the storm outside. Derek cleared

his throat. Those grey eyes were watching her, seeing her, knowing too much.

"Sorry," she muttered. She meant it, but also too many problems were vying for attention in her mind that she couldn't promise not to drift again.

His short, low grunt was his acceptance of her apology. She almost smiled. At least she could count on him to get her.

"We need to find Nate," she said.

Before she could even tense a muscle to move out of the booth, he said, "We do, but you need to eat first."

"I'm good," she lied.

He glared at her. His hair was the longest she'd seen it, and had started to curl at the ends.

"Fine. I'll have something." A solid drink would be good.

"Beer doesn't count." *Fucking mind reader.*

"I'll get soup." It was about all she could keep down. Worry had her gut churning, and much more than liquid was going to get evicted.

The sharp creases at the corners of his eyes smoothed, though the dark marks below them lingered. She wasn't the only one foregoing sleep.

"Do you want to tell me what you saw in that hallway?" The question sounded like it was asked for her benefit. Maybe it was. Maybe he wanted her to unburden. She'd had too many demands this week to take it as such, though.

"Do you want to tell me why you didn't tell me the

cops were looking for you?"

He pulled away for a moment, but eased back toward her just as quickly.

Callie cupped her hand over her mouth until she'd locked down her frustration, and then she spoke. "I'm being the asshole again. Sorry. I need to get her back, Derek."

"I know," the words were soft brush against her cheek.

"You saw the fingers." The hum of the nearby heater almost erased her shaky words.

The fucking fingers. Her mom's fingers. Delivered on a platter—a literal platter—next to Nate's little serial killer handwritten note. He wanted his soul back. He'd taken her mom. Leverage like that fucking worked. Callie was goddamn eager to return his shitty soul. She knew where it was and would have forked it over in seconds if she could find the bastard.

Derek stretched his hand out to her, and she took it. His palm was the warm comfort of cocoa and blankets. She siphoned the softness for a long moment.

"We will get her back." His confidence rang with a steel core of sincerity. Callie couldn't even fake that, but that was the point. Derek didn't falter when it came to her. Thank God.

"If we can go find the corner guy on El Paseo, we can find him." Even to her ears, she sounded convinced.

"Where on El Paseo?"

"Near the Cathedral."

Derek stared at their joined hands, but he didn't react when she squeezed his fingers.

"I don't like it," he said.

Callie let go. "None of this is particularly likeable. It's where Benton said the guy was."

"Okay. Benton's probably reliable."

Callie lifted her chin, but managed not to throw out a *See?!*

"He also doesn't know which guy it is. We're talking third-hand gossip at best. Could be Dougie or Fiona or Adam."

Callie leaned in, surprised how much she needed this plan. "He said corner *guy*. So not Fiona."

Derek nodded.

Their waitress stopped at the table to take their orders. Callie followed through on her tortilla soup promise, but also requested a cold beer in a longneck bottle. Derek slid out of the booth for a quick run to the restroom. Though it was only 10:30 p.m. and Dott's was far from empty, Callie was alone. The temptation to run and continue searching for Nate wasn't as strong as before, but it wriggled in the back of her mind.

She'd been so close to safety. She'd gotten Josh back. He was *sober*. Derek was willing to skip town with her. Running wouldn't solve her problems any more than drinking cured a sour stomach. She still had her boyfriend, but keeping her big brother on the straight-and-narrow and dealing with this mess with their mom and Nate was tricky.

She pulled her phone from her pocket, and texted Josh. She simply asked, "Any word?" because like her he was worked up searching for Zara.

If one wanted to point fingers, they could point at him. He was the reason that Callie even knew who Nate was. It was Josh's meth addiction that had pulled Callie into this world. She'd been blackmailed by Nate's boss Ford. She'd entered the soul magic world because of them. She'd done it because she loved her brother, because he'd bailed her out when she was kid. It's what Delgados do. Family first. Always.

Only these days Callie was beginning to feel like it was family first for the others when it was convenient. Yes, it was her fault Nate was after them. It was Callie who ripped Nate's soul from his body. She'd done it because he'd gotten a kid murdered. She'd been wrapped up in the need for justice or vengeance or something. She hadn't thought about Zara. Her mom wasn't great, but she was hers, and she sure as shit didn't deserve to be kidnapped or to have her fingers cut off and sent to her daughter. Literally no one deserves that.

Josh, though, was happy to keep telling Callie how it was all her fault the few times he texted back. He'd avoided all twenty-seven of her calls and was never home when she went by their mom's place. He hadn't said he blamed her, but he hinted fucking hard. Josh messaged back, "No. You find Nate?"

"Not yet. Have a lead." She didn't want to get his hopes up, but he needed to know she was trying.

"K."

"Has anyone you know seen Nate?" She hated to

ask. She wasn't tossing blame, but the fact was Josh knew these dealers. He knew Nate. He knew where they used to be holed up. He knew their faces, their names, which pockets they hid the good stuff in. He also was several weeks sober and she wasn't trying to wreck that for him. A kidnapped mom already put him on edge, and Callie wasn't sure he hadn't hit the needle again.

"I'm working more now. Lots of construction jobs. They need me. Pays good." He hadn't answered her question.

"I'm glad the job is working out." Callie didn't trust anyone who would hire her brother for manual labor, and the last time she'd talked with Josh about the gig he'd said he was supervising. Junkies don't make the most reliable employees, and you don't put someone with zero experience in charge. Something was up with the job, but now wasn't the time to bring it up.

"Almost have enough cash for a P.I. to find her."

"You don't need to do that. I'm on it," she messaged back.

"P.I. is better than the cops."

She was better, too. Derek even more so. She didn't bother telling him so. At least he was focused. At this point, she'd take the wins when she could get them.

"Keep me posted. Love you." She didn't use to text her family love, but when one's mom gets kidnapped, you start making sure the loved ones know how you feel.

Derek slid back into the booth. His movements

were lithe, but that muscle in his jaw was ticking again.

"You okay?" She so rarely was the person asking that question these days.

He parted his lips, and then closed them again. Flummoxed Derek was a special sight. He filled more than half of the seat across from her. His elbows rested on the table, and if he'd leaned his weight into it he could have tilted the thing. Unease, though, permeated his hesitant motions. He pulled his phone from the inside pocket of his leather jacket, and looked at the small device in his hand. "My brother just called."

"Father Henry?" Callie had met the priest only recently, and he'd been mostly kind to her. Less so to his brother. While he and Derek got along better than she and some of her family, the dynamic of priest and enforcer for a soul magician was, well, complicated.

Derek rolled his eyes. "Can we drop the Father stuff?"

She wouldn't much care for hearing Josh get an honorific title either. "Sure. What did Henry want? Is everyone in your family okay?"

Derek's smile was slow to form, but genuine.

"What?"

"Just thinking about whether he'd asked about family. I suppose he did."

It was Callie's turn to look confused.

"He asked about you."

"Oh."

"Oh?" His smile widened. "Calm down, doll."

She shook off the warm fuzzies attempting to rise in her tummy. "So what did he want to know about me?"

"He was worried."

"What?"

"He's concerned." The way Derek teased the word suggested he didn't need his little brother worrying over his girlfriend. "He said he wanted to make sure you were okay after your last visit to the cathedral."

Callie resisted the urge to ask what for a third time. "That's…weird."

"My brother is weird. Who wants to sign up for a lifetime of rules, rituals, and zero quality time with hot women like you?"

Derek started to chuckle before Callie felt the heat rise in her cheeks.

"I meant why does he want to know?" It was a safer question than 'how much does he know?'

The last time Callie had been to the Cortean Catholic cathedral she'd been with the Soul Charmer. She'd been to the basement. She'd learned how much the church knew about the soul rental gig, and that they were key in keeping the Charmer in business. Souls needed redemption, needed back into our world, and the Charmer had to free them from the well to do so. She'd done it that night. The Charmer had not taken her back to the church again. She was fine with that. The less she had to see that well, to hear those souls, to be a part of the bargain with purgatory the better.

"My brother knows something. He thinks he's too

honorable to tell, but the fact he called means something is up and it's probably tied to the Soul Charmer." Derek was almost successful in keeping the apprehension from rattling his voice.

Cops asking about Ford's death. Zara kidnapped and injured. Nate was missing. Josh hustling work for cash. Stumbling with pulling souls at the Charmer's. Now Henry was worried about her enough to make Derek worried.

Callie didn't bother hiding her fear. She was stretched too thin to be able to conceal much anyway. "Isn't it always? The Charmer's exhausted right now. He isn't invested in Nate, but having that asshole disappear now doesn't make sense. There's just too much bad coming at us all at once."

Nate shouldn't be gone. His boss was gone, the empire for the taking. He had the power to make them bend over by taking Zara. What was the point of making threats if you couldn't cash in the rewards? Which meant either he was fucking with them—possible—or someone even viler was out there. Whoever it was, Callie was ready to plow through them to save her mother. She had to.

Family first.

CHAPTER FIVE

The Cortean Catholic cathedral was remarkable during the day. Stained glass windows depicting saints rising to Heaven warmed and shimmered beneath the high desert sun. At night the jutting peaks of the enormous building became imposing. Artificial light left the whitewashed exterior stark and foreboding. The centerpiece of the faith's stake in Gem City loomed above the squat buildings in the plaza. The city had a firm two-stories-max policy for buildings. Except for the church. Its cathedral's peaks could block the skyline and no one made a peep. You could do that when you held even the mayor's fear of the afterlife in your hands.

For once Callie could relate. Nate held her mother's life in his greasy hands, and that meant Callie was damned in a tangible way. Guilt clamped her insides, and she could picture basic black zip ties—the same kind she'd used to hold Nate—and with each passing second she could almost hear them clicking one notch tighter. Any more and she would go morally septic.

Her car whined when she cranked the wheel to parallel park a block down the road from the church.

"You need to let me look at the power steering in this thing," Derek said.

Her sigh said 'not now' nicer than she could have aloud. "I let you do the spark plugs."

He gave her knee a quick squeeze. "That you did, doll."

She'd let him fix the leak in her kitchen sink because the super never would. The spark plug thing apparently was a big deal, and she'd finally acquiesced when she realized she had enough money to cover all her bills with money to spare for the first time ever. The Charmer paid well, but that didn't mean she needed to go throwing cash out of her pocket. Now was the time to stockpile and rebuild her savings, because eventually shit would hit the fan and she'd need a very green safety net.

She pulled the car away from the halo of the low, hazy streetlamps. That light could keep her car from being jacked, but she and Derek were staying inside. From this darkened side of the street, they could see the three main corners where hustlers shilled their wares on the El Paseo. All of them had worked for Ford, and now Callie needed at least one of them to have stayed loyal to Nate after his boss's untimely demise.

"Hey," Derek whispered. When she turned, he took

her face in his hands. His palms were rough, but familiar on her cheeks. "I've got you."

"I know." Her voice was barely a breath.

"We will get through this together. We'll find her. I won't let Nate get away with this." His vengeance slashed the air with the ferocity of coyote teeth.

He refused to say it, but she could tell he thought Zara was dead. She wouldn't be, though. Callie's aunt had always said Zara was as stubborn as stone. It was more, though, something bright and sharp dug behind her heart at the thought of Zara being dead. Maybe it was a Delgado thing or maybe it was magic or maybe it was God doing her a solid. Whatever it was, Callie believed Zara was alive. What she didn't know was for how long.

"One of these guys has to know where he is," she said.

Derek slid his thumb across Callie's lower lip. "Nate forgot who he was fucking with."

She scoffed with the force of a sucker punch. "He knows the Soul Charmer fine."

"Not the old man. Not even me. He should not have fucked with you, and that asshole is going to find out why."

Callie leaned into Derek's palm. He pulled her forward to meet his kiss. His lips were soft, but the force behind them wasn't gentle. He licked at her lips, and she parted them. Energy snapped between them. Sweet ozone—electricity on the air—wrapped around them. The desire to be closer, to refocus all her fears and worry into something positive and forgiving, had Callie leaning into him. She nipped the corner of his mouth. He groaned, and the sound shot through her belly. The tightness, the earlier pain receded. Derek's fingers slid into her hair at the nape of her neck. Callie shivered.

He pulled back. "I need to remind you that you're a badass more often."

"Mhm." She leaned back in for another kiss that ended too soon.

"Looks like Dougie has a customer, doll." At least he sounded as disappointed as she was.

He let go of her, and she tried to ignore the creeping sense of loss as her skin cooled. "Should we move on them now?"

"Nah. Let's watch both dealers for a bit, and see if either has the good stuff."

"I was kind of hoping we could punch our way to answers today." She hadn't meant to sound so sullen.

The roguish smile he offered her was almost as good as another kiss. "I've been telling you since the day we met, I only punch when it's necessary."

"This situation doesn't count?" Humor laced the words.

His shrug was tight enough his leather jacket should have creaked. "Too important to fuck it up by breaking someone useful."

He'd been right, though. The longer they watched the two dealers, the more they learned. Dougie wasn't smooth. His buyers wore loafers and button downs.

They tugged gaping coats shut, but didn't bother zipping up because their car was idling across the street. The cars were nicer than Callie's by a fucking mile.

Adam was on the far corner across the street from the cathedral. He was far enough away that the crisp floodlights illuminating the statues of saints Antonio, Catalina, and Michael didn't show more than the dark profile of his face. Most of Adam's clients so far had been rail thin and in coats that were two sizes too big. They'd rocked on their heels and their hands jerked with need as they reached to accept a packet from the corner dealer. Callie would have recognized the tweakers hitting up Adam even if she were a dozen blocks away. Her shifts at the ER a lifetime ago had been filled with oxy addicts and meth heads looking for a fix in between hits. She didn't want to compare them to Josh, but she could have done that, too.

A woman in knee-high designer boots, and a long, belted trench coat approached Adam. He shrugged her off. Her hands were flying wide. Even from this distance, it was plain the lady was pissed. Adam pointed her toward Dougie, and she headed toward the other dealer with a huff. Adam offered another, one-finger suggestion once the woman's back was turned.

"I think we have our man," Derek said.

"Why?" Callie didn't take her eyes off the pretentious woman. She drew attention in front of the church, even stopping to give a quick curtsey and make the sign of the cross. She was buying drugs, and had no shame. "Is she a renter?"

"Huh?"

"The woman there. Does she rent from the Charmer?"

Derek paused, and Callie didn't mind that the woman wasn't memorable to him. "I don't think so. Why?"

Now wasn't the time for her to unload her feelings about the people who partook in their boss's services, but Callie could offer a partial answer. "She likes attention, and doesn't seem to be bothered that the priests inside the church might see her buying *whatever*. That cockiness is usually reserved for the people we make pay double."

He nodded slowly. "Sure enough, doll."

"So who's our man?"

"Adam."

"Why? I mean, he's an asshole. So that makes sense for being Team Nate, but both of them are hawking at a pretty regular rate."

"They've got the same number of customers, but Adam over there has pulled in ten times the cash. He's been pulling packets from every pocket. He's carrying a selection."

"Dougie's just passing out weed, isn't he?"

"Maybe molly, too, but yeah. White-collar shit."

"You think Nate would be closer with Adam because he isn't handling the more widely used drugs?"

"It's Gem City. Everything is widely used. But, yeah, Ford's empire was built on selling expensive shit to people who were desperate. Potheads aren't going to knock over a liquor store to pay for their habit, but meth addicts…" he trailed off.

"It's fine. Josh pawned Zara's TV once. Stole the diamond earrings my Tia Cheri gave me for my fourteenth birthday." She didn't look away. She didn't hold back the pain scraping her throat. She wouldn't be ashamed, and he needed to know that. To know she could handle this. "You're right. Methamphetamines make addicts do desperate shit."

He moved like he was going to hug her, and she tensed. He edged back into his seat. She'd loved his hands on her earlier, but the air was no longer laced with hope. Truth was stagnant in the car, and the only escape was to get out and score some answers. Fresh air and some progress could put Callie and Derek back at ease. At least she hoped so.

"Let's pull the car over around the corner on Juniper Street." Derek pointed to the street behind Adam's corner post.

"Less likely to see us coming?" Callie asked.

"And closer if we need to book it."

Callie took the long route around the plaza, and parked the car a block in the other direction. The streets were empty, and her car was the only one parked on this street, but she still took another darkened spot. She could see Adam from here, too. Lights were on in the cathedral across the street. Could the priests see these dealers outside their church every night? Did they not bother to minister to them? Maybe they had. Maybe that's why Father Henry was checking on Callie. Could he know what Nate was up to? Callie shook off the thought. If Henry knew where Nate was, he'd tell his brother. He and Derek weren't close, but she'd seen them together. Their animosity was cultivated from a profound love. You can't ditch that easily. Family doesn't forget what's important, even if you don't like their chosen path.

She killed the engine, tapped her pocket to confirm she had the flask, tugged the zipper on her coat a little higher, and then stepped out of the car. Even in her warmest jacket, the icy wind cutting around the building slapped her hard. She fought the urge to hug herself for extra warmth, but she needed to keep her shoulders back and head high. Even running on fumes, one had to play the part. Derek fell into step beside her. His fingers skimmed hers. Now wasn't the time for holding hands, but the light touch was enough to help her focus.

"We don't rent to Adam, but he's got to be a soul user," Derek said.

She was already so cold, Callie wasn't sure the warning was necessary. She thanked him anyway.

"We going in straight?" she asked, realizing they should have talked about this in car where there was a heater.

"No point in playing a game. Adam's smart."

Callie raised an eyebrow.

"For a guy who slings dope outside the church, he's smart," he amended. "Anyway, he'd know who we are. I think Ford put out the word before everything went…the way it did."

Even now, Derek couldn't bring himself to talk about it. Sure, it wasn't safe to speak the word bombing on the streets, but even when they were alone he couldn't talk about what he'd done. Not in those terms. Was it shitty that she related to that feeling? Was it even more shitty that she liked they had it in common? Callie blinked a few times until the tears welling at her lids receded.

Focus. One thing at a time. Find Nate. Get Mom. Get out of the soul magic business. Like it was that easy.

Adam's eyes widened when he caught sight of Callie and Derek across El Paseo, but he didn't bolt. Hell, from this distance Callie couldn't say the guy had even tensed. His shoulder was angled away from them, but his eyes tracked their movements when they crossed the street. Anxiety prickled beneath Callie's sternum.

"Didn't figure the Soul Charmer's crew needed to hit a corner," Adam said as way of greeting. His eyes would have been a bright green if the ghastly film of frequent soul renting hadn't already begun encroaching on his irises.

Callie shoved her hands deeper into her pockets. She found the flask on the right, and squeezed it. The obsidian inlay pressed against her bared skin took the edge off the chill of Adam's ragged soul. Didn't do shit about the sleet pinging against her back, though.

Derek edged closer to Adam. Her windbreak gone, more icy pellets came at her side, but he also was between her and the dealer. "Ain't here to buy."

Adam shuffled a half step away, but turned to fully

face them. "You sure? Your girl looks pretty uptight."

A laugh punched her gut. No one of the opposite sex had ever suggested she was a prude, but if she was, what the fuck business of it was his? Derek tried to grumble over the sound, but there wasn't a need.

"I don't need your shitty ass molly, but thanks for the offer," she said.

Adam cast a quick glance toward Dougie's corner. The other dealer was doing his damnedest not to look their way. Dougie didn't want to get in trouble. So there must be something to get in trouble over. Score one for the stake out.

"Then what do you need? I'm here to sell."

"Do I look like a cop? I'm not gonna scare off your business." Derek's words were casual, but with each word he edged a little closer to Adam.

The dealer was almost as tall as Derek, but slender. Not the emaciated cut of a junkie, but more like a vegan kid or someone who opted for cigarettes and coffee over real food. He was a con man. The thick confidence Adam was pushing said more about his goals to move up the ranks in Ford-turned-Nate's business. Someone didn't plan to stay on the streets. Callie would have admired his determination if he weren't working for the douchebag that cut off her mom's fingers and delivered them like a holiday ham.

She couldn't side with Adam, but playing the part was manageable. "Having us here helps your business. No one is going to hide ones in their wad of twenties while we're here. We just make people hold up their ends of bargains and return what's owed."

He tugged his coat sleeve down. "I haven't had trouble getting paid tonight."

"I don't care," Derek cut in. His words were far more frigid than the sleet speeding around them.

Adam tucked his light brown hair up under a black beanie. "Then move on." His earlier bravado now shook.

"Not yet. We need to talk to your boss."

"Who says I have one?"

Derek's glare was molten menace. "You make that shit at home with a mail-order chemistry set?"

"Distributors."

Derek hooked a hand around Adam's upper arm. The pop could have been a settling of snow beneath their feet, but the dealer's sharp inhale suggested otherwise. "Where is he?"

Adam tried to pull away, but Derek was gargoyle still and strong and Adam was in his grasp. The dealer thrust a hand out toward Callie, and grasped at her. Derek nudged him back in time. Adam's hand met air. Before Callie could even move, Derek had whirled his left elbow up and around to whap Adam. There was a light snap. When her boyfriend had pulled back again, Adam's right eyebrow was split open. Blood sluiced down the side of his face, and drops clung to his eyelashes.

It looked fucking wicked, but Callie's ER stints gave her the comfort to know that facial wounds could bleed like a bitch. Nothing was broken, and worst case he'd need a couple stitches. Old Callie would have butterflied it for him, but she wasn't that person anymore. That person avoided being a part of seedy conversations on grimy streets with shady people.

Callie stepped forward, and spoke with all the anger churning at realizing she was no longer being the kind of person who would want to help this guy. "Want to try that again?"

He knew she didn't mean the grab. "Nate's off the radar."

Derek eased up on the dealer.

"So Nate's in charge now?" Callie needed the confirmation.

Adam clapped his hand to his forehead. Blood seeped between his fingers, but he didn't notice. "Yeah, but he's lying low."

Callie met Derek's asking glance. She didn't need to tell him the guy was lying, but something about the trust in that look steadied her feet and let her ignore the ice tipping her fingers and the sleet poking her back.

A roar rumbled through the square. The statues across the street practically rattled with the rev of a powerful engine. Huge halogen headlights bathed the corner in blue brightness and momentarily blinded Callie. By the time her eyes adjusted, a muscle car was rolling past them with the back door wide open. Instinct put Callie on the ground. She didn't worry about Adam or the frozen concrete. She hit the deck and prayed she'd be safe. Derek's black boots were nearby.

He still stood. She reached for his leg and pulled. He didn't budge. Adam sprinted past, and leaped into the car. Squealing tires blasted her already battered ears.

She'd never wanted to be a part of this. To talk to men who worked for the mafia. How had she gotten to a point where she thought someone would shoot from a car at her? She'd gotten in so deep so fast.

Derek bent down, and helped Callie up. He had Adam's jacket wrapped around his fist. The tears she'd held earlier began to fall. He yanked her into his chest with more force than before. His arms were tight around her, and he turned them so the brunt of the storm beat against his back. She burrowed her face in her personal human shield, let the leather of his coat warm and soften against her skin, and wept.

CHAPTER SIX

Callie hadn't slept in almost four days. She should have collapsed from sheer exhaustion, but adrenaline continued to spike her synapses. Could someone overdose on the body's natural highs? Could she be felled by cortisol levels? The priest at the church she'd attended during elementary school would have told her the Lord was testing her. Father Henry might have told her the same.

But this wasn't a test. This was the universe fucking with her, and she was over it. Her one fresh lead had bolted into a noisy muscle car, leaving her with nothing but bruised knees and regret.

She sat on the edge of her bed. She'd thrown the jeans in the hamper, but the scrape of concrete over the knees might need more than a good scrub. Callie rubbed lotion over the bruises. It wouldn't heal any faster, but it comforted her like it could. Derek sauntered into the room. He moved with that casual swagger he saved for home. No flexing muscles, no tight shoulders, no grimace.

"Take these," he said, and handed her three brown pills and a glass of water.

Callie accepted them, but hesitated. "You're not trying to make me sleep, are you? If Nate finally calls back, I need to be here, to be coherent."

"You're going to have to sleep eventually, doll, or being coherent won't be an option. But, no, I'm never going to make you do shit. It's Advil. You can see the name on the pills."

Callie tossed the tablets into her mouth, and took a generous drink of water. She pretended she hadn't peeked at the tab for the name first. "Thanks."

The pleased rumble emanating from his chest has the silky warmth of aged bourbon. If only her body weren't on high alert now, she'd drink him in and relax. Fortunately, they were on the same page there, because disappointing Derek was the last thing she wanted to do.

"I've got a contact who can run the plates for me." He was already wearing his jacket again.

"You got the plates?" She'd been focused on the headlights and the tires and Adam leaving with information she needed.

He tapped his index finger against his temple. "Like a fucking camera."

The urge to smile hit her, but even her face was too tired to comply. "Bet there are some great home movies in your head."

He leaned down and kissed her forehead. "Lace is a predominant thread."

Okay, even her wrung-out body couldn't resist reacting to that one. "I love you."

He kissed her again, this time on the lips. "Love you, too, doll."

Derek moved to leave, but stopped in the doorway. He turned back to face her. "I'll be back soon. If you hear from Nate, you call me."

"Yeah. Of course." Calling from the car still counted, right?

"If you're up for it, dig through the shit from Adam's coat. Maybe we can still get decent intel out of him."

Callie nodded. Adam may have slipped Derek's grasp, but his coat hadn't.

She gave herself a few moments alone. The pillows were calling her, but she wouldn't be able to sleep. She'd tried two nights ago. The horror show behind her eyelids wasn't going to abate until she set shit right, until she'd found Zara. It wasn't even the gory gift Nate had left her that bubbled up first now. Now she could only relive her last conversation with Zara. The image of her mother's face when Callie had slammed a beer bottle to her sternum and sucked out the rented soul. The betrayal. They were family. They were Delgados. They weren't supposed to screw each other over like this. The guilt bubbled in her belly, and the fresh pills threatened to make an emergency exit.

She could make it right, though. That's also what family did. It didn't matter if Zara had been neglectful. It didn't matter that she'd rented souls. It didn't matter that she'd demanded too much from her daughter. None of that mattered. Zara was family, and Callie would save her.

Callie let out a long sigh. Her back hurt and her muscles ached. She was probably dehydrated. She drank the rest of the water Derek had brought her, and then headed to the living room.

Adam's coat lay across her kitchen counter. Its drab olive losing its richness against the off-white Formica. She and Derek had already turned out the pockets. The contents rested next to the jacket: Adam's phone, a cocktail napkin with a street address somewhere on the northern edge of Gem City, four packets of heroin, two bags of meth, a tiny bag with a bundle of molly, and a business card.

Callie had been about to flush the drugs, but Derek said they might be a bargaining chip to get information. She tugged the sleeve of her shirt down over her palm, and then pushed the packets to the side until they were almost beneath the jacket.

She picked up the business card. It'd been packed in a pocket next to the meth, but looking now, it was not drug related.

Fuck. The blunt swear blasted the base of her skull. The card was a problem. *Her* problem.

The glossy, black card read "Be Anonymous with a New Soul" in golden script. She flipped it over, hoping to find a name. Someone she could point the Soul

Charmer toward. That would have been easy, though, and nothing was fucking easy anymore. No name, no store, no address, but in blocky yellow was a phone number. It was local.

Callie went back into the bedroom to grab her phone from the nightstand. She stared at the darkened screen in her hand. She couldn't dial the numbers. What was she going to do if these people answered? Diving headlong into the Charmer's bullshit without his request was unnecessary drama. She needed to save Zara, and that meant finding Nate. Someone else hawking souls was a second-tier problem. Nate was interested in soul magic, but his immediate cash had to be coming from a pile of pills and powder.

She brought her phone back with her into the kitchenette. In case Nate calls. Or Derek or Josh messages. Not because she was going to do anything desperate.

The room was stuffy. The storm outside had shifted from sleet to snow, so opening a window wasn't an option. Callie adjusted the thermostat down. She rummaged in the top shelf of her entryway closet until she found an Autumn's Glory candle. She lit it, and hoped the blend of cinnamon, nutmeg, fir, and fire would calm her nerves.

She opened Adam's phone. It was nicer than hers. The screen wasn't cracked, and it weighed less. A small bubble on the screen told her he had thirty-nine minutes remaining. There were around sixty numbers stored in the logs, but no names were attached to them in the Contacts. She skimmed the numbers. Most of them had the same area code, her area code. At least he was talking to people in Gem City. If one of these was Nate, that might help. Except she had thirty-nine minutes on the phone and more than sixty people she'd have to call.

She was about to flip to the messages section, when one of the numbers caught her attention. Callie rarely had a phone number memorized. Work number, her mom's number, and her own number. That was about it. But this number ended in 1456. Her brother's number was like that—he'd pushed her to memorize it when she was still in high school. She could only remember the last four digits even then. Callie flipped open the contacts on her phone and scrolled to Josh's name.

Her chest was tight. Her heartbeat pushed hard against her ribs, expanding, growing, punching. She set the phones next to each other, and willed herself to see something different. She stepped away. Drank another glass of water. Splashed a little on her face. Came back. The numbers still matched.

Fuck that kid.

Josh knew Adam. He could have helped her. Instead here he was in contact with yet another dealer. This phone wasn't old enough to have been from before Josh got sober, before Callie had paid his debts again, before he'd detoxed on her couch. She wasn't sure what part she was most angry about, but the ire throttled through her veins fast enough to burn off the guilt. Angry wasn't better than sorry, but at least it was useful.

Her hands were shaking. Callie tapped Josh's number on the screen of her phone, and then the speakerphone button. The hollow ringtone filled her apartment. Her next-door neighbor had to be asleep, but she still thumbed the volume down a couple notches.

"You find her?" Josh's voice was scratchy, but urgent.

"Not yet." Callie stared hard at the drugs peeking from the edges of Adam's coat. It helped her hold on to her anger.

"Damn, Sis. Do you know what time it is?"

No, she did not. She also didn't care. "Late."

"Or too early. Is it an emergency?"

Callie couldn't do this small talk. She couldn't let Josh act like she was the one who was out of line here. Like she was alone in being a fuckup. "How do you know Adam?"

She heard a mug slide against a wooden table. Probably Zara's coffee table. "Adam who? What are you talking about?"

"Dealer down on El Paseo. Tall guy. How do you know him?"

Josh coughed twice into the phone. "Why do you care who I know?"

"For one, he's a dealer, and you are supposed to be sober—"

"I am fucking clean. You just can't let that shit go, can you? Miss Perfect. Like you're the only one who can make mistakes and be redeemed. You work for the Soul Charmer. You got Mom taken. That's on you. Doesn't have a damn thing to do with me staying clean."

Wow. It wasn't like she wasn't proud of him for staying sober. She was, but this also wasn't the first time. Being the responsible one in her family was getting goddamn old. *He* was the one who slipped back into drug use over and over. *He* was the one who took and took from her. Her help didn't mean shit, apparently. Life got hard, and now it was all on her. Again. The post-detox thank yous were gone, but the least he could give her was honesty. She'd earned it.

"I always have your back. I work for the Soul Charmer because I had to get you back from the mobsters who you owed money for drugs." She let the words explode. "Sorry if discovering you've stayed in contact with drug dealers would worry me. It's not like I let you crash on my couch or paid for your rehab. Nope. I'm completely the asshole here."

Callie was leaning over her phone. She'd gripped the edge of the counter. She let go, and swiped her hands down her face. Her hands were cold, but without the bite of magic. Small fucking miracles.

"I didn't say you were an asshole." Even over the speakerphone Josh sounded smaller, younger. She could almost forget she was the little sister, he the big brother.

"You didn't answer my question. How do you know Adam?" Her tone sharpened with the smack she wished she could deliver to the back of his head.

"From work."

Panic bit her chest. "You slinging drugs now?"

"You just can't help yourself, can you?" he said under his breath. Before she could return that volley, he continued, "No. His brother works with me. Adam comes by to visit. He does more than sling drugs. He delivers materials."

"Materials?" She didn't bother hiding her disbelief.

"It's construction. We use building materials. Really, Callie, do we have to have this conversation in the middle of the night?"

He really didn't get it, did he? "It's important."

Josh was quiet for a moment. "No, it isn't. You're digging into my shit without a cause. You're doing it at three in the goddamn morning. You should be doing something about getting our mom back. Spending your time trying to drag me down ain't fair. Either you trust me or you don't. I'm not the one putting the Soul Charmer before family. I'm not putting an outsider like the Charmer's muscle before family. Could be that's why I'm not the one who got mom taken. Could be you need to remember to put Delgados first again."

"Are you fucking kidding me?" Callie's voice was so quiet, it was a miracle Josh heard her.

Something metal squeaked on his end of the line.

"No. Just. Fucking. No. I'm your little sister, but I've been cleaning up your messes for years. I never say no to you. I never turn you away. You sent Ford to my fucking door to demand I work for him and then the Soul Charmer. I did things I vowed I would never do—and things I didn't even know I was capable of— for you. For family. For Delgados. Mom got herself into this shit." As soon as she said it, Callie knew it was true. It didn't shake the guilt gripping her spine. Truth didn't work like that. The truth had to break you before it could set you free.

"Mom chose to be involved with soul renting. She chose to ignore my advice to stay away. She pushed. I'm not saying I'm blameless, but this isn't all on me. I'm doing everything I can to save our mother, and it would be fucking nice to get some help."

"Oh." Josh swallowed loud enough for Callie to hear.

"I was calling for help. For mom. For our family. But, yeah, Josh, I'm super fucking selfish."

He swallowed hard again. Maybe the bitter truth was caught in his throat?

Finally, softly, he said, "What do you need?"

"I need to find Mom." She sucked in a steadying breath. Before he could bring up his private investigator idea again, she continued, "Help me find Nate."

"I'm gonna get us a P.I. We don't need Nate."

The shiver shooting down Callie's spine had nothing to do with the thermostat. That familiarity. She hated that her brother had ever met Ford, Nate, and the other scary dealers, but she might have hated it even more that he didn't hold grudges against them. Josh had gotten himself addicted. She wasn't trying to put that on the people who distributed the drugs. But Ford and Nate were more than that. They'd kidnapped him. They'd blackmailed her. Those acts *were* on them, and if she could have she would never have spoken Nate's name again. She had to, though. She had to play his stupid game, because he held the cards now.

"Seriously?"

Josh's end of the call offered only the rustle of fabric.

Once again, she had to take the lead here. Had to guide him along. It'd be nice if he could be the same big brother who had protected her as a kid. The one who snuck her out of school for baseball games, who hid snacks under the sink for her when Zara earmarked all their money for Blackjack, who had helped her piece together Halloween costumes, and who had hidden her from bullies. She stifled a sigh, but resignation rattled against her ribs.

"Nate has our mom, Josh. He's literally the bad guy here. Tell me who to talk to, where to go. *Something* for fuck's sake."

"I don't know what to tell you. Honest. I haven't talked to Nate. He's missing, too. That's why we need to hire a guy to find Mom."

Josh was lucky they were having this call over the phone, because the urge to crunch his junk with a kick to the pants was begging for attention.

"Do you at least know of anyone who is close with him?"

"His ex-girlfriend is a cocktail waitress at Rodrigo's." His voice wavered, but the undercurrent of hope didn't escape Callie.

"What's her name?" she asked, trying not to imagine anyone wanting to have sex with Nate ever in the history of time.

"Cindi, I think."

Callie glanced at the clock. It was almost four a.m. Rodrigo's was a T&A joint serving sucky bar food. It also kept nightclub hours. Nights and weekends only. Talking to Nate's ex-girlfriend was off the table for at least another twelve hours. Too long. Adam was on the move, and that meant at least some of Nate's crew knew she was searching hard for him.

She needed another lead, but Josh wasn't up to giving it to her. They said goodbyes, and Callie started scrolling through Adam's phone messages for more clues.

CHAPTER SEVEN

Callie had been staring at Adam's phone for so long, she almost didn't recognize the buzz of her own cell. The rattle of plastic and glass was a reminder of her obligations to the Charmer. If she still worked at the retirement home, requesting leave would be as simple as a form and a promise to keep others updated. She might earn an on-the-books paycheck from the soul-renting gig, but it didn't come with a 401K or any time off.

Becoming an apprentice to the Soul Charmer had not given her freedom from collections duty. She now had more to do without Derek at her side. She missed his casual lethality, and the way it put clients in the mood to remit.

He hadn't returned yet. She texted him. "Any luck?"

Derek's response pinged back almost immediately.

"Plates were stolen."

Well, shit.

"Recent. Am looking into the victim," his next message read.

Derek had connections to get access to the Gem City PD files. He should be able to dig into this without putting himself in danger. At least that's what Callie told herself. Only three people knew Derek had bombed Ford's properties: Callie, Derek, and the Soul Charmer. None of them were going to speak the words aloud, but lying low still felt necessary. Ford's crew—was she supposed to start thinking of them as Nate's?—weren't dumb. They knew who had grudges, and the Soul Charmer was top of that list.

Callie needed to make a move without catching attention. She needed to do it without Derek. He could stay busy on one angle, and she'd take the other more dangerous one. It was about time she started protecting him the way he did for her.

The alerts on her phone showed four overdue souls. Three in the suburbs and one in the Railyard district had her name on them. Her scavenger hunt through Adam's messages gave her an idea. She opened the full log, and scrolled through the locations. Beck had almost as many repos assigned, but one caught Callie's eye. Johnny Rocks—probably not his real name—was one of the hardcore tweakers who still held a fervent belief in God. He was determined to rise to Heaven—just as soon as he finished getting high on earth. Callie and Derek had picked up from him before. Some days Johnny Rocks was docile and an easy pick up. Other days, though? You better know how to dodge punch.

Callie peeked at her watch. Beck usually hit up the Charmer in the early morning. He'd drop off the previous night's collections, and get his face-time with the boss. If Callie could get down there soon enough, she could catch him.

It had finally stopped snowing, but the grey sky was tinged with enough green to tell her this was merely a short intermission. Someone had scattered chunky salt rock on the steps and sidewalk outside her apartment, which would have been nice if they ever remembered the parking lot. Especially as Callie's Chuck Taylors didn't offer much grip. She edged down the stairs slowly, and plotted a path out to her car. Once she stepped out of the breezeway, ice became the least of her problems. A trio of black-and-white police cruisers was parked near building nine. Callie lived in building ten. The cherries atop the cop cars weren't flashing. Uniformed officers clustered at the opening of the other building's breezeway. Yellow and black tape partitioned the entrance, and laid claim on the space. Callie averted her gaze before she appeared too interested. She *was* interested. She didn't spot Grady or Ortega, which meant maybe this didn't have to do with her. Cops at your apartment complex wasn't ever a good sign.

Callie slowly shuffled the soles of her sneakers across the icy patches and into the parking lot. Mrs. Rios stood behind her son's truck. She puffed a cigarette, and watched the police. She nodded at Callie. "You believe this shit?"

"What happened?" Concealing curiosity was more complex than people gave it credit for.

Mrs. Rios, who lived two apartments down from Callie, let out a long breath. Smoke and steam from the cold rushed from her lips before she answered. "That squirrelly guy with the glasses and the noisy car. You know the one?"

Callie didn't know his name either. "Yeah."

"He killed his girlfriend and then himself."

"Damn." How did people get to that point? How did that happen? Callie had done a lot of desperate things, but even at her lowest she couldn't fathom *that*.

"Been listening to the cops. Sounds like the guy's fingerprints don't match his file. He's got a record for something. Guess he's one of the soul users." Mrs. Rios shook her head. "I know this ain't Evergreen Estates, but you'd think they'd do a background check on people before letting the move in here."

Callie mumbled an agreement. Placating her neighbor wasn't a priority. A soul user had killed his girlfriend and himself. If his fingerprints were still jacked, he still had a borrowed soul in him when he died. This was not fucking good. How did the match go so wrong? How did this guy get the wrong soul? The Charmer was careful. He had protocols to avoid this. He wasn't perfect—shit—but this was bad. If they thought the cops were interested in soul magic before, the heat about was about to flip full inferno.

She needed out. She needed to find Nate, get her mom back, and get the fuck out of the soul rental business.

<hr>

Beck was pacing in the front room of the Soul Charmer's emporium. Callie's Chucks sunk into the carpet, but any sound was lost behind the *squish-suck-plop* refrain from Beck's heavy circuit.

"You okay?" she asked out of habit. Everyone asked that question these days, and everyone lied when they answered. Politeness with the promise of abdication. Those who truly knew us didn't have to ask.

Beck slowed his path, but didn't stop. His noncommittal shrug the same lie Callie would have offered. Where Derek was blunt bat with a metal core, Beck was lean muscle wrapped around rebar.

"Fair enough," she said to herself. Louder, to Beck, she asked, "You waiting on the Charmer?"

Even her small talk was salty.

Beck stopped pacing. The floor whined beneath him. "Always these days. He's double-checking the souls I brought back. Like I'd bring the wrong ones."

Beck wasn't as adept with soul magic as Callie was, but he had the ability to use one of the retrieval containers. Its magic did the work for him. She and Beck were the only two who could use the latent magic in the container to pull a rented soul from its host. Derek had tried to take in the Charmer's magic before, and the result was a lot of vomit and a sore stomach. Maybe that's why she understood Beck's frustration. At least she was able to command souls on her own. At least she had some leverage against the Charmer. Beck didn't hold the man's magic in his belly. He didn't burn like vellum in a lantern near an open soul. He couldn't bring back the renter's real soul. Even her flask didn't have that kind of power.

Bursting through a curtained doorway shouldn't have been possible. There was no thud of wood against wall and no heavy thwack of palm against wood, but The Soul Charmer managed to slam the curtain aside with enough force to shock a sharp wind from between the folds.

"Your souls will do," he said to Beck.

The Charmer dropped a flask on the countertop. The jade exterior connected with a dead clunk against the surface. His flask was larger than Callie's, but far less ornate. The green gemstone wrapped around the container in four thin bands between the brushed aluminum. Beck didn't move to touch the thing. His fingers twitched at his side. They were far larger than the stone strips. Would he ever feel the hum of magic stored within the device? A rented soul behind Callie's sternum hadn't felt like anything to her, but even now her flask, with its rich onyx exterior, warmed and pulsed inside her pocket.

The Soul Charmer turned toward Callie so slowly his spine should have creaked. Red streaks shot through his eyes, but his inky black pupils were sharp. Watching. "Calliope. About time you came back. I agreed to take you on as an apprentice, *pay* you, and yet I have more than a dozen souls missing from my shelves. Did you think you could simply steal my magic, and then ignore your responsibilities?"

Callie had never had the Charmer turn an accusation on her, but it wasn't the first time she'd been blamed for bullshit. Zara had been damn good at making everything Callie's fault. What did it say about her that she knew had to navigate this kind of irrational anger?

She inclined her head, a deferential move, and then said, "I came here as usual. I'll get your souls like normal."

Normal. Usual. Fucking lies. None of this mattered, but she needed this magic, this power on her side. She needed to keep the Charmer calm and firmly aligned with her. If Nate asked for more, she'd need that assurance. She'd need access. She'd need souls. She'd need to be able to do whatever was necessary to save Zara.

"The churn is too much," the Charmer whispered. The words meant little to Callie, but she knew better than to ask for an explanation. He dropped a heavy hand onto the counter.

"Bring back everything you can," he said to Callie. Then to Beck he added, "Send in more business."

"I thought you wanted us collecting," Callie said before she thought things through. Yet again.

"*My* business isn't simply retrieving souls. It's finding them homes, hosts." Simple words packed with the punch of memory. The image of souls stretching against the well's barrier flashed to the forefront of Callie's mind. It was gone just as quickly.

"More hosts." Beck nodded. "Got it, boss."

The Charmer was already moving back past the curtain when he called back, "Be back before it gets busy."

It wasn't clear which of them he was speaking to, but both Callie and Beck remained quiet for a dozen long breaths. Tendrils of smoke rose from the tips of the incense on the counter. Steady, slow plumes. Tension bracketed Callie's neck. When the air didn't waver, she relaxed enough to refocus on Beck.

"I didn't think he could be more volatile, but I guess sleep deprivation is that much of a bitch." Callie could muster fake confidence more quickly these days. She sounded unconcerned, even let the corner of her mouth tick up in an almost amused movement. Her heart was working overtime, but Beck couldn't see that.

Beck shoved a hand through his thick, dark hair. "Then he needs to pop a damn Xanax or double dose some melatonin."

She fought the urge to roll her shoulders. To loosen muscles and her mind. He didn't have to hide the harsh halos around his eyes with concealer. When your body exuded physical malice, you didn't need to cover up your flaws. Every mark, even those of fatigue, could disarm the enemy.

"I actually came to see you." Her strained voice shivered.

That got his attention. Hazel eyes fixed on her. "Why?"

Hell. She came here to ask him for a favor. Passing one another in the shop didn't count as knowing each other, though. He rocked on his heels, and she could almost see the way his legs flinched, ready to run. The first time she'd seen Beck he had been coming up from the shop's basement after securing the Charmer's rival Tess. She doubted he remembered what the Charmer had gotten Callie to do then, what she'd done to Tess in that room, why she'd done it. She wasn't sure if that knowledge would help or hurt her today.

"I've got a 'burb retrieval from Jose. You know the stockbroker guy who wears those khaki slacks that the golf nerds down the mountain love?" She was rambling. She needed to focus. "That guy's wife exhausts me."

Beck chuckled, but those eyes remained wary.

"I don't want to go out there. I saw you had Johnny Rocks on your list today. Happy to swap."

"You want that sketchy addict?" He didn't hide his curiosity. Callie had only been in this business for weeks, but she already knew curiosity usually ended with shit on fire.

She edged behind the counter, and pulled out the stash box filled with incense. There were three lit in the front room, and the one nearest the door was burned to the stub. *Hands busy, eyes down.* Faking low-key vibes would only work if she could hide her weariness. Opening the door for him to ask about what was going on, to wonder why she *really* wanted to spend her morning seeking out a couch-surfing tweaker, would only further complicate things. Her life already was taking on chess master-level complexities, and she was purely a checkers girl.

"He likes me. Makes it an easy pick up. Plus no chance of running into Jose's wife Melinda." Callie edged past him to place the fresh incense in the holder.

For the first time since the Charmer's blustery exit, Beck's shoulders eased. "She isn't that bad."

Callie turned to watch Beck from over her shoulder. She didn't have to lie when she said, "Last time she almost hit me with a vase."

"She threw a vase at you?" Wariness melted away, replaced by a keen sharpness. The Soul Charmer didn't hire idiots. You didn't stay out of jail or with your soul long in this building if you couldn't read a person.

"Not at me. At Jose. But I had the flask on him at the time." Amusement laced her words, and Beck bought them. None of this was funny. Jose and Melinda weren't funny, but the story at least wasn't a lie.

"All right, Callie girl, I'll swap the junkie for the philanderer with the angry wife."

So he *did* know Jose. Melinda hadn't been mad about the soul renting. Derek had collected cash from her before. No, Jose's wife was pissed he was using the soul to step out on her without having to confess to their priest. Of all the parts of that situation to be mad at. Callie shook her head at the memory.

Callie slipped out the front door before the Charmer could pop his head out again and demand some fresh absurdity from her. Tracking down Johnny Rocks wasn't going to be quick, but if anyone knew where to find the guys with the good meth, the guys who would know Nate, and who would be legitimately scared of her, it was him.

All she had to do was find the junkie.

That would be easier to do if she'd found him more than once. Last time Johnny Rocks had been beatboxing outside Deco's, a local arcade. He'd told her he liked the lights. He'd tried to pet her hair. He'd been very high. Other than being too touchy-feely for her tastes, he'd been an easy repo.

Once back in her car, she cranked the heater. While she waited for the car to warm, Callie texted Derek. "You still busy?"

She'd planned to do this on her own, but his help wasn't horrible. She wasn't about to admit it to Derek, but not eating or sleeping was taking a toll. Acid churned in her stomach, and her belly let out a grumbling plea. She popped open the center console, and pulled an energy shot out. She knocked back the liquid, and hoped the organic pep shit wouldn't rot her veins.

Derek didn't answer her question, just replied, "Tell me where to meet you, doll."

His devotion warmed something in her. Maybe her brain was going gooey, but she couldn't help but smile. Even with Zara missing, even after Josh was an asshole, even knowing what lay ahead.

"Taco time," she replied, and could already imagine his grin in response.

The greasy little taco shop had a different name, but a dozen years ago ran a promotion with a guy in a cartoon taco suit with an oversized watch dangling around his neck. The little pieces of matching pasts that she and Derek shared aligned in simple ways, but they mattered to her.

Derek confirmed he'd meet her at the south side taco shop in twenty minutes. Callie pulled away from the curb, and hoped Derek could help her find Johnny Rocks quickly. Finding someone who knew Adam was essential. Josh might not be willing to give her a possible address for Nate, but she wasn't afraid to push Johnny Rocks to get her one.

It'd been five days since her mother's fingers had been delivered. Mob medical teams were not remarkable. Zara needed her. Time had to be running out. Callie would not let Zara die. She would not let Nate take her mother from her. Callie gritted her teeth. Now wasn't the time to let blame drip down her bones.

Souls, fire, drugs. Whatever it took to get her to Nate, to Zara, she was going to do.

CHAPTER EIGHT

Tacos couldn't solve everything—they weren't pie—but they sure didn't hurt. Derek had arrived at Alberto's first, and ordered Callie two of the shredded beef tacos. The food was plain, but still decadent in a dripping-grease-everywhere kind of way. Callie ate one of the tacos without question, and Derek relaxed. Seeing his jaw ease and his shoulders soften reminded her how much he was willing to bear. The bombings weighed on him still. His arms would twitch in his sleep, and his lips would curl down in a childlike pout, and though they didn't speak of it in the mornings, she knew he was remembering placing the blast caps, igniting the fuses, running.

She didn't want that life for him any longer. They'd agreed they were getting out from under the Soul Charmer, but that was an easier goal when mobsters weren't disappearing with your family and when you didn't know the people protecting unattached souls.

They didn't speak of these things while they crunched through the fried corn tortilla shells. There was something to be said for savoring the silence. Unfortunately it couldn't last.

Callie crunched the paper taco wrapper into a small ball. She bit the end of her soda straw, but didn't sip. Finally, she said, "I need to find Johnny Rocks."

Derek groaned, and eased back into the rigid metal chair.

"I swapped with Beck," she added before he could suggest he take care of dragging the guy into the shop on her behalf.

He stared at her for a long moment. "Do I want to know?"

Probably not. "We need to find Nate. Adam's phone didn't tell me a whole lot." She paused just too long, and Derek snatched the thread.

"What did it tell you?"

Callie's toes curled inside her Chucks, but she managed not to squirm. Derek wouldn't judge her. Why was this so hard?

"Josh was in the phone. I called him, and he wasn't helpful. And he's all set on hiring an investigator, and wouldn't tell me where to find Adam or Nate, and he knows Adam because he works with the guy's brother, but he wouldn't tell me where safe houses were or give me any leads and it was pointless," she ripped through the truth.

Derek didn't flinch or pull away. He simply nodded.

"I told him it was his turn to help," she added softly, shame squeezing the words.

"Hey." He reached a scarred hand out and lifted her chin until her gaze met his again. "It's hard to tell the ones we love they're hurting us. Hard to call them on their bullshit. I'm proud of you."

Whenever soul renters blabbed about the sensation of taking on an extra soul, they sang about the light in their chest, the lift, the reprieve from whatever crushing concerns held them back from what they wanted most. It was like a guilt-free euphoria, supposedly. Callie hadn't gotten as much as an endorphin high the one and only time she'd had a second soul wedged in her body. This, though? Right now? It was the closest she'd come to that rush. It wasn't that her body warmed so much as that her ribs expanded on a fully oxygenated breath and in that newfound space lightness built scaffolding along the ribs. Each inhale was easier. Callie couldn't remember the last time someone outside the family had said they were proud of her. Fuck. She couldn't remember the last time anyone was proud of her. Derek didn't say shit like that to score points. Tears prickled along her lower eyelids. She sucked in a quick breath through her nose, and hoped her sinuses would get the "hold that shit in" message.

Derek simply smiled at her. "It's okay. I've got you, doll."

"Thanks" might not have been the right answer to anyone else, but Derek's chest expanded and from the other side of the table it sure looked like satisfaction.

"I guess we need to find Johnny Rocks then," Derek said without a hint of irritation.

He continued, "But I want to look through Adam's phone later, too. There might be more info to squeeze from it."

They left Callie's car outside the taco shop, and swapped for Derek's car. He didn't drive it often, but it was too damn cold to be on the motorcycle. It was a basic black and both the right level of new to be quiet and the right level of old to be forgettable. The interior heated more quickly and thoroughly than hers. She tugged off her gloves. The car bumped its way down a two-lane road on the edge of town before turning into Gem City's industrial corridor.

The pawnshop they pulled up to had iron bars over the windows and a neon pink sign in the window proclaiming, "We Buy Gold." Callie's few pawnshop experiences had been about recovering important items her brother had put up for cash. The diamond studs their grandmother had left Zara had cost Callie quite a bit to get back, but heirlooms and legacies were worth the money. Zara had yet to give them to Callie, and considering the way they parted and her mother's current predicament, those earrings might never make it to Callie's hands. Whatever. She shook the errant thought away. Diamonds were nothing compared to her mother's life. She had to focus. Johnny Rocks. Adam. Nate. Zara.

If only it could be that simple.

The door buzzed to admit them. The interior of the shop was bright, and the tile floor polished. She'd often suggested the Charmer's emporium was a pawnshop for souls, but his place was much darker. Callie and Derek edged along one wall covered with an array of guitars, a sitar, two trumpets, and a lone trombone. A quick scan proved the store empty aside from the clerk. He was the most average guy she'd seen in ages. Shorter than Derek, slim build with pudge around the middle, and a short beard. The case behind him held dozens of firearms. Callie's pulse sped, but she figured that was the point. Mr. Average wasn't intimidating, but having rifles at the ready put him in a position of power.

"Can I help you folks?" he asked, not moving from behind the counter.

Derek barely moved. His hands were at his side, but he stretched his fingers back toward Callie. She slipped her hand into his, and he squeezed twice. He'd read the room, too. Callie was fine with letting him do the talking.

"Hey, Greg. We're looking for Johnny. You seen him lately?"

One didn't get into the pawn business if they scared easily or were a shitty liar.

"Johnny?" Greg didn't bother hiding his sneer.

Derek's back vibrated against Callie's shoulder, but this grumble didn't reach anyone's ears. "Johnny Rocks. Found him here a few months back. He's late on owing my boss, which usually means he's looking to sell something good to you."

Derek's eyes were narrowed, and Greg's did the same. Whatever had happened last time, these two weren't friends.

"I don't buy from thieves."

"Didn't say he was a thief. Just said he has debts to pay."

"I also don't do business with people who can't pay."

"Fine. You see Johnny, though, can you nudge him in the Soul Charmer's direction as you boot him out the door?"

Greg offered a slow nod.

Callie started to move toward the door, but Derek squeezed her hand once more and she stopped.

"You want to extend your term while I'm here? Looks like you're a little lacking in employees to cover for you." If Callie hadn't known Derek didn't steal, she'd have thought he was making a threat.

Greg shuffled beneath the counter, and Callie regretted eating the taco earlier. Her stomach plummeted.

Long quiet seconds passed until Greg lifted a hand. Green bills peeked from within his palm. "I've got four hundred. How long will that add?"

Derek released Callie's hand, and walked slowly to Greg. He accepted the wad of cash and shoved it in his pocket without counting it. "The Charmer will let you keep it for another month since you're such a loyal customer."

The front door lock buzzed loudly. Callie and Derek exited. No Johnny Rocks and no souls, but four hundred dollars richer.

Once they were back inside the privacy of the car Callie asked, "What was all that about?"

"He's kept the same rented soul now for months." He turned the key, and the engine fired.

"What? Doesn't that defeat the point a bit?" How would someone be able to escape guilt if it was always in them? Which soul would be absolved at confession if there were no breaks? How did it stay clear which soul was which?

"Whatever he did, he says he doesn't want anyone else to know about it or to feel it if they rent the soul."

"That sounds like a load of bullshit."

Derek's laugh curled around Callie's ears, but his arm slid behind her and pulled her close. The heater began to churn warm air. "It does. I asked the Charmer about it once."

She leaned into the crook of his shoulder. "And?"

"He said sometimes the souls are too similar. He tries to keep it from happening, but they can become attached. The rented soul doesn't want to leave, and Greg's soul is fine with it, from what I understand."

"So we couldn't take the rented soul back?" Only now Callie realized she didn't feel the push of heat from Johnny's rented soul, she didn't hear it calling for a home.

"Charmer could probably force it, but he said it's easier to let the guy keep paying a low rate. Good for business."

"Only the Charmer would fuck up matching the right soul for someone and then still make the guy pay."

"Money's money, doll."

Given that her bank account was steadily in the black for the first time in her life, she wasn't about to argue.

The next three stops went similarly. No guns, no souls, and no Johnny Rocks. The sun began to crawl behind the mountains. Callie would have done another energy shot, but the handful she purchased were inside her car. She stifled a yawn.

"Let's head back to your place for a bit," Derek suggested.

Her place. Ugh. The flashing cherries and the black body bag. "Shit. I didn't tell you."

"Tell me what?"

"A thing happened." Callie hesitated. It wasn't that she didn't want to tell him as much as it was she didn't know if it even mattered anymore. Had Mrs. Rios' known what she was talking about? Derek's brows drew together, and it was enough to make her talk. "So a guy murdered his girlfriend and himself in the complex this morning."

Derek's jaw hardened, but his tone was gentle. "Damn. You know them?"

She didn't know most of her neighbors, and rather

liked it that way. "No, but supposedly the guy's finger-prints didn't match his file."

Derek's slow nod probably mirrored her own. The realization of what it meant. Of the potential impact was creeping into his cortex. "Did the police ask you anything?"

"Nah. I booked it. I only know what happened be-cause one of my nosy neighbors was in the parking lot. The cops didn't see me." At least she hoped they hadn't.

"I'll keep an ear out on this, but we should still hit your place. A little rest isn't going to kill you, doll." The words were delivered with sweetness, but the slash of worry beneath them was poorly concealed.

"We have to find Johnny Rocks. Soul Charmer was worked up this morning," she said, like this wasn't an-other way to solve her own problems.

"We will. I want to peek at Adam's phone. Might give us a lead for Nate and for Johnny." He was con-fident and casual, and Callie realized she could see past both. He wasn't lying, exactly, but the strain in his forearms and the hint of a furrow at his brow said he was worried about her.

"Fine. We can stop for a half hour or so. Then we have to get back out there."

"Do you want to pick up your car?"

She'd almost forgotten. "You planning on leaving me?" She'd said it as a joke, but her chest tightened while she waited for his response.

"Never, doll. We'll get it later."

The police had been long gone from the apartment complex when they pulled into the lot. The crime scene tape only covered the late neighbors' door now. It was almost hidden. Almost. Callie pretended she couldn't see it, and quickly they were upstairs and inside Callie's apartment. Derek nudged the thermostat up a few notches before Callie was more than a couple feet inside the door. She didn't call him on it. Not like they were going to stay in the house that long. She eased off her coat, and laid it over the arm of the sofa.

Derek sprawled on the seat next to her coat. His boots nudged the edges of her coffee table, but he didn't put them on top. "Do you have the phone?"

"Sure. I went through all the messages and the list of his contacts. He doesn't use anyone's name, and the texts were dollar figures and times. Only one close to anything was one asking about picking up burritos."

She picked it up from the counter, and thumbed the screen on. "I probably wouldn't have recognized Josh, but he's had that same phone number since I was a kid."

Callie took two steps toward Derek and then stopped.

One missed call.

One voicemail.

"There's a new voicemail." She didn't recognize her voice. She stared at the small phone icon. Derek came to her side.

"This is good. Anyone brave enough to leave a voicemail is probably also dumb enough to leave details about what they're buying and where."

She held her thumb above the screen. "Right. Shall I?"

When Derek agreed, she tapped the voicemail icon and toggled on the speakerphone.

"This is a message from Nate…"

Callie didn't hear the rest of the recording. The phone slipped from her fingers, and dropped to the carpet. She forgot how her legs worked. Her knees shuddered. Her stomach became stone. High, but packed with gristle, Callie would have known that voice anywhere.

The message was from Nate, but the voicemail was Zara.

CHAPTER NINE

Callie's knees slammed against the floor. The threadbare carpet did nothing to blunt the fall. Her hands fumbled to grab the phone.

Her fingers were unable to find the right button.

Unable to stop the muffled sound of her mother's voice.

Unable to replay it.

Unable to do a goddamned thing.

Derek picked up the phone and tapped the pause button. He sucked his bottom lip in until his mouth was a bitten line of focus. Callie slid back over her heels and let her rear find the carpet, too. About right that she'd end up crawling before she could get Zara back. Pride didn't do a thing when you were already broken.

Tears began to track down her cheeks. Her voice was a ghost. "We need to hear it." *I need to hear it.*

Derek scooted close to her. His shoulder bumped hers. The almost-there movement a reminder she wasn't alone. Most nights that was enough. Tonight wasn't most nights.

She nodded toward the phone, and he started the message from the beginning.

"I am alive for now." Zara's first words were clear, but slow. The syllables were off. Zara hadn't been much for reading aloud when Callie was a kid, and it was clear her practice hadn't gotten better.

Zara sucked in an audible breath on the recording. Callie mimicked the action. She could picture her mother pointing at some scrawled word, and hoping for an out. She must not have gotten one, because her mother continued. "He wants his soul back. Did you really take it?" the second question faster, quieter, and laced with fear. A slap of skin against bone rang. Zara hissed. Her next words were stuttered through heaving breaths. "You can do better than that. You have a big supply of souls at the ready. You'll bring him two extras."

Zara started to speak, and then paused. The sound was a screech of regret Callie could relate to, but not one she'd ever heard from her mother's mouth. Callie began crying in earnest. Derek draped an arm over her shoulders and pulled her tight to him, but they both remained fixed on the phone in his hand.

Adam's phone. Nate's words. Zara's voice.

"His soul. Two backups. Bring them to the cathedral corner by 10 p.m. or..." her mother's voice, shaking and soprano, shuttered.

It was replaced by the sour spit of Nate's sneering. "Bring them or your mommy dies tonight."

The recording was over, but neither she nor Derek moved. The last time Zara had been in this room, she'd been loud, she'd been angry, and she'd been vibrant. The woman on that recording was none of those things. Callie could count the number of times she'd seen her mom shed real tears—con job ones didn't count—and the number of times her mom had been scared was half that. This was worse. She'd never heard this pale, reedy Zara. Her mom wasn't an upstanding citizen. She had been far from the perfect mother. She didn't deserve this, though. No one did. Callie tried to swallow the sick slosh of her stomach ripping its way up her throat, but her body no longer had room for anything but guilt and ire. She stumbled to the bathroom and ditched her earlier food.

Once certain she was steady—or as steady as someone who got her mom kidnapped and just heard her threatened could be—she splashed cold water on her face. Derek stood in the bathroom's doorway. She was thankful he hadn't pushed in, but the ticking vein in his temple suggested he'd been watching and he was thinking.

"Tell me you have a plan," she said with the rasp of hot coals doused with water.

Derek's fingertips turned white against the doorframe. His answer ground out between gnashed teeth until the simple words were bloody. "Give him the fucking souls."

It sounded too simple. Probably *was* too simple,

but Callie needed a direct line out of this mess. "Okay," she started to nod slowly, but stopped a half second later. "One problem."

His brows pinched together in question.

"Flask is empty. I don't have shit to give him."

Derek swore under his breath. "We'll hit the Charmer's."

He had to realize how dumb of an idea that was. "You weren't there earlier today. He accused me of stealing his magic and of working against him. I don't need to get on the Charmer's bad side, too. We can't jack souls from his place."

Derek scrubbed a hand over his face, pausing to squeeze his forehead for a moment. When his hand fell away the hollows beneath his cheekbones were deeper. She wasn't the only one pushing her body to do more with less.

"I need to sit," he finally said.

Derek moved to the couch. Callie stopped at the refrigerator to pull a couple cold beers from inside. She popped the caps, and then came to sit with him.

She handed him a beer. "I'm too freaked out to think."

He drank down half the bottle in a single pull. She curled against him, and they leaned against the back of the couch and drank their beers. The ceiling fan overhead hummed a steady, slow buzz.

"So we need two souls."

"Three. Something has to stand in for Nate's," Derek said.

Callie tried not to squirm.

He turned to face her more fully. Concern etching across his face. "Right?"

"Actually, I have Nate's soul here. I snagged it last time I was in the back of the Charmer's. We were getting so close, and he's so squirrelly right now. I couldn't risk him renting it out."

The worry lines faded from her boyfriend's forehead. "Smart. Where is it?"

"Hall closet." She nodded toward the narrow, shitty, MDF door.

"So we need two souls in—" he peeked at his watch "—four hours or less."

"We need to wring everything we can out of the phone. You said you thought we could make some calls? If Nate knows we have it, we don't have much time."

Derek cut his hand through the air. "He wouldn't have tipped his hand with the voicemail if he hadn't already taken care of that."

"You think he's that smart?" Callie had met Nate enough times to know the guy was a slimy, straightforward kind of sleaze. He wanted in on soul magic. He'd been reading up on old religious texts not long before she'd yanked out his soul. He carried that shit around with him. No shame. He made plain plays for women and drugs and power. No stealth. He demanded his soul back and then fucking disappeared. No smarts.

Derek shook his head. "He ain't dumb. If he really has taken Ford's guys on as his own, someone else would have done that. Maybe even Adam."

Callie finished her beer. She set the empty on the coffee table. "I've got three other markers to hit for souls today."

"Not counting Johnny Rocks?" Derek put his empty beer next to hers.

"Kind of pointless now." Callie couldn't hold back the defeat. She'd finally heard from Nate, but it hadn't been on the right terms. Hadn't been on terms at all. It wasn't that Callie was unfamiliar with being beholden to the whims of assholes, it was that the consequences now were bigger than her. It's one thing to fuck up your own life. It's another when it screws with family.

Derek didn't miss a beat. She wasn't alone. "Who are we after?"

"One in the Railyard, one near the plaza, and one more pickup in The Greens."

Derek groaned, and Callie smiled in turn. "I wish I could have swapped that one out with Beck, too, but it'll be easy."

The Greens was a neighborhood backing up to a golf course. It had gated entrances, full-time security guards, and grass in the desert. It was fucking obnoxious. The people who lived there never returned their rentals, as if part of the cost was her hauling her ass out to their homes. Soul renting was pitched as sidestepping sin, but it shouldn't be so damn convenient.

"We'll start out there." If she didn't know him better, she'd have thought Derek was whining about it. Instead she knew he was running scenarios. The quiet ones had a lot going on inside. Callie should have known that the day she met him.

"If we work our way in," Callie said following his logic, "we'll have the plaza pickup as a last-ditch option if Sharon or Casey aren't home."

They shrugged back on their coats. Callie tucked her flask into her side pocket, and then pulled the jar containing Nate's soul from the closet hiding spot. She didn't know if it was having a plan or drinking a beer in a handful of minutes, but the sharp bite of her nerves had dulled.

Now all she had to do was collect some souls and save her mom.

***

Sharon Wilson's house had enough rooms to sleep everyone in Callie's apartment complex, but a lone SUV sat in the winding driveway. A plump, petite woman with white hair opened the door. Callie stumbled back a half step as icy shards prickled beneath her skin. This woman wasn't Sharon, but she sure as shit was a soul user. A long-time user based on the powerful reaction Callie had. Derek angled himself between her and the woman at the door. Callie used the reprieve to get her hand on the flask. The device purred against her palm and pulled some of the cold from her arms.

The woman turned to lead them into the home.

Derek leaned close to Callie's ear and whispered, "You solid?"

She tried not to bristle. There was no judgment, just worry. "Wasn't expecting that."

He arced a brow.

"Heavy user."

The rough scrape of an "oh" comforted her.

They passed four ornate and never-touched rooms before a well-dressed woman in navy blue stepped into the hallway. Her auburn hair was in a perfect twist. The chill skating across Callie's skin met the heated rush of magic. Her fingertips tingled with an urge for action.

"Now is not a great time," Sharon cooed with the confidence of someone who is used to being obeyed.

Derek's stony visage exuded more fuck you than usual. "We're here already."

"We were just sitting down to dinner. If you could return in a couple hours, I'd be happy to return the item." Sharon's conspiratorial whisper dug into Callie's skin in a way the magic didn't.

"You're already late on returning. I'll take it now," Callie said. She let vehemence simmer plainly. She might be angry and scared because of Nate, but she had no shame at leveraging it with this woman who thought her life, her time was more important than everyone else's.

Sharon gave Callie more attention then. The temptation to call the magic to her hands, to see if she could force some flames, rallied in her chest. That fire was for someone else, and she was really trying to be less of an asshole.

"I said—"

Callie pulled the flask from her pocket, popped the cap, and powered it against Sharon's chest in a fluid movement. The woman gaped and squealed. Callie knew the act wasn't hurting her. The soul leaped into the container. Frost began to nudge its way back over her palms. Callie tightened her grip on the flask.

"The Soul Charmer appreciates your patronage." The saccharine response her own middle finger to Sharon, this house, her boss, her magic, and her goddamn situation.

One soul down, one to go.

CHAPTER TEN

Derek's car idled quietly on El Paseo. He and Callie were parked only a few feet from where they'd watched the drug dealers shop their wares the night before. Dougie's corner was empty, but Adam stood tall in the same place they'd met him yesterday. Callie saw him more clearly now. There was no slouching, gangly frame. He didn't curl his chin into his coat—a new one in shiny black. Smugness seeped with each languid step he took. Even from a block and a half away the cockiness was overpowering.

He had the right to be. He'd escaped last night. His boss had backed him. Hell, now he got to be the one handling Nate's very soul. Whether the mafia boss had told him so didn't matter. They were trusting this guy with something vital. Callie hadn't taken him seriously enough.

Scoring the second soul hadn't been too hard. The

Charmer wouldn't be happy, but that was a problem for future Callie. Making the Soul Charmer mad tomorrow was better than making her mother dead. So fuck it. She'd shove these souls in Adam's hands and take back her mother.

She scanned the steps in front of the cathedral and the pockets of light near each corner out front. "Zara doesn't seem to be here."

"I'm sure Nate's watching," Derek said.

"How can you be so confident?" She wasn't.

Derek licked his lips quickly. "It's what I would do. Smart business to watch over something important like this."

"Oh."

"Well, and he's got a fucking hard-on for you, so he'll be here to see you." Derek spat the accusation. He'd intervened with Nate before on her behalf, but never mentioned it. Now his eyes narrowed. Jealousy wasn't supposed to be hot, but Callie didn't have time for supposed to.

"At least we won't have to talk to him, and he'll have to see you at my side." She added the last part only to see his reaction. He licked his lips again, but slower this time.

"You're not wrong, doll."

Callie rested the flask in her lap, and pulled the jar with Nate's soul from a pocket. The obsidian jar was opaque and the silver cap screwed on tight, but the sickly sweet call from within the container wasn't dampened. It begged for entry into her body. Not a home. Not safety. It wanted to be in her.

She glared at the jar, and focused her thoughts, "Never happening."

Callie reached to open the car door, but paused before pulling the handle. "I can't give Nate the flask."

"Shit. No, you can't."

Callie scanned the car's interior for something, anything to put the extra souls into. Leave it to Derek to have a goddamn pristine ride. "Do you have anything in here?"

He flipped open the center console, and then pulled out a travel sized stick of deodorant.

If it weren't so categorically unhelpful, she might have laughed. "That won't work."

C'mon brain.

"What about the jar?" Derek suggested.

"It's already got Nate's soul in it," she said automatically.

"I've seen the Charmer slip a second soul in the same jar before."

Callie couldn't tell if he was lying. What would happen if more than one soul was stored together? Could the others be damaged by Nate's soul? The dashboard clock gave her fifteen minutes to get the souls into Adam's hand.

"Screw it." Callie uncapped the flask. Her hands heated immediately. The souls were bound in the magic of the flask, but two of them together already had ash sloughing from her skin.

She pinned the flask upright between her thighs, and prayed her jeans wouldn't singe before she could get this completed. She gripped the obsidian jar in one hand, and twisted the silver cap off with the other. Black flakes clung to the cap. She ignored the disintegration of her skin, and focused only on the thin tendrils of white swirling within the container. The soul immediately lurched toward the lid. Flames sprung from Callie's knuckles. She ignored them. She didn't ask or coax Nate's soul. Even if he would have responded to that, he didn't deserve her kindness. She shoved her power at the lid, choked the opening with a command to stay. A pulse of magic wobbled at the lip, and the flames on her fingers died.

Callie wasn't sure how long she could hold this. Beads of sweat made her lower back sticky. She kept her gaze fixed on the mouth of the jar, but dropped one hand down to the top of the flask. She picked it up without leaving too much soot on her pants, and then delicately poured the souls into the jar.

She had to coo soft encouragement to them, but eventually they slid past the barrier and into the jar. Her hand holding the jar flashed a bright blue, and then smoldered with the heat of a cooktop. Her skin started to blacken, but she slapped the cap onto the jar as quickly as possible with her other hand. When it was secure, the flame died out, and her flesh began to repair to a rich brown. If only the wounds on her heart could heal so quickly.

She stared at the little jar. Tried to ignore the pleas from within. She swallowed hard.

"How are we going to do this?"

Derek took the jar from her, offering a reprieve from the worrying calls within. "Together."

Callie and Derek walked around the back of the cathedral before approaching Adam. They didn't need him getting an eye on the car or knowing how they'd exit, if they could help it. Derek's exhales lit the air, a dragon on the war path. The November chill no longer bit at Callie. Simmering magic had staked its claim and denied entry to all other sensations.

Adam turned toward them, his coat shining like wet ink beneath the halo of the low-hanging street lamp. Acrid anger hit Callie at the sight of the cocky dealer grinning at them from a post fifty feet from the church. There was likely a law on the books to drive him further away from holy places and schools. Laws didn't do a whole lot if they weren't enforced, though. Hell, they didn't do much for her. She couldn't turn Nate in for kidnapping her mom. She couldn't send the cops to his door. The cops hadn't touched Ford, and she had no reason to think they'd want to move on Nate either, but more importantly, Nate knew too much. He had leverage. He could turn her in. When you acted outside the law, you couldn't rely on it. Callie sniffed, but it didn't dislodge the odor. Fighting to escape a home where crime was the norm had been hard, but now she was back consorting with criminals. She couldn't even blame someone else for this. She'd taken Nate's soul. No one told her to. No one forced her hand.

Adam preened. Pride practically poured from his ears.

"Where's Nate?" she asked. She kept six feet between them. Out of arm's reach, but also far enough to dampen any soul magic fire or freeze.

"You don't get to ask stuff like that," Adam practically sang.

Good thing Callie had lost all sense of pride in the ER the night she'd been fired. "Whatever. I've got his shit. Where's mine?"

"Can't say. Boss said to be here and collect the souls." The envy in the words made her think he'd rather work for the Soul Charmer, but also that he had no idea he was gathering his boss's soul.

Derek's elbows edged out from his body. It was a subtle swell, both making himself larger to protect her and opening himself up in case of a fight. What had he seen that made him think body shots were on the agenda?

Callie tilted her head toward Derek. "Here's the souls."

Derek pulled the jar from his pocket and handed it over to Adam. The dealer's eyes were on the jar and not on the way Callie edged away from the action.

"They all in here?" Again, that awe.

"Yep. They don't take up that much space." She wasn't about to explain that she didn't know what state the souls would be in after their shared confinement.

Adam pocketed the jar. "You going to return my

shit, too?"

"No," Derek said with finality. "Where's Zara?"

"Nate said to give you this receipt, and that he'd be in touch once he verified the souls—whatever the fuck that means—to return the woman." *The woman.*

Adam handed Callie a long envelope. It was folded in half. While the paper wasn't flat, it wasn't wide enough to have another appendage in it. Thank fuck.

She peeked inside the paper, and almost dropped the envelope. If her emotions hadn't already been pushed to their limits she might have screamed or cried or thrown something. A strip of blood-soaked cloth was the receipt. Beneath the dark red the paisley print of her mother's favorite peasant top peeked through.

Callie stared at the cloth, the message. Nate wanted to remind her not to screw him over. She hadn't planned on it, but now she wondered if Derek had taken out the wrong man.

She affixed her hardened gaze on Adam. "Thanks. I'll be waiting for Nate's call."

Callie turned her back to the dealer, to the cathedral, to fucking Gem City, and walked away.

CHAPTER ELEVEN

The world had a way of halting when you were waiting on an important call. Seconds ached and minutes burned. Hours were stretched over aged cactuses and pierced with spines. Callie and Derek had driven back to her apartment without speaking a word, and now time stuttered.

Inside the one-bedroom apartment with the deadbolt latched, Callie drew the first full, deep breath into her lungs in hours. Tension still trapped her tummy, but the rest of her body was loose enough to collapse onto the couch. Derek sat beside her. His upper lip *almost* twitched every few moments. The rest of his body was stock-still.

A thriller paperback—four days overdue at Gem City Library—rested on one corner of her low coffee table. The back cover promised vengeance, and Callie hoped she'd be able to relate soon.

Derek placed Adam's cell phone on the center of the table. The screen was dark.

"How long do you think it'll be?" The barren room amplified Callie's rasp. The heater sputtered as it kicked on, but even that rattle couldn't cover the desperation behind her voice. Derek wouldn't know any better than she would, but the need to control the situation was biting at her brain.

"It'll be fast, doll. Nate wants his soul back." Derek's certainty couldn't puncture Callie's fear.

"How's he even going to get it back in his body? How is he going to know if I gave him the real thing?"

Derek hesitated for a moment. His fingers fluttering against her leg. Finally, he said, "He was reading that Saint Petro book before. He's trying to figure out the soul shit on his own. Maybe he will try doing it himself?"

DIY soul magic had 'bad idea' all over it. The remembered cries of the souls smushed into the jar alongside Nate's rallied in Callie's ears. "The soul might do the work for him."

Or the others in that jar might shove that asshole's soul out.

It probably didn't work that way. It hadn't at the soul well, but something about the slimy sensation she'd suffered being near Nate's soul made her think it was possible. Maybe some people were so rotten even their souls couldn't be commanded.

"You know, doll, you can be fucking scary when you want to be these days." He'd meant it as a compliment, and the praise mingled with notes of admiration and a more sensual approval.

"We've got time to kill…." She cast a knowing glance toward the bedroom, but delivered the words with enough humor to make it clear she didn't mean it.

"We ain't missing that call." He stretched in a slow, languid movement. He dropped his arm behind her shoulders. "Seriously, I think Adam about shit a brick when you turned your back on him."

"Nate has something to hold over us, but not that guy." There had been a time when she would have buckled under the steady gaze of anyone who stuffed a box-cutter in their boot. Shit had changed. *She* had changed. Confidence was a necessity now. It was an invisible exoskeleton built to brace her from Gem City and its worst. Each strut and brace born of necessity. Shaped steel was dangerous when it was molten, but resilient when it cooled. Callie wasn't as hard as metal, but she was determined as fuck.

"No one gets to hold shit over your head, Callie, not for long. Nate will get his when this is over." It wasn't hyperbole, it was a vow.

Callie needed to stay focused. "We need to get through this first."

"I wish I'd taken out Nate when I had the chance." Regret ripped through the room.

She'd had the same thought. Would saying so change anything?

"No," she said. "This is on me. Stealing souls has consequences."

Derek pulled her close. Her cheek nestled against his shirt. Soft, clean, and warm. Home.

Callie closed her eyes. "We need to quit blaming ourselves, and start blaming the Charmer."

"Long game." The finality, the earnestness in the words was what she needed. She and Derek agreed to get out from under the Soul Charmer. They were buying time. Once they could, they'd get away from soul magic.

Once she had control of her abilities.

Once they had a plan.

They'd ditch all this bullshit.

Adam's phone buzzed. Callie startled at the harsh clunking of the vibration against her cheap-ass table. Derek's one-armed hug steadied her. She picked up the phone. Its screen was bright with a green bubble at its center.

One new message. Unknown number.

Callie damn near choked on her heart.

"It has to be him," she said with reverence reserved for the prayers of the faithful.

The message was scant. An address and a threat.

"'We're done for now.' Are you fucking kidding me?" Callie's incredulity rivaled her anger, and that was saying something.

Derek pulled up the address in his phone. "She's up north. Looks like he left her in the middle of the Pojoaque rez."

Callie blocked the taunting jab from Nate from her thoughts. Zara was waiting somewhere off the highway. "How fast can you get us there?"

Derek pulled off US-84 twenty minutes later, and the car grouched over the sandy dirt road. This spur from the main highway was sparse. No lights or pavement here, just dusty desert and nocturnal predators. They were on the reservation, but nowhere near any residences.

Being this close to Pojoaque and with Derek and a damn plan gone awry was too familiar. They were mere miles from the mystical shop Tess had worked out of. A shop where Derek had been stabbed. A place where Callie's life had changed. She'd discovered how deep her ties to Derek went, she'd discovered what she was capable of, she'd made allegiances. Did Nate know that? Did he know about Tess? Did he know what had happened to her? Why she'd disappeared?

Callie bit the inside of her cheek and dislodged the thought. Nate wasn't that fucking smart, she told herself.

Derek slowed the car. Snow shimmered in the headlights. "She should be here."

Callie didn't wait for more information. She hopped out her side of the car, and then yanked the zipper on her coat to her chin. "Mom?" she called loud enough a coyote should have called back.

The trunk slammed behind her. She spun, hoping to find her mother.

"Flashlight, doll." Derek lifted the device and

clicked it on. The rough, barren desert turned a ghastly grey in the artificial light.

Together they called for Zara. Five minutes stretched into five years. Callie's pleas for her mother became more frantic. Her ribcage seemed to shrink with each passing second until Callie's breaths were coming rapid-fire and her head was going light.

A shadow shifted to her right. "I need the flashlight over here."

Derek was at her side, flashlight at the ready.

Zara.

Mom.

Callie skidded onto her knees next to her mother. Frost formed on Callie's fingers, but she didn't bother reaching for the flask for warmth. Zara was curled in the fetal position. Callie called her name, but her mother barely stirred. Ice shot up Callie's arms, and her hands were now too stiff to articulate. None of that mattered. Her sinuses burned with the strain of holding back tears. She nudged Zara onto her side more fully and away from the lone juniper bush at her side. Dirt caked bloody streaks down Zara's face. Derek stepped closer with the flashlight, and the deep gouge at the crown of Zara's head was apparent. Blood continued to seep from it, though some of her hair was matted to staunch the flow.

"I've got some gauze in the trunk." Derek sat the flashlight against the dirt, and ran back to the car. *Thank God.*

"Mom, we have to get you out of here." Gauze

clung to Callie's icy fingers, but she pressed the clean side against the wound and hoped they weren't too late. Zara's eyelids fluttered, which was better than no reaction at all.

Derek hurried back, and dropped to his knees next to Callie. His breath was coming fast. His hulking shoulders shaking.

Callie hoped the cold from her hands might help slow the bleeding. Hazy purple bruises cut with raised red hash marks scored the right side of Zara's face. *What did they do to her?* Zara's hands were in black, knit mittens. How many fingers had she lost? How long could you go without them and still reattach? Callie had stored them just in case, but her memories of medical anything were blank right now.

Callie's voice was soft. "I know we can't take her to a hospital, but..."

"The fuck we can't. I'm not taking her to our back-up guy. Not your mom. We'll figure out how to deal with it when we get to the hospital." Derek pulled off his jacket. Goosebumps pebbled his skin the second the leather was free. The outline of his pecs was visible beneath his tee, even in the minimal light. He handed Callie the jacket, and then stooped to scoop Zara up into his arms. Callie was once again thankful of his strength because she didn't know how to do any of this, including carrying a wounded and unconscious person without hurting them.

He eased Zara into the backseat. "You ride with her. I'll get us to St. Vincent's as fast as I can."

It was the closest hospital, and Callie was thankful

for that. It was even close to Zara's house, which her mom would like too. Locals only.

Callie grabbed a few fresh squares of gauze, and climbed in next to Zara. Her mother was slumped over. A memory stabbed sharp between Callie's lower ribs, as if trying to skewer her spleen. Tess, again. It'd been Callie's car. The other woman bound on the floorboard. They'd shot her with tranquilizer darts, but she lolled at the same angle Zara did now. A stolen blanket had kept the blood from seeping into the floor mats then. Callie curled an arm around her mother. Moonlight streamed in from the window, turning the thin layer of ice coating Callie's hands into a shimmering blue. Tess had been tortured that night. She'd disappeared in the permanent way shortly after. All for wanting a piece of the soul rental business, for going up against the Soul Charmer. Zara wasn't in the market to take over organized crime. She was a pickpocket and a con woman, but not a team player. Would Nate have treated her the way the Soul Charmer had Tess? The gauze beneath Callie's fingers was already turning tacky, which suggested he had. Callie's cheeks burned, and she realized she was crying. She wasn't weeping over her fear or her worry or even her guilt. Callie tried tears of fucking anger, and each drop that rolled down here cheek was another nail in Nate's coffin.

Zara made a small whining sound. Callie needed to focus. She pressed the gauze more firmly against the wound. At least she was a human ice pack, but they needed real help for Zara.

Derek settled in behind the steering wheel. He was

taking them to the hospital, but that only traded one problem for another. How could they save her mother and still have a chance to stop Nate?

"Wait," Callie said.

The car was in drive, but Derek's foot was still on the brake. "What?"

"Josh."

"We can take her in, Callie. It's okay."

It wasn't, though. If they wanted revenge for this. If they wanted the chance to follow it through. If they wanted any fucking assurance that Nate wouldn't come after Callie's family or Derek's again, they needed to keep the cops out of it. The more police looking at Derek and into the Soul Charmer and into Ford's death, the more likely it was they'd end up in jail. Callie used to think prison would be the worst outcome. Now she feared what would happen to her family, to her city if she and Derek were locked up. What kind of hell would Nate bring to Josh and Father Henry? What kind of shit could happen if he tried to take on the Soul Charmer?

"No—"

"We can call your brother from the hospital." Derek flipped a U-turn and headed back toward Gem City.

"No. I mean, yes, we could, but he also could be the one to take her in."

CHAPTER TWELVE

The parking lot at St. Vincent's Hospital had fifteen lampposts in its parking lot. Callie waited underneath the only one with a burned out bulb. Enough snow had fallen to cover the concrete in the lot. She let the shadows shield her from immediate judgment. The hospital glowed bright as a bastion of hope. She'd worked in a hospital once, and even knowing where the astringent was stored and the sharps were disposed of and even having visited the morgue, the place had never lost its shiny hope.

The people working inside that building were saving lives. They were good people. She used to be one of them. She sucked in the shadows, letting the muddy darkness fill those empty holes in her chest. Now wasn't the time for sulking about missed opportunities. Now was about Zara. It was about family.

Josh had been waiting in the parking lot when she

and Derek arrived. He hadn't asked questions or be-rated her. Derek had extracted Zara from the car care-fully when Josh wasn't certain how to start. Bloody gauze and a few strands of Zara's long black hair had clung to Callie's palm. Her skin was warm again now, the cotton fibers long fallen away.

Josh had taken Zara inside, and about a half hour later had texted that their mom was going to be okay. He hadn't said more.

Not yet.

So Callie waited.

"You want to get back in the car, doll?" Derek asked. His jacket was open, and the heat from inside his sedan teased her through the open window.

"Not yet." She'd asked him to wait in the car earlier. She wasn't certain how much time had passed, but her nose wasn't completely numb yet. She needed the slap of the below-freezing temperatures to steady herself. She wasn't so sanctimonious to suggest she deserved the bitter bite of cold. She just didn't want to feel, and natural cold was far better at killing her senses than the magic-induced frostbite had been.

An ambulance screamed into the lot, and whipped around the corner to the brilliant red Emergency aw-ning. The red and white flashing lights almost touched her, but no one at that entrance was watching the park-ing lot. They had bigger priorities.

Derek opened his car door and stepped out next to her.

"I promise I'll come in soon," she said, her tone

flat. She'd come in once she had a plan. Callie had no idea what to do next. She needed sleep, but crashing out without knowing if Zara was conscious or what all was wrong wasn't an option. She couldn't go raging into the hospital to find out. She couldn't go to work. The Charmer needed souls. Souls she'd brokered to get her mom back. She hadn't even bothered trying to control her magic around her mother, which was a whole other problem. Moving into the car or into the light were her only paths right now, and so she stood still.

"Callie." His hand was on her shoulder. "Your brother is coming."

Sure enough, Josh's lanky, slouched silhouette was gilded from the glow past the sliding glass doors. Callie and Derek were at the back of the parking lot. Josh shouldn't have been able to see them yet, but he headed straight for them.

He scratched his head, tousling his hair. From the messy array, he'd only run his fingers through it before coming to the hospital. He approached quickly, but kept his gaze locked on the ground. "Hey."

Callie rushed forward to meet Josh at the edge of the shadows. She wrapped her arms around him, and held tight. Frost bit at her cheek against his chest and at her forearms embracing him. She willed the magic to *give me a fucking second*. His ribs pushed against her arms, even though his clothes. He hugged her back with a ferocity that squeezed the air from her lungs, and let her forget the magic glazing her with ice, the fear of the last several days, and the consequences of everything. Josh used to be her safe place, and for that half moment he was again. She'd missed that. Missed him.

Her joints were growing stiff from the magic. If only her brother could have avoided the Soul Charmer's wares. If only she knew how to repair a torn soul. She didn't, though, and so she had to back away. The hospital's beacon of light now loomed behind them, a stalwart reminder of how vastly shit had gone wrong.

Callie stepped back far enough to melt the ice on her skin, and to have Derek at her side. She wasn't quite steady yet when she asked, "Is she okay?"

Josh shoved both his hands into the single front pocket of his hoodie. He pushed them down until the rumpled cotton was taut over his shoulders. Only then did he look at Callie. His eyes were bloodshot. Whatever sibling bond they'd revived was already disintegrating.

"Her ribs are busted, and they put seven stitches in her head." He spat into the snow.

Facial wounds always looked more severe than they were, Callie reminded herself. Seven sutures on a forehead were about minimizing a scar, not worrying about big-time damage. Maybe this was something she could come back from. Maybe it's something they all could come back from.

Josh wasn't done, though. "She's missing fingers, Callie. *Fingers*."

Her brother had barricaded his fear, but the claw marks of its attempted escape were obvious in his too tight jaw and hardened gaze. Callie tried to cage her own. Burying the scream chiseling at her collarbone wasn't easy.

"Could they reattach them?"

"Callie, our mom has been mutilated and you're asking about reattaching fingers?"

"I have them," she blurted.

"What?"

"I told you! Nate was behind this. He sent them as a threat."

"You have her fingers?" Each word dripped with more incredulity than the last.

Callie bit the inside of her cheek. She was trying to be helpful, but this was already going sideways. Derek tensed at her side.

"We kept them safe so they could reattach. If you think they still can, we'll bring them," Derek said with more focus than Callie could have mustered.

"I don't fucking know. They didn't ask if we had the fingers—" Josh paced left and right "but who the fuck would have the fingers?"

This was more familiar ground. "Lots of people who hurt themselves in their garages building shit bring in the fingers."

Josh glared at her. "I don't think they will believe Mom was building a table or some bullshit. You don't bust open your head and break ribs building a table."

No, she supposed not. "Fine, but if they want them…"

"Yeah. Got it." Josh was watching Derek now. "What are you doing here? What's your deal in this?"

Derek didn't hesitate. "Where she goes, I go. That's my deal."

Josh huffed, but the wind caught the sound.

They needed to focus. The longer they were in this parking lot, the more likely eyes would be on them. And the longer Zara would be alone.

Josh lit a cigarette. "Told them I was leaving for a smoke."

"Okay. Is she awake?" The words ground against her teeth, leaving sour sand behind.

"Kind of. She's out of it. They gave her drugs, but nothing great because they're monitoring her brain."

"I'm sure they'll give her the good drugs soon," Callie lied. Until they were confident of her cognitive function, she wasn't getting the make-you-sleep shit.

"Are you going to be able to visit her tomorrow or are you still tied up in whatever shit they've gotten you into?" The hostility in her brother's voice surprised Callie more than the abrupt change of topic.

Callie hesitated, but Derek didn't miss a beat. "Don't forget your role in putting her in Ford and Nate's sights. Now ain't the time to be pointing fingers, kid."

Josh took a step forward, but his glower couldn't touch Derek. "I don't remember asking you."

"Stop." The word was a plea, but both men listened. "Josh, thank you for coming to help. We *both* agreed to avoid the cops on this. Mom is safe, but I'm not yet."

"He thinks he can keep you safe?" Josh jutted a thumb toward Derek.

"He will," Derek vowed.

Testosterone thickened the air, stinging her sinuses. "Get over yourselves," she muttered to herself. Louder, she continued, "Look, I need time to make sure I'm safe and to deal with this mess. Do you think you could watch out for Mom for at least another day or two?"

"I have to work, Callie. Not a lot of places want to hire a guy like me." It was the first time Callie had ever heard Josh acknowledge the consequences of his drug use.

It was huge, and she wasn't about to ruin it.

"You're right," she said. Derek stiffened at her side, but didn't interrupt. "Do you think we could get Aunt Lily to come help?"

"Yeah. I could call her," Josh said slowly. He probably hadn't talked to their favorite aunt since he'd gotten clean.

"Thanks. Let me know if she can't help, and we'll hit up Serena or Ray." It sounded like a solid plan even if they were banking on other Delgados to take care of Zara for them.

Josh took a long drag from his cigarette, and then nodded.

"She said you knew Adam." Derek was trying to use his kind voice, but the stress of the situation still scraped his throat when he spoke.

"Like I told her. His brother's a good dude, and so yeah Adam comes around the job sites. He's chill. Nothing to worry about."

Callie tried to ignore the vast sea of differing experiences between she and her brother. Offering trust was a kindness to yourself. The walls one had to build to protect a battered heart were tedious to maintain, but Callie couldn't give everyone that kind of access. Josh shouldn't either. His meth dealer liked to invite him over to play video games. That didn't mean they were friends. That was business strategy. That was come by so I can continue to keep you addicted and sell you more shit that will rot your veins. Even now Callie doubted Josh saw it that way. She couldn't let him go on thinking Adam was safe, though.

"Avoid Adam." Her words were a command.

"You're overreacting—"

"Josh! Look at me. Adam was the bagman for the ransom that got us Mom back. He knew what they had done to her, and was fine with it."

Josh flicked his cigarette out into the snow. "Naw. He probably didn't know it was our mom. He probably thought it was some smack or meth."

"He handed me Mom's bloody shirt, Josh. He *smiled* when he did it. He fucking knew."

Josh paled. Good.

"Please promise me you'll keep as far away from him as possible." *Please please please.*

He ducked his head for a moment. His lips were pursed. When he met her gaze again, he said, "I'm all about a low profile these days. No need to catch his attention."

"Smart man," Derek said with the right amount of approval to earn a half smile from Josh.

Callie hugged her brother again, quickly, but didn't say anything. The problem with being from a family of conmen and thieves? Your family will always know when you're lying. Josh hurried back toward the hospital and Zara in her critical condition, and Callie tried not to worry about what would happen when he next saw Adam.

Once her brother was back in the building, Callie and Derek left the hospital. No one followed them. Derek drove Callie to her car, and then he followed her back to his place.

The bougainvillea beside his front door had already lost its beautiful fuchsia petals. Now, beneath the yellow glow from the lone bulb out front, the branches bent and bowed beneath the increasing weight of the snow. Callie gave the bush a nudge with her toe to shake the worst of the snow away, and hoped the little plant would make it through the winter to blossom again. Derek unlocked the front door, and ushered her inside.

Warm, dry air welcomed them into his townhome. Callie took off her coat and laid it over the back of the couch.

"You want a drink?" Derek asked. He dropped his jacket over the back of a barstool.

Callie walked around to the front of the sofa. It was low and square. The modern styling looked stiff, but she'd found it was the right amount of plush. She sunk into corner seat. Her elbow rested on the back, and she propped her chin on her hand.

The long look she gave Derek must have been an answer.

"I'll take that as a yes." There was no judgment from Derek.

He poured a screwdriver, and brought it to her. "Figured you could use the Vitamin C."

Callie smiled, and her cheeks stung. She didn't know if the sharp pain was from the chap of wind, the ice of magic, or not eating much for days. At this point, it didn't matter the source.

"Thanks," she said before taking a sip. The drink was bright and boozy.

He sat next to her, and sipped his drink. When Derek's eyes closed, she could see the worry cutting around his eyes and tugging his shoulders together. She understood. Fatigue weighed her muscles until every movement felt like an underwater battle. The aching tension in her calves was undeniable and more than just a potassium deficiency. Everything hurt, but at least she wasn't broken. This was temporary.

She sat up a little straighter, and extended her arm until her hand cupped the back of his neck. Derek's warm chuff only encouraged her. She pressed and rolled her fingers against the steel rods he had for tendons. She nudged and soothed and as the minutes ticked by his shoulders began to ease down and his head started to tilt back. She doubted she could relax, but it eased her heart to be able to give him some respite.

Callie took another sip of her vodka and OJ. It was heavy enough on the former to burn her throat.

Derek's eyes were still closed when he asked, "You want me to build a fire?"

"I'm good."

"I know." He opened his eyes. "You also need to sleep."

He wasn't wrong. "You do, too."

He nudged the bottom of her glass with his knuckle. "Finish up."

She knocked the drink back, and let the bite remind her she had survived the day. Derek finished his own drink, and then in a quick motion stood and scooped Callie up in his arms.

"Totally not necessary." Her protest was half-assed.

"You need rest, doll. I am to see you finally get it."

The liquor softened her head and Derek did the same to her heart.

"Fine."

Callie was asleep before Derek even climbed into the bed.

CHAPTER THIRTEEN

The pale glow of daylight brightened Derek's bedroom. Callie rolled over to put the curtained window at her back. Her head throbbed. If the sun had already crested the house to make it to the back window, even the grey fabric Derek had hung over the window couldn't buy her more time.

The bed sagged on her side. "Callie?" Derek's sour tone didn't match his sleep-smashed hair.

Callie brushed her fingertips over his locks. The short strands were soft, and she smoothed them back. "Hmm?"

"I hate to wake you, doll—"

"Then don't. Climb back in with me. Our problems can wait a few more hours." Sleep was good on her. The playful tone in her voice was off from disuse, but she aimed to fix that.

She tugged Derek down, and then arched up to meet him. Her breasts grazed his chest, and his groan was a curse. She pressed her lips to his and swallowed the sound. The dark rumble vibrated against her sternum, making her feel dainty and precious. Against Derek like this she wasn't teeming with soul magic power. No, she was swathed in desire and hope and it'd been too long since she let them override her mind. Bubbles tickled her stomach, and something darker warmed even lower.

Derek's fingers dug into Callie's shoulder. She nipped his lower lip.

"Doll. Callie. Wait," he said between breathless kisses.

"Wait?" She paused, holding a breath deep in her lungs. Holding back the need to push.

His calloused thumb skated across her lower lip. "My gorgeous woman." He sighed like everything could be okay, but this was Gem City. "I wish we could do this now. Fuck. You have no idea how much I wish we could do this right now." His words were half groan, half plea.

She arched a little in a way that made him close his eyes and clench his jaw. His need grounded her. She was safe here, in this bed, with him.

The safety couldn't last.

He wet his lips. "I'm so sorry, Callie. The Charmer called."

That name was cold water to the face. Callie sank back against the sheets. "I thought we agreed not to mention his name in bed?"

Derek didn't take the bait. All levity was gone. "He's called an all-hands meeting."

The hollow depths of his voice conveyed the gravity, but Callie didn't understand the words. "Is that concerning?"

"It means something is fucked."

"How fucked?"

"He didn't demand every person show up armed when Tess was stealing from him."

Oh. This was 'burn the city to the ground' bad.

She understood. She'd experienced the vitriol and the vehemence from the Soul Charmer when he realized Tess was taking souls that belonged to him. He'd demanded Callie and Derek exact results with fire. If that didn't warrant sounding the alarms what did? "What could be...." she trailed off. Maybe she didn't want to know.

Derek's lips thinned. "I'm not going to guess, doll. It ain't fucking good."

Callie sat up. The headache drilling into the back of her head whined. "How long until we have to be there?"

"He said immediately."

"But?"

"But nothing. We have to get over there. I don't want him sending Beck for us."

She didn't either. Fuck. Beck. "I don't have the

Charmer's souls," she blurted like he didn't already know.

"If he's this worked up, he might not even ask about the flask. We could say it's back here. Buy some time."

Callie was shaking her head before Derek even finished. "He's been squirrelly all week about his stash. He's been convinced stuff is missing. Asking why things aren't where they 'should be.' He's going to ask about those souls, and I sure as shit can't tell him I gave them to Nate."

"No," Derek agreed. "If he doesn't bring up Nate, we shouldn't either."

"Look. You go in. I'll figure something out for the souls." Her brain was already spinning scenarios. Could she pick up from others to buy time? How many souls would be enough to keep him from asking questions? No, no, that wouldn't work. She'd be perpetually in the same boat.

"We can't split up." Derek was resolute, and usually Callie loved that.

"I can't have him take my screw up out on you."

"This isn't about you. He needs you. Besides, like I told your brother, these days where you go, I go."

He had said that, hadn't he? Well. WELL. Fuck. "I'm going to pull new souls from the soul well."

"You're what?"

"The soul well. It won't throw off the number he has in his stock. It'll help the church or some shit—I don't entirely get that whole thing, but I think they'll be cool with it." The more she talked, the more she was convinced this wasn't a horrible plan.

Souls needed to be extracted from the well beneath the cathedral. The Cortean Church needed the service of the Soul Charmer—or her. So they said. The priests wouldn't be pissed if she popped in to pick up a couple souls, and the Soul Charmer didn't need to know.

Derek was less convinced. "What about the souls he wants?"

"We'll get them back eventually. If we can appease the Charmer today, we can focus on getting some payback on Nate and that includes taking back the Charmer's souls."

Derek's frown was full body. Even his black tee shirt appeared to give her a disapproving stink eye. Finally, though, he said, "I'll take you to the cathedral, but we have to be fast. The Charmer said as soon as fucking possible and that's never been more than an hour for me. If we take much longer he's going to know something isn't right."

Callie pulled on a pair of jeans and had her hair swiped up into a ponytail in record time. Five minutes later, she and Derek were out the door and on their way to the Cortean Catholic Cathedral. Her stomach was surprisingly settled.

The sky was a brilliant blue. No clouds could hinder the sun, and so the town of Gem City was vivid with every outdoor surface shimmering in sunshine. The temperature hovered just below freezing, but at least it looked pretty. That was the only bright side Callie could muster as they drove to the same spot on El

Paseo for the third time.

The dealers weren't center stage on the corners at one thirty in the afternoon, but Callie couldn't help but scan the crowd of milling tourists for Adam or Dougie or any of Nate's other flunkies.

Derek moved to follow her into the church, but Callie stopped him. "Do you want to wait out here?"

He arched a brow.

"They aren't going to let you in *there* without one of these." She tugged down her sleeve to expose her nighthawk mark. The simple black lines made it an elegant tattoo to everyone else, but Derek wasn't just anyone. He knew that was a magic brand. A mark that granted her passage to the soul well. An identifying icon he did not bear.

"I get that, but there are too many eyes here. I'll wait in the vestibule."

"It's fucking weird to hear you use church terminology."

They headed up the steps together. "Did you think I didn't grow up in these places just like you?" He fought to hide a grin and failed.

"Maybe Henry's your family's black sheep and everyone is embarrassed at his chosen profession."

Derek wrapped an arm around her waist. "Please tell me you'll ask him if that's the case next time we see him?"

Callie didn't bother agreeing to that. "Did you always come to this cathedral?"

"Not until Henry was ordained."

"That had to be a trip." Callie might have had to tiptoe into sketchy parks at night to find Josh and had spent enough time outside the front of the casino when she was nine to know the Blackjack dealers on sight, but at least no one in her family could toss out 'holier than thou' and truly mean it.

"It was over two hours of liturgy."

"Ouch."

"Exactly." Derek held the door open for Callie. "I'll wait here. Remember, we need to move quick."

Like she could forget.

The sanctuary windows were glowing with the midday sun. The saints watched her walk toward the confessional booths. Every church was big to Callie. Something about the tall ceilings always made her want to shrink, but the cathedral actually was behemoth in size: ornate sconces, intricate artwork, and a delicate weave in the carpet. She walked along the right edge of the room. The border on the carpet laid out the story of Saint Stephen and his martyrdom in gold thread against the rich garnet background. His sacrifice spilled in shimming grandeur and lost to the edge of the well-worn path. If it were her place to say such things, she'd advocate using money on feeding the homeless and increasing access to rehab and mental health in the city instead of weaving shit people were going to walk on, but no one cared what she thought.

Father Henry stepped out of the confessional closest to her. He was dressed down in a simple black button-up and his ever-present white collar. "Callie?"

"Didn't mean to startle you," she said.

"Oh, no, it's fine." He tugged his shirtsleeves down. "Is my brother with you?"

Callie inclined her head toward the entrance. "He's waiting for me outside."

"In that case, how can I help you today? Did you need to take confession?"

Judgment slicked over her, its oily residue choking her pores and going a long way toward explaining why Derek wasn't a big fan of his brother. "No confession, Father Henry. I need access." She tried to force the right amount of meaningfulness into the words without sounding like a creep.

"Come again?"

Damn. She held her wrist up. "I need to go below." She was not going to say soul well. Not in the open. Not with someone she barely knew. Definitely not someone who implied she needed to confess her sins. He wasn't wrong that she'd made massive mistakes, but she'd owned them. They were hers.

The priest hesitated. He glanced around the room. The two of them were alone with the echoes of God and his saints. "Are you certain?"

This was getting old. She didn't have time to parlay. She didn't have time to get her boyfriend's brother to like her. She needed those souls and she needed them fast. The flask in her pocket trembled against her hip as if in agreement. "Completely," she snapped. "I'm in a bit of a time crunch. Can you let me down there, or do

I need to ask someone else?"

He wrung his hands, but his voice was steady. "I can let you down there. It's only that the Soul Charmer is not a godly man." *No shit, Sherlock.* Father Henry glanced over his shoulder yet again. When he continued it was in a scant whisper. "Regardless of his…help. He is not on our side. I don't know what made him that way, but I don't want that for you or for Derek."

At least the guy was being honest. She'd give the priest that. "I'm not trying to get into the game, but I have obligations. I have to protect us—me and Derek—and that means I need to get down there right now." She didn't spell out the consequences, because she wasn't entirely sure what they'd be. Whatever would happen if she failed, it would hurt them both. That hadn't been a lie, and Father Henry knew it.

"Okay," he said with more certainty this time. "I can't go down there with you. I don't have the approval yet, but I can unlock it for you. Do you know what to do?"

She had no clue how this would go alone. She'd had a hell of a time when she'd been here before, and there hadn't been anywhere near the pressure. Henry didn't need to know any of that. Burdening him with her fears or her problems or, shit, even her sins was too much. Too much to put on her boyfriend's brother, no matter how judgmental he was. They might not be close now, but family mattered.

"I can handle it." She tossed the words casually in his direction and hoped they were the truth.

Their footsteps were muffled by the plush flooring,

but pale blue light glimmered only on Callie's shoulder. The sickening sense someone was watching rotted in her gut, but then maybe that was church. She'd been gone so long she no longer was used to the awareness within these walls. She shook off the thought before Father Henry turned to face her again.

He pulled a lone, oxidized silver skeleton key from his robes. The metal didn't match the warm wood of the confessionals, but the outline of a bird in flight at the tip of the key did. The hawk was echoed in the scrollwork on the last confessional, the one Father Henry now unlocked. The one marked with the same predatory bird she bore on the inside of her wrist.

"May He be with you, lift you up." The words were standard.

The rote response bubbled to Callie's lips, but she denied them. The priest wasn't offering a standard goodbye. The words meant more now. They were real, and Callie took them as they were offered.

"Thank you. I'll be quick." Or at least she'd try.

She stepped into the booth. The door closed behind her, and Callie took the first terrifying step onto the landing. The smooth black lines of the hawk on her skin began to shimmer and sting. She reached unseeing to her right. Her hand met the slick wood. She trailed her fingertips lower, lower, lower until she found the switch. A single sconce lit at her side. A lantern and a matching lighter sat on a small table a few feet ahead.

She started to move closer, but a high-pitched whine pierced her ears. She gnashed her teeth together. Caught the inside of her cheek. Iron. Rust. The air thickened. It pushed and pushed closer to Callie. Her bones ached, and her skin tightened until she half expected her skeleton to leap out for a reprieve. She would have screamed if her jaw could move. It hadn't been this bad last time. God. Please. She would have remembered this. What had the Charmer done before? The priest? What was happening now? She fought to still her mind, to ignore the way her body began to bow. Her muscles and flesh always returned after magic ripped at her. She would recover from this, too. She pushed aside the pain, and imagined every thread of soul magic flickering beneath her skin. Pulling them together in her mind was quick, weaving them into a wall of sense and power.

Her power.

Last time she'd been here, she'd pushed. That wouldn't be enough. Callie shoved her power forward, imagining the wall hovering a foot in front of her. It was a glorious, glowing shield, and she kept a tight mental grip on the reins.

The air quickly dissipated to a standard oxygenated blend. She reeled the magic back into her body, and then doubled over breathless.

Once she caught her breath, Callie lit the lantern and began her descent down the winding staircase. As before, she couldn't sense how deep into the earth she was going. She tried to count the steps, but even that distraction failed her. Her mind wandered. Derek was waiting. Now Henry was probably waiting too. Her mom. Her brother. The Soul Charmer. She needed to do this, and she needed to do it correctly.

That was the burn. She arrived at the wood-paneled hallway. The soft hum of the well already teasing her forward. Those souls deserved more than what the Charmer could give them. Why was the Cortean Church okay with this? Was it really a safe move for someone like her to take them? Without supervision? Was she damning them? She'd been told they understood the consequences. This was a volunteer gig. A round of rentals as an act of contrition. That knowledge didn't assuage her guilt. Maybe nothing ever would.

She approached the well. The hawk at her wrist began to glow white. The flask was oddly silent.

The grey and green dome atop the well pulsed in time with her heartbeat. Was she imaging that? What had the Soul Charmer told her last time? She needed to let them call to her. There were so many voices. Soft coos and plaintive pleas and charged promises bubbled from the mystical space. The portal stretched and morphed before her, as if the souls on the other side could see her. She ignored the needles pricking along her spine. They couldn't see her. They couldn't hurt her. She had the power here. Or she would if she could channel it.

I got past the barrier on my own, I can get past this bullshit, she reminded herself.

Callie pulled the flask from her pocket, and thumbed off the cap. She wished it could offer a swig of something potent, but the act steadied her nonetheless. She pushed out with her senses again, and gained the space to breath, to talk, to focus.

"Okay," she said aloud. "I've got room for two."

The cacophony of cries redoubled. If her ears could have collapsed closed, they would have.

"It's a rental gig. You're going to be riding with… not great people." She wasn't sure why she told them. These souls knew the deal, and no matter what she was still shuttling them to the Soul Charmer. Maybe it was finally getting a night's sleep that was urging her to keep her conscious at least a little clear.

Black lava rocks were stacked in a perfect circle around the well. Each dark brick glistened even in the low light. Callie took a step closer until her knees almost touched the stones. The energy in the room began to swell. Sparks like fireflies flashed in her periphery, but when she turned for a better look they had disappeared. The golden filigree at the top of the well faded in one second, and was brighter in the next. The simple scrollwork shimmered, and then reshaped itself into words in a language she couldn't place. A steady *ba-bum ba-bum ba-ba-ba-bum* began beating against her soles. The room widened and narrowed in the same syncopation. It was breathing, but not in time with her. The room was brighter now. Callie squinted.

It was moving too quickly. She didn't have jars with her, and her breath was gasping to keep up with the galloping room. Her chest burned, but no flames erupted. She checked. Too much relied on her not fucking this up. If she could do this, the Soul Charmer wouldn't have to know. Henry wouldn't need to tell his monsignor.

The soul well continued to slosh and writhe. She didn't have time to be cautious, or to worry about what came next. She stepped close, and listened. A gruff *take me* hit her hard, and she replied okay. She focused on the harsh call as she held the flask over the tumultuous sea. Gossamer threads tracked past the gate and into her flask. It was so quick. Callie let a little tension slip from her spine. One more. Voices screamed and light battered against the viscous threshold. Callie tried to push that aside. Another soul caught her attention. It offered no words or supplication, but it stretched toward her in such a way that tears began to well in Callie's eyes.

"Okay. You," was all she said, and swiftly the soul pierced the veil and slipped inside the flask.

Two souls trapped. Two souls to trade. Two souls that weren't hers.

CHAPTER FOURTEEN

Callie couldn't get out of the Cortean Catholic soul well fast enough. The fresh souls stowed in her flask shouldn't have prickled her senses, but every fine hair on her forearms was at attention. The thick layer of magic coating the top of the stairwell didn't choke her this time. Maybe it tried, but the flask controlled her attention. The sensation wasn't entirely new. The same pressing awareness rode her the first dozen times she'd stuffed Hostess products in her cargo pants at fourteen. A girl had to eat. She hadn't cared about nutrition at that point, just a full belly. She hadn't stolen these souls officially. She'd been given access. Father Giles and the Soul Charmer had forced those fucking vows on her to tend the well and maintain the balance. They'd told her to take souls from the well. Said it needed to happen. Neither of them knew she was here, though, or what she'd done. She needed to keep it that way. Lying had a way of making above-board moves feel a whole lot like stealing. Doing so beneath a house of God did not help.

Callie thrust the confessional door open, and it thunked into Father Henry. His *oof* was high enough to unveil his unease, but his baritone was enough like Derek's to make her do a double take.

"Callie. You're back. Everything done?" He didn't glance around the empty hall, but he'd dropped his weight into his heels. Father Henry had been in fights, and his body remembered.

His tone was too close to a narc to allow her to say much. She wasn't his parishioner. "Thanks for your help."

Callie didn't wait for more small talk. She didn't have time, and honestly didn't think any of the conversation with her boyfriend's brother was going to improve her current situation. Henry stepped forward, his face drawn tight.

"Yeah?" She didn't bother to hide her discomfort. She was done pretending she was fine.

"Is he…just…." Father Henry let out a long sigh. "Try to keep Derek safe, okay? He needs more good influences."

Callie wasn't about to touch that. She was not a good influence. Some days she wasn't sure she was good. Good people didn't steal others' souls. Good people didn't know mobsters. Good people didn't get people kidnapped or killed. She couldn't lie to a priest, though. No matter her issues with the church or her faith. So she said the one true thing she could: "We keep each other safe."

Her wrist prickled. The hawk mark fizzled, and black ink seeped over the white lines. By the time she returned to Derek in the vestibule it looked like any other tattoo. Any physical touch of what she'd done, of where she'd been, had disappeared. Could anyone tell what she'd done? Derek gave her that same steady gaze she'd seen all day. He took her hand in his, and led her back to the car.

She couldn't resist touching her wrist again. The skin was smooth. The line work a crisp black. No longer a raised, white brand. Still her nighthawk, though. Still from magic. She wouldn't—couldn't—forget.

The heater in Derek's sedan worked well enough Callie could ditch her gloves within minutes. She peeked at herself in the side mirror. She didn't look any different. Hopefully the Charmer wouldn't think so either. Whatever had him fired up couldn't be the well, which was about as bright side as she could get right now.

"Do you think he knows?" Callie asked.

Derek didn't take his eyes off the road. "Knows?"

Callie paused for a minute. What did she really want to know? Was this about her? Them? Were they safe? Derek wouldn't have those answers, but he did understand the way the Charmer's mind worked.

"About Nate's soul. About the others I gave him?" The truth of those questions was almost too much. She had gotten good at sharing with Derek, but this exposure terrified her. Her lower torso began to squeeze and slowly the tightness gripped its way up the rest of her stomach and chest until her organs were sure to asphyxiate her.

"I doubt it. He has a lot of eyes and ears throughout Gem City, but he wouldn't call us all in for that. He would have demanded to see you. Hell, he wouldn't have wanted me there. I've made my stance on you crystal fucking clear."

A bubble of lightness rose in Callie's chest. "Thanks for being on my side."

"Where you go, I go. That's the deal, doll." The emphatic nature of his words only further underscored the safety in sharing her secrets with him. It might not get easy, but at least it was starting to feel less wrong.

She leaned over the center console, and rested her head on his upper arm. The dark rumble from low in his throat said he didn't mind. The plastic partition between them bit at her hip, but she embraced the mild pain.

"You know, I love you," she whispered.

"I've heard that."

She glanced up, and his smile was broad and genuine. The road beneath them began to jostle the car. Brick paving meant they weren't far from the Charmer's. Once again their boss killed the joy in the room.

Callie watched the dashboard clock click over to 1:13. The day was both moving too fast and too slow. "Have you ever seen the Soul Charmer like this?" A moment ago it might have been a brave question to ask. Before she'd reminded him she loved him. Before she let him know her secrets.

His biceps tensed beneath her cheek. "Once."

Derek was quiet long enough Callie thought he couldn't tell her more. She understood the kind of memories one stored in scars. The crimson pasts and the ashen secrets. Excavating them was a task in itself, but cobbling them back together to share aloud was a second kind of pain. She wasn't about to force that abuse on Derek. She closed her eyes, and focused on slow, even breaths. His breathing mimicked hers when they lay entwined at night. Maybe this could help.

The car slowed. Tourists staggered out in front of the car. Derek hit the brakes, but didn't flip them the bird. They waved and laughed, but didn't ask for directions. When the car was moving again, Derek finally spoke.

"The Charmer used to have competition. Did you know that?"

Callie relaxed against him. "Maybe? I didn't pay much attention to the Charmer other than to offer an ambitious side eye to the nurses in the ER who talked about trying out his wares."

She was perpetually thankful she hadn't had to collect from any of them. Nothing says look how far I've fallen like hypocrisy.

"Within a few weeks of opening his shop a few others popped up. They weren't like Little D. I mean, they weren't Charmer-level scary fuckers, but they had more skill than that."

Soul magic had a steep learning curve. "How did they know what to do?"

"A guy the Charmer knew taught them. He doesn't talk about him in the same way he doesn't talk about Tess."

"Gotcha." Callie could guess what Derek meant by that. No one was talking to that guy anymore.

"Anyway, so other people open shops, too, and he didn't handle it much better back then. These other soul magicians hired enforcers."

"Ford?"

"His dad, I think, but the Ford family."

"That explains a lot."

Derek shrugged a single shoulder. "Well, I think the other magicians originally paid for protection. Standard racket from the Ford family, but a couple got it in their heads to push out the competition."

"They attacked the Soul Charmer? What kind of idiot would do that?" Other than Tess, but she had some weird woo-woo feels about the souls.

"The kind of idiots who didn't think he had back-up."

"Oh."

"Yeah, *oh*. Boss wanted a show of force. This was about eight years back. So there were only three of us. Plus the Charmer."

"What happened? What did you do?" She'd told herself not to ask that question, but the absurdity of the situation had sucked her in.

"No other free-standing shops have lasted since. No one goes up against the Soul Charmer of Gem City and wins. That's what happened."

Wow. It's not like she was new to being terrified of the Soul Charmer. He'd done a magnificent job of showcasing his callousness and his power. He'd cultivated an aura of prince meets serial killer. Understanding he'd treat every threat as critical, though, changed the game. That something had hit him hard enough to bring everyone in for the first time in eight years? Motherfucking nightmarish.

Calm breathing was bullshit. The alleyway leading to the Soul Charmer's emporium came into view. Callie sucked in tiny breaths faster and faster.

Derek put the car in park, and then wrapped his arms around her. "Doll…Callie…it's okay. You're okay."

She pulled the flask from her pocket, and held it in front of them. "He'll know these aren't real."

"They're real." Derek was emphatic.

"But they're not his. He'll know. He'll know and he'll do something horrible, and I don't know how to fix it."

Derek stroked Callie's hair. His touch was firmer than necessary, but it helped. "Calm down. It'll be okay. We'll get the souls back for him. We're just buying time."

"But what if he already knows?"

"He's not God, Callie. Whatever we're in for, it ain't because of anything you've done. Could be about the shit that went down at your apartment with the soul renter. Could be fresh pressure from the cops. Could be a lot of things." The hard edges of the words matched the sharp planes of Derek's cheeks. Color rose from his jaw. Here she was breaking down about the souls and Nate when the cops were after Derek. When he'd killed a man. Did the Charmer know Derek had done it with her safety in mind and not because of his loyalty to him? Probably, but would that be enough to protect them?

Callie nodded slowly. Her heart rate didn't slow to a standard resting pace, but at least she wasn't hyperventilating any longer.

"We've got this," she said, and wished she had Derek's power of convincing confidence.

"He called us to help solve his problems. Just remember that when we go in, and you'll be fine."

Was he reading her mind these days? Was that some couple shit?

"He always calls us to solve his problems." The derision in her voice was real, but somehow it helped ground her. She could hold herself together a little longer.

"So it'll be routine, doll. In, out, and at Dott's in time for dinner."

If they could be so lucky.

CHAPTER FIFTEEN

The Soul Charmer's shop had never been bright. The entrance was set back down an alley with limited lighting and even less foot traffic. Callie and Derek approached the building. Sour tendrils of warning coiled around the base of her neck. The front door, slathered in layer after layer of weathered and cracked black paint, stretched in front of her, ominous and overwhelming.

"We got this," Derek said. He took her hand and tugged her forward with him.

It wasn't fear of the Soul Charmer that made her stagger. Not now. A sharp pain slapped her cheek. Gusts of wicked wind rushed through the corridor and whipped behind her back. A jagged block of coal grated against her belly, the wrongness of the moment coalescing in her mind in tangible pain. Callie dug in her heels.

"This is wrong." Fear leeched all tone from her voice.

She repeated her words. This time Derek stopped, too.

His scowl hardened the longer he watched her. "Callie." Her name. A plea.

The coal she'd sensed in her belly shattered on the pavement. Soot marred the front of her coat. Another magic trick. She was about to apologize for getting caught in another of the Charmer's traps when Derek clamped his hands onto her hips and yanked her toward him.

"What the fuck?" Derek stared at the brittle briquettes of black on the ground.

"You can see them?" This was more than some nighthawk bullshit. The flames on her arms were always visible, but the power protecting doorways and the heavy pressures had always been just for her. Derek had never seen them.

The bits of coal disintegrated quickly until only smudges remained.

"Fuck yes I saw them." He turned his attention back to Callie. His hands tightening on her hips. "Are you all right?"

She could tell he wanted to give her a once over, but when it came to magic they were both at a loss.

"No damage done." Probably.

"Has that happened before?" Worry sharpened his question.

"That? No, but…"

His hands eased until they were more comfort than confinement at her waist. "You got an idea, doll, I want to hear it."

It was a guess. "It felt like a warning."

"What kind of warning?"

A bad fucking one. Not that she could tell Derek that. Not after she'd broken down in the car and dumped so much of her baggage in his hands. "The kind that says we should watch our steps. We need to find out what's happening." At least that wasn't a lie.

Derek nodded once, the movement final. "Right. I go in first. Anything goes wrong, you're going to fucking run, right?"

And leave him? Not likely. She pushed up onto her toes and lightly pressed her lips to his cheek. The scruff tickled, and reminded her there was more to the future than simply magic and murder. "No heroes over here."

He didn't push about bypassing the agreement. Instead he stepped toward the front door. He licked his lips quickly, unnecessarily. "Let's get this over with."

Mildew and patchouli assaulted Callie's nose. She coughed and sputtered, but stepped fully into the Soul Charmer's client space.

"Who the—oh hey." A tall, broad woman greeted them. The black pistol in her hand was tilted toward the floor, but Callie wondered how quickly the woman could raise it. How quickly could the threat become a promise? Callie struggled to swallow, but held steady.

"Savannah." Derek's tone wasn't soft.

"Hey. You Callie?" Savannah asked.

A nod and an awkward, fake smile later, introductions were over, and the three of them were alone.

"Where's the Charmer?" Derek asked.

"That's the question, man," Savannah said. "Beck and Miguel are in back."

Callie wasn't about to trust this new woman to hand her information now anyway. Too much was on the line. Soot still clung to her clothing. Even the Charmer wouldn't want her talking magic with his other employees. Derek must have agreed, because he took Callie's hand again and moved toward the back.

The nighthawk mark began to simmer as she stepped close to the gateway to the back office. She started pushing her magic forward and out, following Derek through the doorway without a misstep.

It was in the back room where it all started to go wrong.

Her foot caught on something low and blunt jutting from the edge of the doorway. Callie still held her magic out in front of her. She whipped her hands up to block her fall, and the magic offered a pillow for her face. Her knees and shins, though? They smacked hard against the tile. The crack reverberated in the tiled room. She pushed herself up from the floor. Blood smeared beneath her. A slice of smoky grey glass was wedged into her palm. She plucked it, thankful the puncture wasn't deep. She pulled a wad of gauze from her coat pocket, one of the few pieces she hadn't used on Zara, and pressed it against her hand. Her right hand was bloody, too, though. She skimmed her thumb over the pad of the palm, but there were no cuts. Just blood.

"Callie." Derek had clearly said her name more than once. He stood a couple steps ahead of her in a pool of dark red liquid.

She got her feet beneath her, every intention focused on running to him. He held up a single hand. The faded pink ridge of an old scar rose beneath the flashes of light from a flickering fluorescent bulb.

"Pretty sure you need to stay back, doll." The words were casual, the tightening of his lips was not.

She remained near the door, but scraped her gaze over every inch of him: the splatters of red readying to disappear against the black of his boots, the edges of his phone creating an extra crease from within his jeans' pocket, the forced stretch of his fingers locking them into rigor mortis level stiffness, and his jaw clenched tight beneath skin two tones too pale. He wasn't bleeding. Her brain urged her to rush him, to touch, to confirm, to protect, but she had to trust him. If he said she needed to stay back, she did.

She swallowed the fear clawing into her mouth. "Are you sure you're okay?"

His mirthless laugh did nothing for her worry. "None of this is okay, doll, but I'm positive you need to stay back from that." Derek pointed to the far wall. She hadn't even considered looking at anything else here. The blood on the floor, her boyfriend adrift in it, the glass in her palm.

Oh.

Oh, fuck.

The far wall held all the storage for the Charmer's souls. At least within this shop. Two of the bookcases-turned-soul-cases had black steel shutters locked over the front of them. Callie hadn't seen them before, or even known there was a locking mechanism for the soul cases. There were handles at the bottom of the heavy duty and rugged material. But it wasn't those barricades that had her cursing. It was the third section. It wasn't blocked off, and it was nearly barren. Slivers of obsidian littered the fourth shelf. A silver metal lid sat lonely on the third. The other nine shelves? Empty.

The Charmer was meticulous about the storage process. Every soul had a place. Every one was marked, measured, and secured. This shelf hadn't contained the purest souls. It hadn't held the recent returns, either. The Soul Charmer liked to have the recently used souls sequestered. Said they needed a moment before going back into a host. Callie had thought this was about the Charmer controlling the supply, but after seeing the well she thought this might be an actual rule. Not that he'd fucking told her. None of that mattered now. The souls that were missing were the most rented, the ones burdened with the most sin. Those souls had seen some shit.

The Soul Charmer was a shitty mentor, but some truths were too important to hide from her. When they'd been alone, he'd told her about the filthy souls and made her promise to never repeat it.

She'd reached out to grab one of the souls from the

tainted shelf. He'd slapped her hand before she could touch it. "Not that one."

"Why not? You said you wanted anything under 900. This is labeled 775."

"You must always read the whole label." His tone had been cutting.

Callie had held back a curse. "I thought I had. What did I miss?"

"It used to be a 775." He retrieved the jar, and rotated it. Down the right side of the label were other numbers and dates. "It's now a 104."

"I didn't know you had souls that low." Callie read the checkout log on the side of the jar. "Has this soul really been rented thirty times?"

"Twenty seven."

She hadn't known what to say to that.

"After ten, most souls are no longer capable to producing a good match. Most of these rentals were to the same person. You don't make that call. All you need to remember is that any soul we rent out more than ten times goes here. They can only be placed with the right host, which means you don't pick them out for my customers."

The command in his voice caught her in the chest, but not hard enough to stop her from trying to squeeze more information out of him. "What happens if one of these souls is put in the wrong host?"

Most of the time the Soul Charmer's talk about matching souls was about getting the most cash out of the customer. This was different. His conviction was real. His eyes had narrowed until only black slits peeked back at her. He'd clacked the bulky gold and emerald ring on his index finger against the jar. "Some souls have been through too much. Rising to Heaven isn't in their future, but the weight of sin can do more than keep one from celestial paradise."

Callie understood sin. She understood right and wrong, and consequences that haunted a person. These were the rented souls, though. They were supposed to be the Cortean Get Out of Hell Free Card. This didn't sound like an escape at all.

The Soul Charmer hadn't been done. "When it becomes more sin than soul, the rental may try to take over."

"Take over?" She knew this shit was shady.

"Not always the way you mean, Calliope. Yes, it could override the host, but more likely it would take over to ruin him. Suicide, car crash, murder. It'd get the host caught or killed to find an escape. Sin can drag a soul down just as the lack of it can raise one up."

Callie tried to shake the memory. At the time, she'd cracked jokes about the Soul Charmer's theological past. That had been before he'd taken her to the soul well. That was before she knew some souls were here as part of purgatory. Before she knew a mismatch could lead to murder. Now she looked at the empty shelf and only saw dozens of missing souls that were done being used.

Sin can drag a soul down just as the lack of it can raise one up.

"Someone had to have taken them," she whispered. Those souls were dangers to nearly anyone who rented them. Those souls were ready to move on and face consequences.

"That's Problem B," Derek said.

"What's Problem A?"

"Some of those pieces are broken shards, right? If you come closer, we might be in a situation."

A short, staccato laugh popped from her chest and disappeared just as fast. "I hadn't even thought of that." She did now, though. She pushed with her magic. Nothing rumbled near her. She took a tentative step toward Derek. Still no flames. She edged closer to him and around the blood. No souls shimmered in the room.

"We're alone."

"No, Beck, Miguel, and the Charmer are supposed to be here."

She'd meant the souls, but saying so aloud now would be awkward. "Where are they? Where is he?"

Derek glanced from the scattered papers on the desk to the back hallway. "Whoever did this, I pity them."

The last time she'd been in the basement of the Soul Charmer's emporium, she'd tortured a woman. She'd forced Tess to give answers. A room set up for interrogations was beneath their feet, and she had no desire to go there again.

"They have to be downstairs." Defeat tasted bitter.

The rear door of the office led to a small hallway. While it was normally Callie's path out of the building, it was also the only way to get to the basement. Derek opened the door, and swore.

"What?" Callie pressed against his back, but his bulky frame filled the doorway. "What's wrong?"

"More glass," he muttered.

That couldn't be enough to unnerve him. She nudged him until he acquiesced, finally taking a step to the side so she could see. The picture frames were shattered. Every single one. None were stolen, but fractals in the remaining edges of the panes suggested a small hammer had been taken to every one.

Derek crunched his way over to the second door, the basement door. "We'll clean it up later."

Callie started to agree. The Charmer was probably seething that she and Derek weren't there to listen to his tirade yet, but something about the narrow space stopped her. It wasn't the thick magic in the air. She wasn't pushing her ability out. The standard warding of the room no longer pressed against her eardrums. The magic wasn't the only thing missing.

"Where did they go?" she whispered.

Derek's hand held steady on the doorknob, but his eyes darkened and followed her. "He's probably got them downstairs."

"Not whoever did that. The pictures. All the pictures are gone." Each frame was bare. The glass on the floor made sense, but the images were gone as well.

Derek let go of the door and stepped closer to Callie. His arm slid around her waist. His hand on her hip grounded her. She could do this.

"Souls and pictures? Did these guys even look at the till?" Derek left off the *assholes*, but Callie heard it.

"The glass isn't gone enough for them to take the photos. They should be here." This wasn't right. It didn't make sense. Benton's picture had been on this wall, and now he was gone. His picture. Maybe the soul he rented. Darkness skittered in her periphery, but when she turned there was only broken glass and dust bunnies.

"Fucking weird, doll, but we need to get downstairs."

A hard crack and a painful moan reached from beyond the basement door.

"You're right. Sorry. Savannah's got the upstairs covered." She even managed not to be bothered by trusting a woman she didn't know. That was probably a lingering effect of sleep deprivation.

The rickety stairs might have unnerved Callie at another time, but not now. Regret sank its fingers into her belly, and with each swaying step down into the basement it twisted and curled. Her own fingers itched with the memory of flames and burning flesh. Remorse rolled her insides. Callie bit back a groan.

Another whack and clatter stretched from beyond the short hallway. Beck had led her down this hallway last time. To the lone room at the end. She'd found Tess—who had been stealing souls from the Charmer and siphoning bits of souls from unsuspecting chakra massage clients—bound to a metal chair. Callie wanted to believe magic had overrode her moral code that day. Tess had been packed with borrowed souls, and the flames had come easy and fast. The truth was Callie had done what she'd needed to. Protecting Derek, getting the Charmer off her back, those had been her priorities. She needed to be a better person, but walking across the dusty, cracked concrete floor of the cellar that was a regular player in her nightmares, she doubted today was that day.

"At least there isn't blood here." Derek's voice was low, but none too quiet. He wasn't concerned about what the Charmer was doing inside the interrogation room.

Yellow light spilled from the open doorway.

"This is bullshit," a male voice said. His words were followed by a spectacular crash. A wide shard of wood shot through the doorway and clapped against the wall behind them.

Callie paused and simply looked at Derek. *What the fuck are we getting into?* His subtle nod said he got her.

Derek eased around the corner first, and paused inside. He blocked the light, shuttering the hallway into shadow. Callie took a moment to ground herself. She shoved at her senses, and stretched her magic forward into the room. Derek straightened his spine, and his hair almost grazed the top of the doorframe. Callie wasn't sure if it was the magic bypassing him or what laid beyond, but she pulled the magic back. Power wasn't rippling from the room.

That couldn't be right. The Charmer never dropped his wards.

"Derek," Callie said his name softly, but the wariness in her voice rattled the syllables. He didn't acknowledge her. She rested her palm on his back. The leather between them was cool. She said his name again. He took in a big breath, and his muscles moved and tightened beneath her hand. This was off. Derek was listening, but not moving. Power wasn't throbbing through the basement. Derek was blocking her view on purpose. He was protecting her, as always. The regret in her belly shoved back until it knocked her spine. She bent her knees and hoped she could hold steady a little longer.

With only enough volume to reach Derek's ears she asked the big question, "The Charmer isn't here, is he?"

CHAPTER SIXTEEN

Beck picked up a shard of wood—what had once been the leg of a stool—and smacked it against the wall. The brittle wood, already fractured, splintered. Pocks of white dotted his reddening face as the wood flakes fluttered to the floor in a blast of furious snow. "How the fuck does she know the Charmer isn't here?"

Good question. Callie pushed forward past Derek. He didn't stop her, but he didn't make the task easy either. The nine by nine room was littered with broken bits of furniture. Even the lone metal folding chair in the corner had dents warping the back and the seat, and the legs were akimbo.

Beck glowered. His ire wasn't focused. His nostrils flared, ready to pick up the scent of war. Callie wasn't about to step into that path. Derek stayed close at her back. Given the disheveled room and its occupants she wasn't about to complain. The other man in the room hardened his gaze on Callie, though. He slowly opened his mouth until a resounding pop echoed. It was a stretch of the jaw, a move she'd witnessed before in others. Here, though? Now? It was ominous. It was the snap of broken things, a threat of separation, and a warning in a lone, jarring act.

"Better question is where the fuck is the Charmer." Derek's voice was a slap of cheap whiskey against a sore throat.

Beck blustered up to Callie. Derek leaned forward until his nose was level with the other man's eye. "No. I get she's your girl now, but we ain't skipping over how the fuck she knows."

"The room is fucking empty. She's smart." Derek's closed fist whacked out to his side and against the drywall. The wall coughed dust.

The urge to preen was unfamiliar and awkward in this room, but the delicate shimmer in Callie's chest wasn't unwelcome. She stifled it. "The walls he puts up around this place are jacked. It feels wrong."

Explaining the way the walls should steal from her—sapping her energy and requiring her focus—wasn't a skill she had. She had never been in for the woo-woo shit, and that made it damn hard to tell others it was real. The vocabulary for emotions was tricky enough, but layering on the pulling and the prodding and the focus and the fear was not a task she was up for.

Unfortunately, Miguel wanted that. He was an average guy; not too tall, not too skinny. Simple haircut.

Basic, black clothes. He'd cultivated an appearance to blend in, but when he spoke something skidded beneath the soles of Callie's Chuck Taylors. "Explain. How does it feel?"

Callie grappled for the right phrases. Her senses snapped out throughout the room combing for energy, but nothing raked back against her nerves. No wall halting her reach. "Overwhelming and underwhelming at the same time," was the best she could muster.

Miguel's boot heel clapped against the concrete floor. Dust kicked into the air and when it fell, he was a half step closer to Callie. The chilly swirls streaming from Miguel put metal in Callie's mouth. The bitter sensation only crept outward when she forced the magic close to him. Her skin didn't ice, but his soul was lacking enough pieces for its bitterness to bite at her. His soul didn't sing over the room, and she didn't try to call it forward, but her magic roiled unchecked.

"Why does that make you think the Soul Charmer is not here?" he asked.

It might have been the right question to ask if one was on the other side of the conversation. Callie didn't know shit about what was going on, and she doubted the guys did either. The problem wasn't Miguel's question. It was the entitled underscore. The pressure on her to perform, to explain, to appease. She gnashed her teeth together, and started to imagine using whatever souls were nearby to build her protection. That wasn't the answer. She unspooled the coil of fuck you in her chest, but kept hold of the end. She was the only one in this room who could snatch souls. That shit mattered.

"Doesn't matter why. Where is he?" she asked.

"Doesn't matter—" Beck sputtered.

"She's right. Tell us what happened." Derek stepped forward, and a broken block of dark glass popped and pulverized beneath his steel-toed boots.

The two other soul collectors looked to one another, but didn't bother hiding their defeat. Neither was ready to push Derek. They should have been more concerned about pushing her. Being underestimated didn't chafe when she could craft her secrets into a shield.

Beck spoke first. "We don't really know."

The defeat in his voice helped Callie ratchet down her anger. These two had information she needed. "Let's start at the beginning. When did you both get here?"

"I was only fifteen minutes away when I got the all-hands call." Miguel shoved his hands in his pockets. The edges of his wallet and phone disappeared. "Place was empty when I got here."

"Same here," Beck said. "Charmer wasn't here. He didn't answer when I called him."

"Was everything busted already?" Derek gave a pointed look at the bits of broken furniture scattered around the room.

A hint of pink dappled Beck's cheeks, but his lanky limbs remained loose. No apologies. "This door," he pointed at the one Derek and Callie now blocked, "was smashed to shit, but otherwise the basement was clear."

As if a broken door was their biggest concern. Did

they not understand the implication of missing souls? Did they not see the trashed storeroom? The Soul Charmer's souls had been stolen. They may have been broken out of their holding jars. The consequences were monumental, and these assholes were down here throwing shit and whining about an empty room?

"And upstairs?" she prodded. Holding back the fire was getting fucking old. An echo of the Charmer's magic nipped at her spine in slow waves. She ignored it.

"Back room was smashed," Miguel said, and then quirked his lips.

"That shit?" Callie pointed overhead. "It's not funny. Do you understand what happened upstairs?"

Miguel began to amble toward Callie. "You didn't want to explain how you knew he wasn't here, and now you're telling us you know what happened? Charmer's Pet better start talking."

Miguel shot a hand out to grab Callie's upper arm. The layers she wore did nothing against the harsh grind of his fingers. Derek's arm snapped out and up. A wet *crack slap snap* later Miguel staggered back on unstable legs. He toppled to the floor. Blood slipped from the corner of his mouth, and the deep raspberry building along his jawline said the meeting with Derek's uppercut was going to turn black and swell to holy hell in the next few hours. Violence shouldn't have been attractive. She'd spent years escaping the fight till you die mentality, but right now that didn't matter. If she weren't terrified the Soul Charmer was ready to call her on giving away his souls, if the threat of the missing souls on her wasn't a legit worry, and if her entire body hadn't been locked in constant red-alert status, she would have tackled him. Her chest tightened for a moment, and her belly warmed, but she let both reactions fade.

Beck helped Miguel into a sitting position. "You didn't have to punch him."

"We'll have to disagree," Derek muttered. He slid a hand around Callie's waist and pulled her close.

She needed the steadying buoy. "I don't know what happened here, but I can tell you it isn't fucking good. Several shelves of his soul stores are gone. Some were broken, but more were taken. That should fucking concern you. Not how his or my magic works."

She didn't tell them about the rotten souls. She didn't tell them that people could be hurt. The Soul Charmer hadn't hired these guys for their empathy skills. They weren't about to be motivated by the threat of souls in the wrong hands. They did, however, report to the same man she did. The Soul Charmer might be able to hold magic over Callie's head, but he had something else on these guys. She didn't know what, but she did know he could steal their souls. If nothing else, that had to keep them goddamn scared.

"Charmer wouldn't let anyone *take* those souls." Beck's shoes didn't move, but he leaned back. If only escaping this was so easy.

"No, he wouldn't." Derek agreed.

"So where is the boss?" A raspy whistle accompanied Miguel's s's.

Callie almost flipped him off. Instead, she said, "Exactly."

Beck and Miguel both avoided eye contact with her. Derek let their awkwardness settle before asking, "Neither of you saw The Soul Charmer since he called, right?"

Both guys shook their heads no.

"Did he say anything on the phone?" Callie didn't have much to go on, which is why she'd thought this was about Nate. The Charmer hadn't said shit to Derek, but maybe that was because his anger was going to be focused on Callie.

Derek's hand tightened on her waist. "He said all hands to me."

Beck sucked in his lower lip. When he released it, he spoke. "He had a guy down here."

Callie hadn't expected that. She hadn't expected them to know more, but now her mind snapped through the scene they'd arrived to. The shattered glass, the missing soul…. "And the blood upstairs?"

"I figured it was from the guy he had downstairs," Miguel said. He cradled his jaw for a moment, and then added, "Maybe it wasn't."

"Hold up. Who did he have down here?" Derek's fingers pressed harder against her hip. It was her turn to steady him. He'd been the Charmer's go-to guy. So why didn't he know someone was in the building for interrogation? Callie wasn't about to pose that question in this company.

"Charmer had me drag in a guy trying to sling

souls outside of that Thai food place near the industrial park." Beck offered a single-shoulder shrug. "Guy was easy to find, and didn't put up a fight. He was a hundred pounds soaking wet. Can't see that string bean taking out the door."

"Or getting the drop on the Soul Charmer," Callie said. Their boss was too clever and too powerful for one guy to take him out. If it'd been that easy, Ford would have forced the Charmer to give him souls long before Derek bombed the mobster's house.

"He had you bring in a corner guy? Why not just put some fear into the kid?" Derek's hardened gaze settled on Beck. The other soul collector looked at the far wall, and then the floor, and then Miguel. Anywhere other than Derek.

"I just did what he asked," Beck said.

Callie brushed the tip of her shoe across the floor in front of her. It knocked the bits of glass and wood shards away, and brushed the top layer of dust clear. Aside from the debris, the floor was clean. "Where's the blood here?"

"What do you mean?" Beck asked.

"Had you already questioned the guy?" she asked.

"Not yet. I brought him in, and bound him like normal."

Like normal. Bile burned in her belly. She rubbed her hands against her pant legs. The memory of searing flesh and sharp screams in this room suddenly too vivid to contain. She choked back the sickness, and curled her fingers around the flask inside her pocket. "There's no blood in here. All the fighting happened upstairs."

"Maybe not all of it." Derek turned to examine the battered door. "This was definitely hit from inside the room, and it'd been bolted. It's not an easy latch to power through."

It was like her boyfriend was a forensics investigator merging the clinical and the plausible. Callie half expected him to ask who had installed the bolt.

"Did you use zip ties or rope," he asked Beck.

"Zip ties." The *of course* was unspoken between the colleagues, but the familiarity rankled Callie.

"Where are they? We need to know if he was cut free."

If he hadn't been, then they had a bigger problem. Had he slipped the bindings, had he hidden a tool on him, or had he been set free?

Everyone began skimming the floor. Miguel found the black bindings quickly. They'd been cleanly cut. The men began to talk about the cable ties as if they held all the clues. Fucking plastic wasn't going to solve this.

An edge of black peeked from beneath the seat of one of the wooden stools. Callie tossed the wood to the side, and picked up the three by two card. The glossy sheen had been scuffed, but she couldn't forget the slogan etched in delicate gold swirls: Be Anonymous with a New Soul.

"Guys," she called.

"He used a piece of glass," Miguel said, ignoring

Callie.

"Glass would leave blood. No blood." Derek answered Miguel.

Damn it. The card was cool in her hand. "Derek," she said his name with the force only a lover could leverage.

His attention snapped to her. He held one of the cut cable ties in his hand, but dropped it to his side, and walked to her. "Everything cool, doll?" he said quiet enough for only her ears.

She lifted the card. "I found this. Adam had one of these in his coat."

Derek hand out a hand. "Can I?"

She passed him the card.

"This makes more sense," he said only to Callie. "The Charmer doesn't use this room unless it's something big."

"Tess level big?"

Derek nodded. "If the mob crew is carrying these anonymous soul cards around, it means whoever is behind it is gunning for the Charmer."

"Business cards and shit? That's a lot of organization for a little time."

"You're not wrong." Derek shot a sharp look over his shoulder. The two other men were still arguing about the zip ties. "At least this means this isn't about *you*."

No, this might be worse. The Soul Charmer had another rival. One brazen enough to drum up business with key criminals, one willing to steal directly from the Charmer's stores, and one with the means to escape this interrogation room.

"You two going to share with the class?" Beck asked, already moving toward them.

Derek held the card aloft. "We've got a fucking problem."

The group climbed the rickety basement stairs together, and walked single file back to the storefront. Savannah had hopped onto the glass counter while they were gone. A bead of sweat slithered down Callie's lower back—from the stairs or the stress, she wasn't certain. Savannah wasn't even goddamn dewy.

"Any customers show up?" Derek asked.

"Nah." Savannah swung her legs enough to let her heels bang against the counter at an easy cadence.

How could she be so casual? Next time they shouldn't pick her as the lookout. She wasn't on alert. Maybe she hadn't ventured past the curtained doorway into the back room. Maybe she didn't know the place had the tornado-level wreckage of a three-day weekend kegger. Maybe Savannah was good at her normal gig for the Charmer. Maybe she coaxed people back into the building efficiently. Didn't matter now.

"Do you know anything about the guy they had downstairs?" Callie didn't bother faking casual.

Savannah looked to Beck and then Miguel. When the latter nodded, she said, "Just another troublemaker.

You know how it is. The Charmer points, we shoot."

The other woman had muscle. There was no denying she could probably stop a runner from the store, but right now Callie simply didn't believe her. The words were true enough. Callie and Derek had been on the other side of that equation.

"I picked him up solo," Miguel clarified.

Savannah scowled for a half second before flashing back to basic and bored.

"What do we know about him?" Derek asked. The soft *flick, flick, flicka-flick* of his thumb against the business card didn't register with the others, but Callie understood. Derek was planning.

"Everyone I talked to called him Vega." Miguel was all business. Thank God. He paused, and pulled a small spiral notebook from his pocket. He flipped back a few pages. "Almost everyone up in Green Heights knew him. Only around the last few weeks, but *making* the rounds."

Beck sidled around the back of the counter until he was closer to Callie and Derek than Miguel and Savannah.

"Anyone renting from him?" Beck asked.

Miguel shrugged. "No one copped to it, but if that many people knew him, there had to be a problem."

Derek could have extracted the truth from them, but pointing it out would only complicate things. If Derek didn't need to avoid the police right now, the Soul Charmer would have sent Derek. For the first time ever having the scrutiny of the Gem City PD was working out in their favor. How the hell had that become her reality?

Derek lifted the Anonymous Souls card for all to see. "Did anyone try this number?"

The low-wattage bulbs peering from worn shades at the corners of the room couldn't reach the black surface. Lighting was unnecessary.

Three sets of eyes narrowed on the business card.

On the blocky yellow digits printed on the back.

No names, slogans, or promises.

The back of the card held all potential clients would need: Ten simple digits and an understanding.

Derek was done with the preliminary dance. He'd been watching the others, too. She'd seen the shuffling, and the collaborative looks. Had he seen more?

"Your girl just found the card, man. When would we have called?" Miguel angled himself toward Savannah. Like she could help him.

"That a no?" The hollow depths of Derek's voice promised a solid threat.

Beck shot his answer quickly, hands open and high. "I ain't called the number."

Derek stared at the other two. Hard. That steely look made mobsters' knees knock together.

Savannah scratched behind her right ear. "Why are you looking at me? I don't recognize the stupid card."

"He didn't ask if you recognized the card," Callie said, her voice skating close to a sneer. "He asked if you'd called the number."

Derek raised his chin a smidge, his jaw holding that same stark line, but beneath it she saw the pride beaming. His eyes caught hers, and in their light grey sea she saw only the welcome of acceptance.

"If I've never seen the card, how would I have called the number?" the other woman shouted.

Miguel rested a hand on Savannah's knee. "Chill."

"Are you saying none of you have heard of this Anonymous Souls before today?"

Beck offered , "Nah," but the other two merely nodded.

Derek's chest puffed, but Callie could handle this as long as he was at her back. "Doesn't make sense. You dragged in Vega who is associated with this anonymous group, but didn't know he was a part of it?"

"We bring in who the Charmer says," Savannah snapped.

"I get that. I also know how he works. I know his tirades and his rants. I know he doesn't give a shit about some scrawny dude promising souls and not delivering. He cares a whole fuck of a lot about someone setting up shop. Someone printing goddamn business cards. Someone who would have the balls to trash his fucking store. He didn't send you to pick up anyone. He sent you to handle a threat." She didn't bother pointing out they'd failed miserably.

The Charmer wouldn't stand for this. If he were here, his magic would be slamming them against the walls, fire would be licking Callie's torso, and someone would be giving up a soul. Only he wasn't here and that was possibly even more terrifying.

Savannah launched off the counter. The invisible shield that popped the other woman in the chin and knocked her back against the wall wasn't planned. Callie didn't have the forethought to imagine using the soul magic in such a manner. She hadn't given it *any* thought, actually. Maybe it was the stress of going from a missing mother, to a hospitalized mother, to stealing souls, to picking through blood and glass, to a missing boss, but her emotions were too close to the surface. It wasn't safe to let her guilt and anger out of the black lockbox within her ribcage.

Not that Savannah cared how complicated Callie's life had become. Not when she was bent over, gasping and coughing.

Derek brushed Callie's hair back behind her ear. He whispered, "It's okay, doll. I've got you."

Her fingertips vibrated in time with Savannah's rapid breath. The other woman's soul was responding to her magic. She hadn't erected a magical wall between them. She'd simply shoved the other woman's soul back. The body went, too. Callie straightened her fingers, released her control of the soul, and then shook her hand out. Anise filled her sinuses and the bitter bite of guilt coated her tongue. She wasn't this kind of person. *Couldn't be* this kind of person. She wasn't someone who grabbed other people's fucking souls. That was horror-show shit reserved purely for the Soul Charmer. He did it with purpose. She'd done it on accident, and that was probably worse.

"What the hell was that?" Savannah said between gasping breaths.

The need to apologize pummeled Callie's gut with a one-two punch combination. Before she could do so, Derek spoke. "A reminder we all work for the Charmer."

Savannah bristled, and then Derek added, "And to mind yourself around Callie, too."

He made her sound like a badass. Callie was merely a woman pulled a dozen different ways, but doing her damnedest to keep going. Apparently that now included taking hold of others' souls and shoving them about a bit. Callie let out a short, derisive snort. The Soul Charmer would be practically cooing with praise if he'd witnessed this. Funny how her best improvements with the magic he'd placed in her body were won when he wasn't present. If this smash-and-dash move was intended as a teachable moment, she was going to be pissed.

The others may have grumbled or perhaps the floor was merely whining. Beck stepped between the two factions with referee poise. "So it sounds like we need to call that number."

Callie nodded. "If we're going to assume no one here knows anything about this group, we need to learn as much as we can."

"Answers before the boss gets back are top priority to me, too," Beck said.

Miguel sighed. "You assume he's coming back." Not a question.

"He'll be back," Beck and Derek said together.

"Did anyone talk to the Vega guy?" Callie asked.

Miguel held up two fingers.

"Good." Callie nodded. "We'll call the number and see if you recognize his voice. If Vega answers, this gets a lot simpler."

"He answers, he's probably behind the Anonymous Souls. He doesn't…" Derek stopped himself from pointing out the situation could get worse.

He was a good guy for trying to protect her, but Callie was intimately familiar with the universal truth that shit could always get worse.

CHAPTER SEVENTEEN

Vega didn't answer the phone.

Even through the echo of the speakerphone, the gruff, "How much you need?" wasn't familiar to anyone in the room. Miguel shifted his thumb to end the call, but that wouldn't do.

"A little something through the weekend." Callie's affect was close enough to the regular customers to make her suck her teeth to dislodge the taste. Everyone was watching her, which only made it worse.

"You got cash?" the man on the other end of the line asked.

"It's not like you take cards." Faking this shit was hard. Derek arched a brow, and she could only give him a melodramatic sorry shrug. She was supposed to be ditzy, and antagonizing the source wasn't a good way to get info. She tacked on a fake trilling laugh.

"Is that a yes?" he finally said.

"Cash isn't a problem." Souls were.

"Bring three hundred to this address—" he rattled off an address somewhere in the Railyard. Beck jotted it down. "Be there at six, and we'll hook you up."

"That's a lot of money for a weekend. The Soul Charmer is cheaper than that." Well, he could be. If someone was soul slumming.

The room went silent. Miguel and Savannah were wide-eyed. Beck was holding up a single hand in the international sign of HOLY MOTHER OF GOD STOP. Even Derek was holding his breath. Had she borked this whole thing?

After a half-second longer of awkward silence, the man on the phone said, "The Soul Charmer is screwing you. If you want quality, be there at six with the three hundred. If you don't, good luck renting from that Plaza dwelling asshole."

Callie fell over herself apologizing. It's what one of their "upstanding citizen" customers would do. She also couldn't lose this chance. No matter what she'd done with the collected souls before, no matter what she'd traded to Nate, if Callie could find out who was behind the Anonymous Souls and who stole the Soul Charmer's wares—probably the same people—he'd get over it. He'd exact a price, because he was that kind of person, but it'd be a cost she could bear.

The soul broker hung up first.

"What the hell was that?" Miguel sputtered.

"Looks like she got us a fucking lead," Derek said.

Beck's smile slipped into a toothy grin. "That was

the start of a good plan. Understandable it's unfamiliar to you, M."

Savannah was white-knuckling the edge of the counter. "Har har. Now they know we're on to them."

Was she kidding? "What part of that made you think he was on to us?"

Before Savannah could explain, Miguel said, "Whatever. It's done. Now we have to go get the soul from him and let him stick it in one of us. The Charmer is not going to be good with that."

"The Charmer isn't here," Beck said.

"You're not the one going," Derek added.

"I brought Vega in. The Charmer put this on me," the third soul collector argued.

Who the fuck fought over doing the Charmer's bidding? What did their boss have over them? This wasn't loyalty. It was fear. It had to be.

"First, that wasn't Vega on the phone. Unless you were lying." Callie waited for Miguel to tell her she was wrong. When he didn't, she continued, "Second, you didn't keep Vega here. So fail there. The Charmer is missing, which we all know is batshit. Souls are missing, which is actually even worse. Finally, we work for the bastard and he's going to blame all of us."

"That we can agree on. None of us have forgotten what happened to Gerard," Savannah muttered.

Miguel's harsh whisper sliced the room. "Don't mention him. Not now. Not ever."

Gerard's name didn't slap Callie the same way it

did the others. She hadn't known the man, the soul collector. He was gone now, though, and from the ever-darkening vibe in the room, the Charmer was to blame.

Savannah stretched, and then stepped forward, and Miguel followed.

The five Soul Charmer employees huddled together. *Okay*, Callie thought, *time for a plan.*

"I have to go get the soul. Beck and I are the only ones who can retrieve directly." Callie did not mention that she could pull souls from bodies or force them into jars. The Soul Charmer was shit about sharing information with her, and she hoped he was with the others, too. Until they proved themselves to be more than threats, there was no reason for them to know what she might be capable of.

"Why you?" Beck asked with genuine curiosity. She appreciated the lack of bravado.

"He spoke to a woman on the phone."

"I doubt he'll be the one making the switch," Beck countered.

Derek leveled his best 'back off' look at Beck. "Probably not, but he'll have the details of who is coming. Even if it's just that she's a lady and will have three hundred bucks on her."

"Fine, but I can't just sit around waiting to hear how this goes," Beck said. "I doubt the big man can either."

The infinitesimal tilt of Derek's head suggested he was on the same page, but doing his best not to fight Callie's battles. It was moments like this that she did not regret telling him she loved him.

"I know the Charmer's haunts. I'll hit them and see where he's holed up." Miguel made moves toward the door.

Callie caught his arm. She released it quick enough to avoid being iced in place, but frost hardened in small rings around her fingers. "It's too risky to go after him now."

When it looked like an argument was brewing behind Miguel's tight lips, Callie added, "If people see us looking for him, they'll know he's gone. If someone did take him, they'll also think they're winning."

Miguel deflated. "Good point."

"We need quality souls back in this building. Beck, Miguel, Savannah, can you three hit the high-level targets and get those souls back in this building? We can't have people cutting out on us right now." Everyone looked at her like she knew what the fuck she was doing, and it took a moment to realize that she just might. At least she had a good gut sense of how the Charmer would react.

If the Anonymous Souls group was bold enough to take souls from within the Soul Charmer's emporium, they would be brazen enough to jack souls from his clients. Tess had tried that, and had experienced immolation-level pain for her troubles. That was without robbing him directly. The blood on the back room floor was still wet. Whether it was the Charmer's or Vega's didn't matter. The Soul Charmer was built like an apocalypse-proof insect, and Callie had no intention of failing him. She liked her soul and her skin right where they were.

"We already have a handful of pickups scheduled for today, but I know a few regulars who only rent the pure shit." Savannah checked her phone. She nodded at the screen. "We can rattle five or six of them and push them in here, if you're here to collect the soul."

"Have them here after seven. The Charmer may have returned by then, but if not I should be back from the soul drop off." Callie found herself nodding along like the plan carried at a steady beat.

"If Derek's going with you, then do we put a closed sign?" Beck pulled a drawer from the chest against the far wall. These people were ready to help. Holy shit.

"Is there a closed sign?" Savannah echoed.

Closing shop was not an option. The Soul Charmer had never closed his doors since he'd opened the small space ten years ago. She hadn't seen his living quarters, but he slept somewhere nearby. Obviously he slipped away for some Z's, and to tend the soul well. One of them had always been here, though. The image of her arm ablaze lit her memory. *Let's not do that again.*

"No closed sign. Derek and I can stay here until I have to leave for the drop site. Derek, will you keep the clients distracted until I can get back?"

She winced in preparation for the impact, but all he said was, "No."

"No? We can't close the shop." This was one of those times when she wished he could read every worst-case scenario flitting through her mind. This could go sideways in a hurry, and they couldn't risk being caught in it.

"You can't go alone." Those four words were the granite foundation for an upcoming argument, if Callie didn't fix this fast.

"I've got this. It'll be quick." She wiggled her fingers at him, a reminder she had a magical backup.

"It isn't safe for you to be out there alone, especially not with them. Not now."

Not now? she mouthed.

"Zara."

Oh. Oh oh oh. Later she'd need to thank him for not spilling her secrets all over the soggy carpet. Telling these strangers that her mother had been kidnapped and mutilated recently was too dangerous. The less they knew of her weaknesses, the safer she and Derek would be.

"You need to lay low right now," she whispered, "but you're right. I won't be alone."

Beck was close enough to hear her hushed words. "I can go with her."

"Where you go, I go." Each time Derek had said those words to her, she'd gone a bit gooey for him. This time the promise hurt. He wasn't holding her back, but by tethering himself to her, he was once again shoving himself into more danger. They needed to take turns on the danger shit. It was her turn.

"I can't lose you now," was all she could manage to say soft enough for only him. It was all she could manage without tears. A little louder, "Beck could help us."

Beck took his cue, and infused it with earnestness. "It'll be a short run, but I can make sure no one tails us and no one tries anything handsy."

Handsy was the least of their problems, but he didn't need to know that. Derek must have agreed on that front. "All right, Beck. You go with her. Stay close to her, and if she comes back with so much as a bruise, what happens to you is tenfold."

Derek clapped him on the back, and Callie tried to ignore the fact they were praising one another over taking care of a woman. Derek wasn't that guy. He was thanking someone else for helping him, he was not doubting her. Magic skills were good, but when it's five on one, an extra set of hands matters.

A broken, tired chuckle was all Beck could muster, but he nodded his agreement.

They had a plan.

Get one soul from the Anonymous crew, and hope it led to more. If they were lucky, they might even get the Soul Charmer back. Lord help her. Since when did anyone want that asshole back?

CHAPTER EIGHTEEN

Beck promised to be back at five thirty to go with Callie to grab a soul from the Anonymous folk. He, Miguel, and Savannah left. It was still early in the afternoon, and that left Callie and Derek alone in the Soul Charmer's shop.

The throaty rumble of a muscle car faded away slowly. When it was quiet, Callie asked, "What now?"

Those two basic words bore the weight of a massive question. She wasn't asking how to kill the time.

"It's an out." His gravelly whisper was the kind of sound reserved for back seats of cars. While better when the conversation was dirty, the intimacy was not lost on Callie.

Stretching her neck for long seconds to the right, and then the left didn't loosen the muscles bracketing her spine. "Maybe," she said finally. "It can't be this easy. We can't just walk out."

He turned meaningfully to the door. Their escape. Their answer. "Why not? That's the plan, right?"

Did he doubt that she wanted him, wanted out of this? "Of course it's the plan. We can't let him hold us here, let him keep ladling on the fucking guilt like hot fudge on a Friday night."

"You worried about rising to Heaven now, doll?" His eyes held no humor.

"I didn't used to worry about sin, but now I'm bearing more and more. His and Josh's and Zara's and it's a lot."

"Hey." Heavy arms and soft leather wrapped around her.

"I'm not worried about Heaven, Derek. I'm worried about here."

He tightened his arms around her. "I'm good. I've got you."

"I need to keep you." Why did honesty always catch in her throat?

"Not going anywhere, doll. Unless you want to book it, and then we go together."

God, she wished it were really an option. The plan to ditch this place was in its infancy, but that hadn't made it less real. Derek was willing to do it. The realization hit her hard behind the knees. His embrace held her steady now, but even he couldn't stop the Soul Charmer's wrath if they bailed on this. If hellfire was real, the Soul Charmer could wield it.

"I wish we could." Callie shot a furtive look around

the barren room. The tapestries wavered when the furnace kicked on, but otherwise only her and Derek's energy filled the center of the space. "This whole thing is off, though. He puts magic walls up over everything."

"Yeah. I know, but you said they're gone. He's gone, so maybe that makes sense?" Derek kissed the top of her head.

"But they aren't actually gone. Not all of them. It's changed, and I don't know how to explain it, but there's more at play here. You saw the coal." It wasn't a question, but part of her needed the validation she wasn't alone.

His thumb worried in a small circle at her shoulder.

"Right?" she prodded. Tell me I'm not losing my shit.

"I saw the coal, if that was what the black stuff was. I saw it melt into the ground or disappear or I don't know what that was, but yeah, Callie, I saw it." A man that size shouldn't sound reedy. She didn't care. The truth was there between them, and if he could at least see that much magic, it might be okay.

"Okay. Well, that coal was his magic. Only…"

"Only what?"

It wasn't? It left a tang pinching her taste buds and pressure in her ears, and neither of those things was tangible when it came to explanations. "I don't know…it was his magic, only messed up."

Derek rocked his weight back into his heels, and Callie swayed with him. His voice was sturdy, his words stronger. "If his magic has rotted, all the more reason to leave Gem City."

"If his magic can turn, so can mine." She hated the soft squeak of her voice.

Derek took her face in his hands. His grey eyes met hers with steely resolve. "You are beautiful and strong. He's a shit stain, and so his magic is ugly and wrong. That isn't you. I know it isn't."

In a flash his lips were against hers, warm and fervent. Callie tried to take in his ardent belief that she was so much better than the Soul Charmer, that her magic wasn't tainted. That nasty voice in the back her mind—one that sounded too much like her mother after a half dozen whiskey shooters—reminded her she'd ripped a soul out of man's body, that she'd burned the flesh off a woman, that when push came to shove, she wasn't afraid to get ugly if it protected those she loved.

Derek's fire smoldered, but he pulled back. "There's more, isn't there?"

Humor expanded in her chest. "Are you asking because shit always gets worse or because I'm being the mood killer?"

"You're not killing the mood, doll." His gaze lingered on her lips. His hand slid around to cup the nape of her neck. The simple, possessive act pushed all tension from her back. "You wouldn't be willing to stay here if there weren't more. I'll keep fighting here with you as long as you want, but now would be a good time to let me in."

He so rarely pushed that Callie couldn't be bothered by the request. It was fair for him to want to know why. She hadn't demanded he align himself with her, but that didn't change the fact he had. He'd helped her saved Zara. He'd helped her save Josh. He'd helped *her*. Derek was damn near family, and it was time she started trusting him like it.

"The souls back here?" She pointed toward the curtain like he didn't know where the fucking souls were stored. "What's left are the good ones."

Derek watched her. Waited. She bit her lip, and he inhaled sharply. "Why did you send Miguel and Savannah to pick up the good ones then?"

He said it so plainly. "I did send them, didn't I?" She no longer had to hide her awe.

Derek's lips found hers again, and this time she let herself fall into the moment. The air between them sparked with potential. Callie leaned into the static between them until her breasts were crushed against Derek's chest. It was her turn to be soft and pliant against his hard and sturdy. Everything she needed. She deepened the kiss. Derek dug his fingers into her hair. She stepped backward, and pulled him along.

Her butt bumped against a sideboard table. It was an inch over hip height, and Derek easily lifted Callie to sit atop it. The dark wood disappeared in the minimal lighting, and Callie with it. Her knees fell wide, and Derek rushed forward between them. The dual layers of denim between them failed to hide how much they needed this. Derek pressed the hard ridge hidden behind his jeans against Callie. She gasped, and arched forward. Her mouth slipped down his neck until she was almost to his shoulder. Sweat shouldn't be this sweet. It was. *He* was. Derek surged forward. The sideboard clapped against the wall. Every nerve ending low in Callie's abdomen fired, tightened, demanded at once. She bit down on Derek's shoulder. His groan could have shaken the snow from the mountains.

Callie shoved her hands between them. She began to unfasten her jeans, but Derek's fist in her hair stalled her. She flipped direction and began to unbutton his pants. He angled his hips forward until she could barely move her hands. She nudged him back, but he refused to budge.

His lips left hers, but he held her hair wrapped between his fingers. "That's a cheat, Callie."

"What?" She wanted him. How was that a fucking cheat?

His chest rose and fell in double time. He shouldn't have been wearing a shirt. "You're dodging my question. Please."

Fuck. She needed to give him the truth, and instead she was thinking with her heart—and maybe her lady bits. The realization of her accidental asshole move was as good as ice cubes down her back.

"Sorry. Not intentional." She hadn't even meant to divert. Maybe that was a Delgado gene.

"So why are they after the good souls?" He didn't even sound disappointed with her. She was too fucking lucky.

"'Good souls' is relative, but I wasn't lying that we need those. If these Anonymous people take the high-value ones the Charmer will go apocalyptic."

He waited. Maybe lucky was the wrong word. That bastard knew her too well.

The hem of his shirt had ridden up during the momentary make-out session. Callie rested her hand against the smooth skin at his hip. He let her, and the access reminded her they were a team. "The case back there that was empty held the heavily used souls."

Derek's grip on her hair released. "How much is heavy? The Charmer said it's ten rentals max."

"Over twenty." *Ish.*

"That could kill someone," he snapped. Derek's eyes were wide, panicked. Callie brushed her thumb against his skin in slow circles. She wasn't the one who was dealing those souls, and he needed to remember that. A breath later he was steadier. "You saw what happens with a bad match."

He didn't have to remind her of the trip to the hospital. The rented soul needed an escape, and it thought taking out its host would get it there. Now that Callie understood some of the shop's souls came from purgatory she understood. Maybe the fight wasn't worth the get for some.

"I remember." She pressed her index finger against his lips. It wouldn't hold back the details, but he understood. "The Soul Charmer warned me about those souls specifically."

"Do you think he knew someone was after them?" he said against her finger, a breathy kiss.

"I hadn't considered that." Honestly. "It was more like he was batting my hands away from a hot stove."

His eyes softened.

"Okay. Yes, he probably would let me touch a hot stove, but the analogy stands. He was warning me not to bring those out for renters. They were only for specific people."

"People he wanted to kill?" Derek asked the question Callie could only think.

"He didn't say that." But would he?

Derek eased back. The space between them growing, but never cooling. "Do we think they were stolen on purpose?"

"I'm not sure it matters. If they knew they were buying the most tarnished goods, then they're out to kill people. If they thought they were crashing and pocketing whatever they could reach, they won't know enough about the magic to avoid damage anyway. One way or another the idiots who rent from us are going to get hurt. Those souls won't be enough to pick up the slack. Either they come back for round two or they have to start stealing from people to fill the demand."

"You think people will die?" That question coupled with Derek's unwavering gaze would have made her bolt if she didn't love him. Thank God that intensity was directed at anyone who would fuck with her.

"You don't?"

He shrugged, but there was nothing easy about the motion. "They always die. I just need to make sure *we* don't die. If someone did plan this, it won't be the end."

"The magic around here is off. I don't know if it was the Soul Charmer or someone else, but I think I can keep this place secure."

Derek grabbed her by the hips and yanked her forward. He leaned close until his mouth was next to her ear. "Hell has a special place for anyone that would go against my Callie. We can put up a good front together, but as soon as we're out of this, you're mine."

She arched against him with pure intent. "I'm yours now."

"Fine. Once this is over, *I'm* done with the Soul Charmer."

She rolled her hips toward his, and found his interest had only grown harder. "Ah, so you're saying you get to be fully mine?"

"Consider it done, doll."

———

Fucking in the front of the Soul Charmer's store was both just right as a screw you to the boss and just wrong as a key romantic moment. Callie took one look at Derek, his elbows braced on the counter and a sated smile on his lips. It had been the right call.

Callie pulled on her jeans. Her phone toppled from the back pocket. Two messages from Josh were displayed.

"Docs say Mom will be OK," read the first.

"Going to work. Aunt Lily is driving up tonight," read the other.

His meth days really did make her brother short on the text conversations. Callie pursed her lips like the act would purge the pill of guilt she needed to swallow.

"How's Zara?" Derek asked.

She relayed the message contents to him, and tried not to think about her mom being alone in a hospital.

"It's bright outside, and we have a couple hours until the soul pick up. Go visit her." Derek was so fucking sincere sometimes it stung.

"I can't—"

"You can," he cut her off. "You'll feel better knowing she's solid and safe. The backroom needs a serious scrub, and I can do that."

"You shouldn't have to do it alone."

"Don't start stealing my lines." He nudged her toward the door. "Nah. You can't go back there. I don't want that blood on you, but also we need that room to Charmer level crazy."

Callie cranked her side-eye shade to eleven.

"I've worked here a long ass time. I can make Miguel believe the Charmer magic godmothered that shit back there."

Callie's laugh was real and from the belly, and so out of place in this den of depravity. Well, if she could screw in it, she might as well be able to laugh here, too.

The suede swagger Derek was throwing didn't fool her. She was a bird one couldn't hold too tightly, and he was smart enough to know that stopping her from going places wouldn't end well. Since his heart was in the right place and he hadn't fought to go with her, she'd accept it.

"I'll be quick," she said, and then barreled into him for a bear of a hug.

"And I'll be here, doll."

CHAPTER NINETEEN

Cold air and the sharp edge of astringent welcomed Callie to St. Stephen's Hospital.

An orderly bumped into her. "Sorry, ma'am. Do you need directions?"

A faint cooing caught the air. Callie looked down the bright hallway, but only saw hospital staff and a couple patients awaiting triage. No toddler sipping milk.

"Ma'am? Do you need help to the ER?" The woman's gentle tone mirrored the coo.

Callie stretched her magic until it grazed the woman in pink scrubs. *It's okay. We'll help you*, was the response she got. The pleased hum was from this woman's soul. Why the hell was Callie hearing people's souls who weren't on her list? This lady wasn't even a renter. The soul chattering away was kind and generous and completely intact.

"Oh, no. Sorry. I'm here to visit my mom." God, the truth tasted good. "Little dazed."

"Completely normal. Do you want me to look up her room number for you?" The woman was attempting to corral her toward the emergency triage.

Callie edged out of arm's distance. "No need. She's up on the fourth floor."

Concern flashed on the orderly's face, but she quickly shuttered it. "I hope she recovers quickly. Elevator banks are ahead on the right."

Callie thanked her, and hurried forward. She jammed her thumb against the Up button, and waited. The directory between the two elevators let her know the fourth floor housed the intensive care unit. Josh hadn't said anything about the ICU. He said Zara was stable. A soft chime announced the doors opening. Callie swore under her breath and charged into the elevator. A violent blast of cold pushed Callie back against the side wall. Her hands froze into tight fists. She shifted her arm up, and heard the subtle fissures of splintering ice.

The two men inside the elevator didn't tug their jackets closed or tighten their stances. The icy air was only for her. The older of the two raked her with a rude gaze. Callie didn't want to reach for his soul. She didn't need to sense it to know he was the kind of man who kept a pair of sweatpants in the trunk of his car for emergency stops at strip clubs.

The other man was closer to Callie's age, and managed a bored affect as he asked, "Floor?"

Three tiny pinches at her ribs warned her not to tell them. It was a fucking floor, but in Gem City nothing was ever simple. Not even pressing a button on an elevator. "Five," she lied.

The older creep edged to the center of the space. He walked hips first. She wasn't going to fall for that dare. The small screen reading out the floors was the only place she was willing to look.

Frost clawed at her neck. How many times had these guys rented to be throwing off this kind of chill? The screen said they were at the third floor. Creep-O stepped in front of the doors, but turned to face her. That shit was not an accident. Only ax murderers and assholes made eye contact in an elevator with uninterested strangers.

The nasty wisps of his soul began to catcall. Which circle of Hell was dominated by men who catcalled? Was there a deeper one for those who bore their misogyny so deeply in their souls that even it couldn't resist rasping the filthy, unwanted things it'd do to her? She fucking hoped so.

Her voice box was locked in a cage of ice. Her grating attempt to speak only earned her a prurient grin of cracked lips. The younger man was pointedly staring at the panel of buttons. He'd get a stellar seat deep below, too.

Her magic prickled beneath the frosty layer. She didn't need to speak to stop him. She didn't need her hands to shove him. These men had tattered souls, though. They didn't need to know what she could do. The screen displayed a bright, red five. Creep-O didn't move, and his companion didn't acknowledge the intimidation.

Callie inhaled and pulled the energy around her in close. It coalesced into a cobbled cloak, every bit the patchwork quilt her grandmother had atop her bed. The chill began to ebb. Her limbs broke free and she stepped forward. She met the douchebag's eyes, and delighted in the panic. He narrowed his gaze, and his arms locked. He was readying for something, but she wasn't about to find out what. Her magic barrier bumped his soul back, and she slipped past and onto the fifth floor.

She wouldn't give him the satisfaction of looking back. Her magic, though, stretched behind her until the man's soul could no longer be sensed.

Callie ducked into the stairwell before she could run into another soul user. She didn't care if they weren't hostile. She needed a goddamn second. When the heavy, fire door clapped shut behind her, she let out a long breath. Hospitals used to be her favorite place. It was the kind of truth she never said aloud, both because it made her sound like a masochist and because it meant admitting she'd lost a key part of herself. Her life had been on track to saving people's lives. She'd been living an above-board life. Now she ripped souls out of people, doled out the equivalent of celestial cheat codes, and had done enough bad shit to earn her twenty to life. Not exactly an upward trajectory.

She began descending the stairs to her mother's floor. This visit wasn't about her. She wasn't here to reminisce. No one was rubbing the loss of potential in her face. She'd came here on her own. It'd been a few years. She needed to move on, and, honestly, it could be worse. No one had chopped off any of *her* fingers.

Hospital's fourth floor was quieter. No one was lingering in the hall when Callie entered. For the best. No one would peg her as the "let's just take the stairs" type. The television in the waiting area was on, but no one was watching. Callie used the brief moment to gather herself. She watched the news loop on the screen. The world's problems could dwarf hers. The ticker proclaimed one of the blow-hards in the Op-Ed department of the local newspaper was calling for congress to act against soul renting. Congressmen were commenting on potential legislation holding those who pawned their souls responsible for the crimes committed with them. Good God. They had no idea how soul magic worked, and they were still trying to control it. The last thing she needed was the Soul Charmer on national television being questioned about the nature of soul rental and how to regulate it against crime. How long would it take the local diocese to get involved and quash this?

So much for a distraction. Callie refocused on the hospital, on finding Zara.

Double doors were down to her left. The red glow of the card reader told her it was the ICU before any signage did. The nurse's station was also on the left. Callie checked her phone. No new messages. Josh hadn't given her the room number.

Three nurses were behind the desk. Two were busy with charts, but the one seated at the desk offered a wan smile. Callie didn't recognize any of them, and the brick of shame she'd been carrying crumbled. None of these people knew her past. Today she could be normal—a woman who was worried about her mom.

She stepped up to the desk. A brushing chill hit her, but the subtle stiffness of her knuckles was nothing after the elevator event.

Callie offered her own tired attempt at a hello. "I'm looking for Zara Delgado."

His smile faded. "Are you family?"

Either they were suspicious of her mother's circumstances or the family parade was in town. Knowing her crew, it really could be either. "She's my mother. My brother Josh was here earlier. He called me." Was she talking too much? Did this nurse suspect she'd seen her mom before the hospital?

Maybe the nurse's stare was the result of hour eleven of a twelve-hour shift.

"Is she okay?" Callie added, and shot a pointed look at the doors to the ICU.

The nurse nodded. "She's stable. They've got her down in 443."

He pointed to Callie's right.

"Thanks so much." She hurried away from the desk before he could ask more questions. She was running on limited time, and she needed to see Zara was recovering for herself.

"Visiting hours run until four," he called after her.

She couldn't stay here that late anyway. Callie

turned left twice more before she found room No. 443. The door was slightly ajar, but Callie rapped a quick double tap on the wood as she passed. Old habits and such.

Zara was never a full make-up kind of person. Sure, she'd slather the shit on when necessary for a con—especially one at a casino—but when not hustling someone it was solely mascara and moisturizer. Her hair, though, was another matter. Every fly-away was perfectly tamed, each end even and uniform. The woman lying in the bed didn't look like either the larger-than-life hustler or the space-y hippie. This woman was frail. Her skin was too tight over her cheekbones. Rings of red, purple, and black rippled over the rest of the cheek. Her hair was slick and flat. Her forehead glistened around the edges of white gauze.

"Did you dunk me in bleach? This place smells horrible." Zara's eyes were closed.

"Not really up to me." Callie strived for a light tone, but seeing one's mother like this sliced a sliver of your heart away.

"Callie?" Zara still didn't look at her, but the lilt in her voice was enough welcome.

"Yeah, Mom."

Silence stretched. Police officers hadn't been stationed at the door, but that meant nothing. The divide, though, wasn't just out of self-preservation. It wasn't about lying low. The chasm cutting through the hospital room was one of mothers and daughters. It was one of family and disappointment. Callie needed to apologize for the things she'd said, for what she'd done.

The last time they were together, she'd slammed a beer bottle against her mother's sternum and sucked out the rented soul.

"I was worried about you," didn't cover it, but it's all her heart could afford.

Zara opened her eyes. They were bloodshot. "Clearly I'm surviving."

Surviving. In another time, she might have spat the word back. Callie had warned her how dangerous it was to dabble in soul magic outside of the Charmer. She'd told her Josh had gotten in bad people, and that Ford's goons were never done with potential revenue streams. "Heard you had to get stitches."

Her mother began to nod, but a wince stopped her. The steady blip of the heart rate monitor jumped. "Stitches aren't a problem."

The accusation that *she* was the problem was a standard Zara move. This woman might have a dozen wires slipping away from her body, but there was no question this was her mother. Because she was her daughter, though, Callie couldn't help herself. "What is the problem?"

The electrocardiogram needles twitched. "This is a bit of a fucking problem." Zara lifted her left hand. The skin was hidden behind a mount of gauze, but the shape was too short.

Callie had been ready to fill the gulf between them with all her anger. It would have made it easier to pretend this wasn't her fault. Tears glimmered, unshed, in Zara's eyes. That did it. Fuck the sea of issues between them. Callie would just leap over the water.

She took her mother in her arms. The machines whizzed nearby, but nothing that would send a nurse to check on them. "Mom. Mom. Mom. I'm so sorry this happened to you. You didn't deserve this."

And that was the truth of it. Zara was a shitty mom, and probably a shitty person. She was still family, and Callie couldn't stop loving her. She'd tried. Even with all that, Zara didn't deserve to be tortured for Nate's leverage.

Zara's good hand wrapped around Callie and pulled her close. Warm tears fell on Callie's shoulders, and it was enough to let loose her own tears. The two women cried in close comfort. The last time Zara had held her like this, Callie had to have been six or seven. The realization had her tightening her hold on her mom.

"You magic people aren't normal," Zara said between shaky breaths. "Josh will get us revenge, though."

Of all the idiotic ways to see this. Callie released her mom, and then let loose her frustration, too. "Those weren't magic people, they were drug people, Mom. Which of your kids would know them?"

"Those men made it clear why they were taking each finger, and your brother's name sure as shit didn't come up."

Callie opened her mouth to dive into a real argument. Her emotions were too close to the surface. She'd let her wall crack, and Zara had wedged a spear right where it counted. The cloying cleansers in the air caught Callie's attention. Centered her. She looked at her mom again. Saw the other woman. Saw the Demerol drip. Saw the other bruises. Zara was a victim here, and she wasn't in a place to be having big conversations. Much less ones that could implicate her children in crimes. "Let's…not. I'm sorry I brought it up. For now let's focus on getting you better."

"The hospital staff are for that."

"Low blow, Mom."

Her mother's defiant shrug had to have tweaked the busted ribs, but Zara didn't flinch.

"I just wanted to know you were okay. I'll let the hospital staff take care of you." She wanted to end it there. Storm out. Pretend she gave zero fucks. She couldn't. "Aunt Lily will be here tonight. You don't want me here, and that's fine, but Josh and I will make sure family is here for you."

Zara had closed her eyes again. "Family first. At least you remember the words."

Callie turned to leave. A large bouquet of bright lilies, mums, and roses was tucked in the corner of the room. "Who sent those?"

The Delgados could be counted on for bail money, but not so much for floral arrangements.

"A nice guy named Adam brought them by. He's a friend of Josh's. Nice ass, too."

Callie tried not to choke on her own saliva. Adam had been here. He name-dropped Josh. Nate was behind this. Even after she'd delivered him his soul and then some. He wasn't done with her? Fine. Once she got through this shit with the Soul Charmer, she'd exact vengeance.

But first she had to make sure family was scheduled to monitor Zara around the clock until this bullshit was under control—or buried beneath the ground.

CHAPTER TWENTY

Callie was out of breath when she reached her car. She'd taken the stairs down—four goddamn flights. Being felt up by a soul might have turned her off elevators for life. Even with the heater on full-blast, it took her car several minutes to get warm. Callie waited. She told herself it was to fight the cold, but it was bullshit. The hospital visit had rattled her. She'd expected the eerie envy of the men and women in scrubs. A life she'd lost. She was almost getting used to existing on the darker edges of society. The realization her magic had protected her from the men in the elevator was heady. If she hadn't heard his soul, would she have been scared? Absolutely. She didn't need to hear the perverse language to know Creep-O wasn't familiar with the word consent. His companion wouldn't have helped her. If she hadn't been able to erect the wall to shield herself, those extended minutes in a tiny box could have marked her for eternity.

Callie nudged open her car door, and vomited. Even energy shots and water couldn't settle against that fucking truth. A couple people bustled past her parked car, but none gave her a second glance. Locals didn't gawk. Thank God. She closed the door again, and swiped her sleeve across her mouth. Was that why she'd been so volatile with Zara? After what her mother went though, how could Callie have let anger override her common decency? She could have taught a master class in taking care of belligerent mothers, but you wouldn't have known it by today's behavior. She flipped open the center console and rummaged past cables and an inch-thick stack of fast food napkins until she found a small bottle of the energy drink. She knocked it back. Her stomach punched back up, but not hard enough to expel the liquid.

She put the car into drive, and headed back toward the Charmer's shop. She hadn't been thrilled about backup for meeting the Anonymous Souls dealer, but after today's encounter it no longer rankled to have Beck tag along. She glanced at the clock—it was almost five already. She toed the accelerator a little lower. The sidewalk traffic increased the closer she got to downtown, but thankfully the streets were fairly clear. Dirty snow was clumped on either side of the road. Callie turned onto a side street, and the steering column whined. Derek would want to fix that, too. She bumped along the hodgepodge road of brick and concrete. She was only blocks from the Soul Charmer's store when she had to slam both feet onto the brake.

A man in a grey parka staggered into the street, his back to her. It was twice as wide as she was. At least he was hard to miss. He lifted a bulky, black camera and angled it toward one of the low lampposts. It had to be something fancy and expensive to have the long lens and the bright flash. If he could afford that, you'd think he could afford some basic life skills like 'don't step out into oncoming traffic.' Callie slammed the heel of her palm against the horn. He startled, and then spun toward her. She couldn't hear what he was saying, but he had the sense to look abashed. Callie wouldn't try to guess where the tourist was from. She simply hoped he didn't find his way to the Soul Charmer's. Idiot tourists were a pain in her ass before she had to worry about getting back the rented goods before they left the state.

Callie parked near the back of the shop, but walked around to the front door rather than taking her usual route inside. Even if Derek had the blood and glass gone, she wasn't ready to test the lingering magic there. Her nerves were fried and whatever the Charmer left for her was not going to help the situation.

The anteroom was empty. The gentle hum of the furnace welcomed her. She waved at the conquistador woven into the tapestry on the north wall. He did not wave back, which given this day was a good sign. The slick surface of the countertop had smudges of black ash at the edges. She swiped a finger through one pass. The soot was smooth against her skin, but a half second later the material began to bubble and fizz until it was gone. It didn't evaporate as much as slip into her pores. Scrubbing her hand against her pant's leg did not quell the lingering tingle in her fingertip. It also didn't leave dark smudges on her jeans.

"Is anything in this place real?" she muttered to herself.

"Yo."

Callie shot a look over her shoulder to see Beck stepping into the shop. A wicked wind gust blasted in behind him and had the conquistador art shivering, too. Beck waved at her with two fingers.

Maybe he hadn't heard her talking to herself. "Hey."

"You ready to see how the other side lives?" He tugged off his gloves.

"Ready to be done with this and have the Charmer back here."

Beck didn't bother hiding his grin. His smiles were all teeth and all light. Must be nice. "Bet you didn't think you'd say that."

He had her there. "True enough."

"If it makes you feel better, I was surprised to miss the fucker, too."

"I wouldn't go that far." Her playful tone masked the unvarnished truth.

Derek emerged from the curtain. The white cloth in his hands was stained with dark reds. "Where are we going?"

"To rent a soul, of course." Beck sang the words like he was about to hop on the Yellow Brick Road.

Callie could play along. "I tried renting before and

didn't get the hype."

Beck laughed. Derek's brows lowered. He wiped his hands on the cloth. If menace had a signature look, this was it. "Not a time for joking." He wasn't talking to Callie.

"Doom and gloom doesn't make this shit any easier. You of all people should know that." Beck shoved his hands into his coat pockets, and the fabric puckered at his shoulders.

Derek dropped the rag on the counter, and then took two mammoth steps toward the other soul collector. "This isn't a joke. Protecting her isn't a game."

"Got it, man, but I can't go into this with us looking terrified. She's supposed to be some party tourist idiot wanting an escape for a weekend high. If she shows up with me all broody badass with her, it ain't going to work. Fuck, that's one of the reasons you're staying here. You're good at scaring the shit out of people. We need that here, remember."

"Hold up." Callie had to shout to be heard. "He's here because he's the one who can handle this shop, but know if the Charmer were here, Derek would be with me and it wouldn't be an issue. Do not doubt his ability to do whatever needs to be done." She would not ask about that rag.

"Whoa." Beck's shoulders lowered. "Guess I know why you two are together. Fucking A. Yeah. Fine. Derek's a ninja and you believe in the power of love or whatever. Can we just get this done?"

Derek ambled to Callie's side, and the testosterone

in the air began to dissipate.

"You're right. We need to focus." Callie hadn't consumed enough calories to multitask for long anyway.

"Agreed." The heavy boulder Derek loaded on the word shook it until everyone felt the weight.

Callie cast him a side-glance, and hoped he could see the question in it. Was there more? Was it something that could be shared in this company?

"Still no sign of the boss?" Beck asked. His gaze skittered from them to the wall and back. It was almost as if they were making out hardcore in front of him, and he didn't want to be the perv who watched. Which was great except no clothes were being shoved to the side.

Derek shook his head, and then added, "He didn't show, but the cops did."

"What?" Callie's stomach hollowed out, readying for a second blow. The Soul Charmer had shielded Derek last time, but no one was here to offer magical protection earlier. If she hadn't spent quality time with her mom, she would have been here. Not that she knew how to hide her boyfriend in plain sight, but she could have distracted someone. He was still here, though. No police had been stationed at the door when she returned. Callie hissed on an exhale. "I mean, what happened?"

"And what about the storage room?" Beck added.

Shit. She hadn't even through about the hell scape that was broken glass and sticky blood covering the room behind the curtain. It didn't matter how persuasive you were, or how crooked a cop was, ignoring a room covered in blood was a hard sell.

"I dealt with it." Derek's hard tone might have made Beck bristle, but Callie wasn't scared. The more she thought about the intrusion and the danger, the more outraged she became.

"What happened? What did they ask? Are they coming back?" Her rapid-fire questioning didn't give him a breath to butt in.

"They showed up and wanted to talk to me." If he gave her that 'no big deal' shrug again, she was going to slug him.

"Talk to you about what?" Beck asked. "Are they looking for the Soul Charmer? Do they know?"

Derek rested a heavy hand on Callie's hip, but he spoke to Beck. "They're always looking for the Charmer, but they didn't know he was missing. I didn't clue them in either."

Did Beck know that the Charmer was behind the bombings? That Derek was involved? She had to play it safe. The fewer people who knew what Derek had done, the safer he'd be. "What did they want to ask him? More of the same?"

"They had questions about how he sources souls. Made some threat about how our business was going to be illegal in a few months, and how I should look for another income stream."

"The news had something about an idiot calling for people who pawn their souls to be held liable for the actions of whoever rented it, but it wasn't a politician." Didn't that shit take time? She'd been more interested in biology than political science in high school, but she was pretty sure legal shit took forever. Debates and lobbying and other bullshit meant to rack up billable hours.

"I'm sure you're right," Derek's tone was gentle for her. "They wanted an excuse to rattle him. Rattle us."

"And that's all they wanted?" She needed the assurance.

He gave her a subtle squeeze with the arm wrapped around her waist. The hint of bleach hit her over the stale Nag Champa in the air.

"That's all these cops asked about." Different cops then. Just what they needed: more cops stopping by for little chats.

Beck watched the volleys between Derek and Callie with too much interest. You didn't get to be trusted by the Soul Charmer by being an idiot. Callie needed to remember that.

"Any trouble with the back?" Beck asked.

"They didn't want to search the place, but the back is clean. Downstairs is still a fucking shit storm, but I figured you broke it, you'd clean it."

Beck stretched a hand over his shoulder and pressed his fingers against his traps. When he let his hand fall back to his side, he gave his head a subtle shake. "I don't even know if you're kidding anymore."

Derek's half-hearted shrug didn't offer much, but it

made Beck snort.

It had taken Derek time to get comfortable enough to jest with her. How long had he known Beck? The tension in the room was beginning pinch Callie's nerves. Or maybe it was residual magic.

"You've been working here too long," Beck said.

While Callie agreed, neither she nor Derek said as much.

She checked the time on her phone. The digits helped her for once. She needed an excuse out of this room, and time was a good one. "We should get going."

"Right." Beck turned toward the door.

"Do I look like I'm angling for a good time?" she said to Derek.

The storm clouds billowing in his gaze parted. "I hope not, since you're leaving with him."

She bumped her elbow against his ribs without any force. "For the pickup—"

"I know, doll." He reached forward, and tugged the hair tie from her ponytail. His forearm brushed her jaw. She started to lean into the touch, but caught herself at Beck's cough. Derek brought her hair forward over a shoulder. His fingers lingered in her tresses for a moment. "Hair down is better. Ponytail is your get shit done look."

She huffed. "Ponytail is my fuck blow-dryers look."

His deep, bourbon-drenched grumble would have

made her stay, if this wasn't so important. She took hold of his tee shirt, and tugged him forward with it. Their kiss was hard and far too short, but it was a promise and a threat. *Come back or I'll come for you* met *I'll return for more of that and more of you.*

"Thanks," she whispered. He trusted her to do this alone. He wasn't going to fight her battles for her, because sometimes she needed to be the one who handled shit. Sometimes she needed to protect him. Doing what it takes was in her DNA. Like called to like there. He lifted his chin toward the door, his masculine endorsement of the plan. That man was better at nonverbal communication than she was at words.

Beck pulled open the Soul Charmer's door, and Callie stepped through first. This place had brought nothing but torture, murder, and depravity into her life, but it'd also brought her Derek. For the first time, she was eager to find a soul and return to the Soul Charmer's shop in downtown Gem City.

CHAPTER TWENTY-ONE

The Railyard was one of the few areas in the city that tourists would frequent at night. The designated pick-up point from Anonymous Souls was in front of a pottery place in the bustling district. The sidewalk wasn't packed, but a steady stream of people hurried past Callie.

Ruby's Ceramics, though, was packed with people painting and laughing. The pottery shop was part gallery, part bring your own booze and make shit classrooms. This evening it looked to be heavily leaning on the latter. Almost every table had two bottles of wine on it. Callie hadn't painted pottery before, but with a solid buzz she'd be willing to try. That is, if she ever got to have a normal night that didn't involve clandestine meetings and missing people.

Callie and Beck stood outside of the small studio and waited for their dealer to arrive. Icicles stretched from the lower points of the street lamp, but the lamp's steady golden flow wasn't hindered by frost. The snow had stopped, but the temperature was steadily dropping. That's how the desert worked, even in the winter. Getting colder was part of the package. Callie tugged her scarf higher to touch her chin. Derek had given her this one. It was thick, knitted wool the color of a cabernet wine in a dark corner. It wasn't what she would have picked for herself, but it was perfect. It was cozy and vibrant and carried enough of Derek's scent to remind her he'd have her back even if he weren't here.

Beck cupped his hands over his mouth. Steam slipped from the edges. "Hope these people are punctual."

"If they're trying to steal business from the Charmer, you'd think they would be. If they're too late, people will go to someone else."

"Maybe. Some people aren't the biggest fans of our boss."

Understatement. "Some people? No one likes him, but there's never a shortage at his place and he's always there…" Callie's mouth moved ahead of her brain, and the last words trickled out as she mentally twisted off the tap.

Beck knocked his shoulders back. His chest was broader; he was bigger. The hawk on Callie's wrist probably did the same thing. That proud puffing could be a good deterrent to a fight. Not that she was trying to start one.

She quickly changed the subject. "Do we look like we're planning to party later?"

Callie bounced on the balls of her feet, hoping it looked like she was keyed up—from excitement or coke, she didn't care. Either way it diffused the jitters.

A puff of smoke carried his staccato laugh into the night air. "I'd buy you were ready to hit a bar and dance."

"I wouldn't mind a drink, if I'm honest." Focusing on their conversation helped steady her nerves. Or maybe a swig or two from one of the bottles of wine inside the pottery joint.

Her magic was mingling with the crisp air, and she stretched it behind her. The men and women hurrying along the sidewalk steered clear of them as a result. The people were far enough from her to keep unnatural ice from coating her skin. She was at peak cold, and could really do without magical bullshit. However, she did catch snippets of sensation from the passing souls. Guess the Charmer had been right about hearing them. None were saying enough to grab her, but the subtle chatter was enough to remind her of the stakes here. If the Anonymous Soul team *had* stolen the Soul Charmer's wares, any of these people could die. They could rent a soul to not feel guilty about cheating on their taxes or for having some no-strings-attached sexy times, and die as a result. As much as she found the whole celestial loophole a gross cheat, the penalty for use sure shouldn't be death.

"It's six," Beck said.

A moment later a black van rolled up to the curb. The passenger side window rolled down.

A thirty-something woman leaned toward them

from the driver's seat, shadows hiding her face. "You order Anonymous?"

Callie put on her best imitation of the customers she hated the most. "That's me! So glad you found it."

"We set the spot."

"Ha! Right! Well…" Lord help her if this woman wanted her to get inside that van.

"Hold on." The woman's three-pack-a-day rasp slid past the window before it rolled back up.

The engine cut, and soon the woman rounded the van. She had at least a head more height than Callie, even as she hunched forward to trudge through the hard-packed snow at the edge the street.

"You have the cash?" Callie wished she could fake that kind of bored disinterest, but the woman's eyes were sharp. She tracked every movement Callie and Beck made.

"Of course. Three, right?"

"Yeah." The woman keened her head to the right until her ear nearly grazed her shoulder. She made the move look graceful and disaffected. Her naturally curly hair offered the air of polish Callie didn't have. Hell, maybe this lady was ready for a night out for real.

Beck proffered the money. Once the dealer had the cash in hand, she said, "You want me to check your chakras first?"

A punch to the nose wouldn't have rocked Callie as much as that statement. She tried to maintain her excited affect, but this woman was too familiar, *those words* were too familiar. Tess had built her business on chakra massage, which had turned out to be her siphoning snippets of her patron's souls. Classy shit. Gem City had its fair share of woo-woo shit, and aligning chakras wasn't that weird. And yet those words, that affect, flicked against her collarbone. The *rap-rap-rap* of memory begging to be let in.

The dealer shoved a lock of hair away from her face in a blunt motion. Aquamarine flashed a hello from the woman's wrist. The speckled stone was familiar, too. Callie could forget plenty in the wake of stress and soul magic. But chakra massage and gaudy ass jewelry? The thwack of remembering hit home, shook her sternum, and fired the truth to the front of Callie's mind.

This woman had worked at Cedar Retirement. She'd been one of the massage therapists who hit up the retirement home a couple times a month—back when Callie still had a reputable job, back before her apprenticeship killed that. Insurance didn't cover chakra whatever, but this woman had stood by as another therapist sided with Tess. Whoever this Anonymous Souls driver was, she wasn't new to the shady side of business. Massage therapy must not pay like it used to if she was hustling souls out of a van.

Had shit gotten bad enough for this lady that she wouldn't remember Callie, too? The whole plan hinged on Callie being the mark, being the dumb girl who wanted some consequence-free sinning. If the driver recognized Callie, it would all fall apart, and Callie was really fucking over things falling apart.

"We just need the rental so she can have a good time this weekend," Beck answered, diverting the chakra question and pulling the attention to himself. He said it like he was a bad influence and ready to give Callie a weekend of pure debauchery. Either he was an ace liar, or he'd given into the chaos party life at some point.

"Your loss." The dealer didn't double take at Callie, and didn't hesitate to continue the transaction.

"Whatever, I'm ready to get the goods and get to the club." Callie's voice squeaked, and she hated herself a little bit more.

"Cool. I'll give you the soul. Sunday morning you need to call the number on the back of this card," she handed over one of the Anonymous Souls cards, and Callie took it. "Tell the guy that answers where you are, and we'll come pick it up or we'll agree to meet somewhere like this again."

This soul rental company hadn't been in business long, but this dealer's indifference was concerning. She rattled this process off like she was a bus driver calling out the stops on a commuter line. How could this already be rote for her? How many souls were Anonymous Souls slinging?

"What if we don't meet up?"

That got her attention. "Excuse me?"

"I mean like what if I'm hungover or whatever and oversleep."

"She won't oversleep," Beck quickly interjected.

"If you don't call in, we'll come find you. We have

tracking on all of our souls."

Callie blanched, and it wasn't an act. Tracking the souls was impossible. This woman was full of shit. Right?

"Purely a safety measure. Keeping rented souls too long can have some side effects." While that was true, this lady didn't know the half of it. It was another repeated phrase with no substance behind it.

"Oh, okay," was all even fake-party-girl Callie could muster.

The dealer slid open the van's side door, and returned with a small tin. Callie didn't have to stretch her magical muscles to hear the soul within. The material wasn't enough to fully contain the soul.

It was screaming.

Blood curdling caterwauls blasted Callie's eardrums. Her chest began to shake, but she wasn't hyperventilating. Her heart lurched. Her stomach heaved. Her magic hit.

Callie wouldn't bother faking. Her hand was engulfed in bright blue flames. She took the tin from the other woman's hand. The dealer yelped. Her skin puckered where Callie's had touched hers. Good. Slinging tainted souls without a single care for the consequences? You get what you deserve. Callie certainly had to swallow her lumps.

Now the dealer was shrieking. Beck barreled forward and into her. He and the dealer collapsed through the open van door. Callie's focus was the searing of her own skin and the source of the problem. The tendon in her thumb was quickly becoming visible as her skin and muscles succumbed to the soul fire. Callie used her good hand to pull the flask from her pocket. She popped the cap, and brought it close to the tiny tin in her ruined fingers. *Go*, she ordered. This wasn't a soul she could be sweet to. Those screams were not pleas for help. They were not a request to escape the rental services. They were pure agony without context. Callie wasn't sure how to even handle the soul, but she'd figure that part out later.

The raging soul leaped into the flask and Callie capped it inside. She watched her muscles and skin regrow. Once her magic was snapped back inside, she took a slow breath and ventured a glance over her shoulder. The ceramics class was still going, and the women and men inside were laughing and drinking and clearly hadn't watched her burst into flames. Score one for the distractive powers of wine.

That boozy haze inside the pottery place would only extend so far. The soul dealer's screams were muffled, but her block-heeled boots banged against the van.

"Little help here." Beck huffed between each wrenched word.

Callie shoved the flask back into its snug pocket. "Sure," was the automatic answer, but could she actually assist him? How many souls were in that van? How many were in poor containers ready to split? How many were vile, broken souls? How many would claw for escape? How many would scratch her?

Beck dropped a heavy forearm at the woman's

temple. She groaned, but her hands continued to dig at his side and the back of his arm, the open van door exposing the struggle to the sidewalk. "Any time now, Callie." His raw words raked the air.

She'd stepped to the curb, but couldn't make herself move closer. Snow seeped into her sneakers. The canvas shoes sinking into the packed snow enough to let the chilled moisture soak her socks. It wasn't the potential souls holding her back. It was the woman at the door of the van. Kidnapping was depraved. Only she'd done it before. She'd taken Tess to the Charmer. Now here she was again with another "enemy." Could she really be a party to another kidnapping? She wasn't supposed to be this person. A couple men crossed the street to avoid the ruckus. Their privacy wouldn't last long. Mobile phones in hands meant the police would be on their way soon.

They needed this lead. They needed this woman. They needed answers. They needed to protect Gem City from the tainted wares she was peddling. Callie needed to find another way to do this without allowing Beck to beat up on the dealer, though. If she could erect a barrier to block souls and she could shove souls to get space, could she do this a better way?

Callie focused on the snapping of magic beneath her skin. She grasped the radiating warmth in her chest and called it to the forefront. Magic pooled in her palms. The shimmering white nebulas were only for her. She lifted her gaze to the dealer. "Beck, let her go." She sounded so far away.

Beck's death glare was legit, but he staggered when

he saw her. The sharp line of his jaw blurred, and the rosy red of his cheeks chilled. He didn't look to her open hands; he couldn't see the power in them.

"Move," Callie reiterated.

He acted immediately.

The Anonymous Souls employee levered herself upright, muscles tight and ready to bolt.

Callie whispered so quietly the wind itself couldn't hear her words. "Sleep. You'll have to speak the truth soon, but now sleep."

Swirling streaks of white stretched toward the dealer and slipped around her neck, up her nose, and into her mouth. The woman coughed twice, and then fell back against the van's thin carpeted floor with a heavy *thud*.

Callie blinked, and the world slapped back against her mind. The street was too loud, her skin was too tight, and the nighthawk on her wrist vibrated in a steady hum. Beck's eyes were still wide, and his lips were parted just enough to let her know whatever she'd done had scared him. *Same here, dude.*

"We need to get out of here." Playing this off as normal was the only option. She could freak the fuck out later. Each day soul magic was becoming easier. While that was convenient in the moment, she wasn't sure it was a good thing. Actually, she knew it wasn't a good thing; any act that brought her in commonality to the Soul Charmer couldn't be a good thing.

Beck's hesitation burned off quickly. He tucked the woman's feet inside the van, and slid the door closed.

"How do you want to do this?" Where his eyes had offered challenge before, now only deference could be found.

Again she was in charge. She could picture her five-year-old self dressed up in Zara's heels. Playing the part of an adult. Beck's focus said he didn't see that. Playing along was the only option. "I'm not sure I can go in the van," she said truthfully. "Can you drive it over the Charmer's? We can regroup there." *And I can ask Derek what the fuck we're supposed to do now.*

"Yep." He tossed her the keys to his car. "You can drive a stick right?"

"I'm good."

At those two words, Beck turned and hurried around to the driver's side door. If he wasn't going to wait for more instructions, she shouldn't either. The wail of a siren in the distance had her pulling her feet from the snow bank and heading down the street. Beck pulled away, and she doubted he looked back.

Callie tucked her chin inside the lush scarf until the fabric grazed her nose. She focused on getting back to Derek and hurried down the street. She wouldn't try to guess if those wails were a fire engine or Gem City PD. She didn't need to be anywhere near them.

She tugged her phone from the front pocket of her jeans, and shot Derek a quick text of warning. If Beck arrived before her, she didn't want to risk the two getting into another blow-up over this. Derek wouldn't be bothered by the dealer being brought in for questioning, but Callie suspected Beck arriving alone was going to result in a broken bone. That was, if he got there first. Callie jumped into the muscle car, and didn't even bother tinkering with the thermostat. She gunned the engine and set out to make record time back to downtown.

CHAPTER TWENTY-TWO

Callie's phone drilled a steady plea in her pocket. She stopped for a red light. Beck's car lurched. New brakes were touchy as hell. She checked the phone screen. There were a half dozen "Call me" texts in a row. Josh hated talking on the phone almost as much as she did.

She tapped his name. The line rang once and then he answered, "Thank God."

"Is Mom okay? Did something happen?"

"Yes." His breath crackled against the mouthpiece.

"Yes to which one?" The light turned green and she hit the gas too hard. She flew through the intersection. The back end of the car bumped against the high hill in the center of the cross street. Callie pulled the car to the side of the road, and slammed it into park. She was less concerned about fucking up Beck's beastly car, and a whole lot more concerned that she was driving the wrong direction if her family needed her.

"Mom is fine." He coughed, and his voice became clearer. "Something happened at work."

"Something?" She dangled the lure because asking why his work issues required a phone call would come across as hostile.

Fabric rustled. That didn't tell her shit. "Josh? What's going on?"

"He's here." The hollow whisper was one Josh used for secrets. He must have his hand cupped around his mouth.

Anxiety pooled static at her waist. The potential bite waiting for more information. "Who?"

"Nate." The name a filthy word forced out in the front pew of Sunday Mass.

The static shifted to sharp spikes poised to pierce the skin. "Has he seen you yet? What's he doing?"

"I didn't think it was a big deal, Callie. Adam's such a good dude. He showed up with sandwiches for the crew at lunch. He asked about Mom, and I wasn't thinking…"

Prick prick prick at her belly. "Are you safe?"

His words were strangled. "I don't know, sis. I told him Mom was in the hospital, and didn't think about how he knew she was injured. I didn't miss work or tell any of the guys here yet. We don't talk about that kind of shit at the job site."

"Is he still there?" Callie put the car back into drive, and pulled out from the curb.

"He's been in the boss's trailer with Adam for a while."

The Charmer's troubles would have to wait. The soul dealer would have to wait. Family came first, and Nate had already endangered her mother. Callie wasn't about to let him get his hands on her brother again. The Delgados were done with these goddamn gangsters. "I'm on my way. Are you at the same job you told me about a couple weeks ago?"

Josh confirmed the address. "It might not be safe to come here," he added.

Safe was a long-lost relic in her life. She wasn't about to find the arc of the covenant either. "I'll be there in a few minutes. Just focus on working until then."

Josh's sharp inhalation worried her, but he didn't argue.

Callie disconnected the call, and immediately placed a fresh one to Derek.

"Callie?" He used her name. At least she didn't have to tell him to be on high alert.

How much could she say on the phone? If he knew she were heading to meet Nate, he'd probably beat her to the job site. It wasn't safe to leave the Charmer's place unmanned, though.

"I'm going to be a little late back to the shop." Not a lie.

"What's wrong?"

So much. "Josh called. I need to make a quick pit stop."

"Zara?"

"Thankfully no. Adam showed at his work, and I'm going to make sure Josh understands why he needs to avoid that asshole." Enough truth to keep her from going full dirtbag. Building trust was arduous, and slipping was not an option.

"Where is his job again?"

Callie gave him the address. Because honesty.

"That's not too far." He was probably mentally mapping the best path to get there.

"I don't think I'll be long. Beck should be back any second, and he's bringing a present."

Derek's short grunt kicked her chest. He could read her so well. "If you're not back in thirty minutes, I'm coming for you."

"I figured." He couldn't see her smile, but she was fairly certain he could hear it.

"Be safe."

The construction company Josh worked for had been hired to renovate one of the lush resort hotels downtown. The building had once been a Cortean monastery. Why people paid hundreds of dollars to stay in a cramped room made for a person with no earthly possessions was beyond her. They did, though, and now Josh was helping replace support beams and update bathrooms. He might have been able to convince her it was honest work if the trailer parked out front wasn't holding Gem City's new crime king and his lackey—

and if those men hadn't recently mutilated her mother.

The workmen were working on updating the gazebos off the patio. Wood peeked from the edge of tarps. Callie edged past the trailer, and hurried beyond the stacks of lumber. Josh was off to the edge of the patio. He was far from the clamped lamps, but his long, lean frame was unmistakable. At least to his baby sister.

He lifted his chin. The bro move was a welcome and a warning. She didn't continue winding back toward the shadows, but instead paused near one of the heaping blue tarps. Josh met her there. He tugged her around the edge of the lumber pallet. His hand was surprisingly strong on her arm. At least he had to be eating again to be regaining strength. The wildness in his eyes, though, suggested his internal reserves of strength were waning. The flood lamps cast his cheek in sharp relief, but let her only catch the wide halos of the whites of his eyes.

"Who drove you here?" his whisper snapped.

"What does that matter? You had an emergency and I hauled ass."

His steel-toed boots tapped a tiny trill on the brick, but he only stared at her.

Fine. "I drove myself."

He stopped the drilling glare and started surveying the construction site. "You get a new car?"

Josh had a way of avoiding his problems, even now after he'd called her in a panic. She couldn't let him toe into this problem.

"No. Circumstances required me to borrow a

friend's to get here." He'd better not ask about who her friend was. Now was not the time to explain the Soul Charmer's staffing issues or why she'd be spending time with another guy from there. That would lead to talking about Derek, and Josh had yet to be on board with the whole boyfriend thing. Funny the stereotypical big brother impulses he had even when she was here to help him clean up messes. Easier to deflect than to own his shit.

She needed him focused. "I don't have time to talk about the car, Josh. What happened? Is Nate still here?"

"He's still here." Her brother's body shook, but his voice held steady. The Delgado fake-it-till-you-make-it gene in action.

"Okay," she said like she actually had a grip on what the fuck was happening. "What exactly did Adam say to you?"

"That's the thing. He was really chill about it. He showed up with hoagies and brought me one. Told me he heard I was doing good here—which is true, sis."

Lord. Now was not the time to dredge up his rehab. Her boss was missing, and she had a rival's employee waiting for questioning back at the shop. She was not living her best life, and shit kept sliding down from above to splat squarely on her shoulders. "I'm glad to hear it's going well," she said because she had to. "But what did Adam say?"

"I was getting to that." The more riled he got, the less the twitching was noticeable. Progress? "So he asked how my mom was doing. I told him she was hanging in there, which is true, but not the whole story."

Yes, she knew that part. She nodded, and he continued.

"He said he knew Zara. Said she was cool."

Callie couldn't stop the snort from slipping. Anyone who hadn't been close with her or Josh growing up thought Zara had been the mom they'd always wanted. Like hitting the casinos on the regular was the kind of party life that was perfect for a single mom. Like kids would love to spend hours in the car outside said casino. Idiots.

"Yeah, well, he said he'd heard she was in the hospital and was hoping she was healing up."

"Did you ask who he heard that from?"

"No, Callie. Why would I do that? We were eating sandwiches and he was checking in on my mom."

Her cheeks heated and it had nothing to do with the slap of the wintry air. "Because your mother was just kidnapped and tortured and who the fuck would be talking about that other than the people involved?"

"I called you, remember? You don't have to get all preachy princess to me. We come from the same place."

"I know that. That's why you should know better than to trust these people." Whisper yelling was still yelling, and a couple of the workmen shot dirty looks in their direction. Callie sucked in a big breath of thin, frigid air, and then coughed it back out.

"Well, do you want to know what happened or do

you want to bitch at me?"

She didn't have time to placate him. "Just fucking tell me."

He huffed, and white smoke rose from his mouth. Her beanpole of a brother transformed into a snow dragon. "After I told him she was out of intensive care, he left for a while. He came back with Nate, and that's when I called you."

Josh wasn't about to say that's when he realized he'd screwed up. Admitting guilt wasn't something the Delgados did. They stockpiled their guilt around their organs until their liver kicked back or their stomach burned. It was unhealthy, and knowing that didn't change anything.

"Did Nate see you?" Maybe this wasn't as bad as she'd originally feared.

Josh looked toward the singlewide trailer at the edge of the building. Callie followed his gaze. The windows glowed with the warm yellow of agave in bloom. There was nothing ominous about the office, but her brother hollowed when he looked at it. His shoulders sagged and his jaw slackened. The white in his eyes—so vivid a moment ago—disappeared to darkness. She'd seen Josh's skin sallow and pocked, and she'd been the one with a warm cloth wiping vomit from his chin and cheeks. This was different than his drug desperation. This was knowledge biting him. This was being near those same people who sold him drugs with a clear head, and the realization that those same people who had tossed him a free taste here and there were the people who had stolen his mother for days, who had taken her fingers, who had terrorized his sister, and who were ready to treat him with the same vile callousness.

It was a lot for anyone. Fuck knew Callie hadn't handled her cannonball jump into this world well. It was more for Josh. He'd been trusting. He'd been the party guy. He'd been addled and avoiding. Now he had to confront it, and Callie worried the only thing keeping him from scoring meth now was the realization he'd have to go to those very people to get it. The thought soured her stomach and the sharp tang of regret filled her mouth.

"Josh?" This time it was she who grabbed his arm. Where his touch had been firm, hers was gentle. The tattered pieces of his soul called to her magic, but she shoved back against the plea. She didn't have time for the ice to lock her hands. She coddled his soul without thinking, and the ice failed to form on her fingers.

The contact was enough to reel him back from the memories haunting him, if only for the moment.

"Nate offered to hook me up." His reedy rasp was going to break her.

Callie tightened her grip. "He—"

"Not meth. He offered be a taste of a soul." Josh's lips barely moved.

Fuck. Fuck. Fuck. Fuck. Fuck.

There were not enough curse words in the world for this moment. Was this a ploy to mess with her? Had Nate brought along the bonus souls he'd demanded of Callie? Was he foisting souls she stole from the Soul

Charmer back onto her own family to make her life even worse? Or was this something else? Something more? Her grip on her soul magic wobbled. Frost slapped her hard enough that it should have left an imprint.

"Callie?" It was Josh's turn to look worried. If she weren't being assailed by ice, she might have cracked a joke about their taking turns breaking down these days.

The trailer's door slammed open. Callie staggered back into the shadows. Josh followed her. Nate lingered in the doorway. Either the white bomber jacket or the ocher glow behind him made Nate look bigger. No. Callie wouldn't let herself go there. Up close he'd be the same acne-scarred weasel as before. He'd asked too much then, and he'd ask too much now. Her knuckles ached to move, but the web of ice was woven too tightly to allow her to stretch her fingers.

What was Nate doing here? If he'd only been here to screw with Josh, then why the long meeting inside the singlewide? Ford's family owned slaughterhouses and land throughout Gem City. Was Nate actually taking up a role in the Ford mob business, and not just slinging dope? Callie once would have said Nate wasn't smart enough to run a business, much less a surreptitious one. Then she'd found him with the journal of St. Petro, a holy book with a whole lot of details about soul magic. He'd been studying. She'd taken his soul, and put herself in this whole goddamn mess.

Nate hopped down the two steps to the curb. A tall woman followed him out. She had a wide nose and broad shoulders, and was very clearly a woman you did not want to get into a fight with. Nate gave the woman his least creepy leering smile. To her credit, the woman didn't blanch. Callie had been on the other end of that look before, and it stained. Nate extended a hand. The brilliant glow from the open office door didn't allow for secrets. Pinched between his first two fingers and his thumb Nate held a shiny black card. Even from her frozen hiding place, Callie couldn't have missed it. That slick material and the promises it made were etched in her mind.

Anonymous Souls.

Nate was involved in Anonymous Souls.

Of course he fucking was.

The woman accepted the card, and gave Nate a curt nod. Adam rushed out of the office to join Nate, and the two walked in the opposite direction of the job site. Whatever they were here for, they'd accomplished it.

The woman returned to the office, closing the door. The construction workers continued bustling back and forth. No one else had seen the exchange. No one else would have had the sense to be scared. That was the burden of knowledge. Innocent moves like handshakes and card exchanges took on another light when you understood the real business being brokered.

Callie stepped out from the darkened hiding spot. The flood lamps hit her, illuminated her, and blanched her skin. No hiding. She couldn't let Nate keep coming at her family. Messing with her one was thing. She deserved it for what she'd done, but we own our own shit. Zara and Josh hadn't stolen Nate's soul. They hadn't denied his advances. They hadn't done shit to him. The urge to sprint after him, to remind him of how the world worked hit her. If he had a problem with her, then come after her. This tormenting of her loved ones was weak.

She only made it a couple steps before the realization hit her: She couldn't go after Nate now. He knew what hospital Zara was in. He knew where Josh worked. He knew she'd given him souls that didn't belong to him—and was, she realized, not so dumb as to ignore the obvious dotted line that she'd stolen them. He had Adam with him, and back up like that carried weapons. She couldn't very well pull Josh into that fight. She curled her fingers into a fist and squeezed until her nails dug into the meat of her palm.

"I work here, you know." The uneasy tremble made Josh's attempted joke fall flat.

"I know," she whispered, still watching where Nate and Adam had stood moments earlier. "You going to be okay?"

"Kind of feel like I should be asking you that, sis. You good?"

Far from it. "If you can avoid them for awhile, I will be."

That might have been a lie. She'd be closer to good if she didn't have to worry about him. She needed time to regroup, to figure out what was happening, to make a plan. Once again, she found herself missing the Soul Charmer. He'd have shoved her into this sand pit, too, but at least he would have handled all the machinations. He'd have had some strategy. He could have frightened people into compliance. Until then, she needed to find out what the Anonymous Souls dealer knew about Nate and his operations. She also was going to have to tell Derek about this, because if there was any hope of forcing Nate to back down it was going to require some leather-clad teamwork.

"He's got nothing for me anymore." Josh's earnestness hurt.

Callie extended her magic out to protect his soul again. It was cold and crying and she somehow understood her brother better in that moment. The jagged scars from growing up too fast were stippled across the whole of his soul. The ragged edges missed who he once was—before the drugs, before Zara had become self-involved, before adulthood—and there wasn't a plea for a home or for a rented soul to mask the pain. Deep down, her brother's soul wanted only to heal. A shimmer of hope fluttered in Callie's chest. Unfamiliar, but welcome. She let her magic coil around his soul. It kept the chill from assaulting her, but also gave him a moment of peace. His lips parted on a slow breath. Callie stepped forward and hugged him. He smelled like home and hope. Tears pricked hot at her eyelids. She sniffled once, released him, and steadied herself.

"Aunt Lily is staying with Mom at the hospital. I'll go by after work." Josh's rasp was gone.

"Visiting hours will be over," she said automatically.

"Since when do we care about visiting hours?" Mischief sparkled around Josh. The good kind.

Delight percolated beneath her diaphragm for a moment, and Callie almost laughed. "Since never.

Give Aunt Lily a hug from me."

"I've got them. You do what you need to, sis." This was the Josh she remembered from when she was fourteen and hungry.

Callie wished she could cradle his soul a little longer. After this was over, she'd have to find out if there was a way to repair broken souls. She gave him another quick hug. "Thanks."

She took two steps away before reeling her magic back in. She pretended she didn't hear his harsh gasp, and kept walking until she was back inside Beck's car.

CHAPTER TWENTY-THREE

Callie parked Beck's car outside the mouth of the alleyway. It was close enough to the streetlight not to get jacked, but also as close as she could get to dart inside. Electricity in the dry air made the night sharper, and she was not about to get cut.

The alley was empty of people, but full of garbage. The quick meal place on the corner had started leaving their trash bags next to the dumpster. Not that she'd ever rat on someone to the landlord, but it did make the journey to sinful escape a whole lot less desirable. The Soul Charmer said the seedier, the better when it comes to offering an out on guilt. If the competition was willing to roll up to wherever you were with a van full of goods, though, laziness probably trumped the visceral delight in doing something dirty. Speaking of vans, the black one wasn't parked on the street, and it wasn't tucked around back as best she could tell.

She pushed the dilapidated door to her workplace open, and found Derek waiting for her alone. He was leaning against the counter, a single boot pressed back on the front surface. It would have been a casual rebel pose, if his eyes hadn't flashed to her with heat and danger. Derek didn't scare her, but in that moment she could see what their clients did. He was a mountain. This bulk of stony muscle. Every limb poised to strike, every angle of his body aggressive. His jaw clenched and released. She watched the muscle tic in slow motion. This customer-facing room still bore the Soul Charmer's hallmarks of Cortean artwork, overwhelming incense, and aging everything, but it wasn't the same room she'd left. The miasma of worry and violence and fear and regret in this room singed her sinuses and shot burning rubber behind her tongue.

Others would have bolted from the room. Callie launched herself forward. Her chest slammed into Derek's. His torso was unforgiving. She didn't care. His arms dropped around her body. Her lungs strained to take a deep breath, but she didn't dare tell him the hug was too tight. Whatever had put him on edge, he needed this. She nuzzled his chest, as if she could somehow get closer to him. He chuffed.

"Thought I was going to have to come find you." The sound vibrated against her cheek before she could process the words.

"Thirty minutes or less. Your girlfriend promise."

"Better than a pizza." He released the embrace, but took one of her hands in his. Soft, steady, and undemanding contact was exactly what she needed.

"Did Beck not make it back?" she asked when she thought he could handle the question.

"He's downstairs."

She nodded like those two words were more helpful than they were. "Where's the van?"

"Moved it four blocks up. We don't need Lexi's crew to find her too soon."

"Lexi? Is that the woman's name?"

"That's what her wallet says." Derek didn't bother hiding his amusement at someone working a dealing job carrying identification.

"What has she said?" Was this woman another plant sent to fuck up Callie's world? She shook off the thought. The card in the basement hadn't been left to Callie, and they hadn't called from her phone.

"Not much. It was hard to wake her." Derek shot a furtive glance toward the back curtain. When he spoke again it was in a low rumble. "What did you do to her anyway?"

How was she supposed to answer that? She'd reached the bottom of her barrel of fucks to give, and now she'd started making demands of the magic. The Soul Charmer was MIA and it was like her abilities decided it was time to pick up the slack. The Charmer had infused her with the skill. Maybe this was him? Maybe he was dead and she was getting residual magic? She had no fucking clue. "Honestly? I don't know how to explain it, but I knocked her out."

His brow furrowed like she'd handed him a calculus problem. "You punched her?"

"Not exactly. Maybe? It was more like a mental shove."

He nodded slowly. "Like what you did to Savannah?"

This had tasted different. It'd been on purpose. Examining that decision now wouldn't help her mental state. "Close enough."

"She was damn hard to wake either way. Beck is keeping her company for now. He might have gotten something out of her." Derek's lack of optimism wasn't a good sign.

"As long as she can answer questions soon, that's fine." She needed to know what Nate was up to, what this woman knew.

"You going to tell me what happened earlier?" He squeezed her hand, and that's all the push he'd give.

He deserved truth. "Adam showed up at Josh's work. Asked how Zara was doing in the hospital."

"Josh told him?"

"Josh didn't realize it was fucked until Nate showed up. After that he realized maybe his sister was right— like always—and he should have been avoiding Adam all along. So he called me."

Derek took a half step backward, and met Callie's eyes. "And you went to meet Nate and Adam alone. Without telling me."

"I did no such thing." She placed her hand on his forearm, the touch as light as her words were firm. "I told you Josh had called. I told you to come for me if

I wasn't here in a reasonable timeframe and I did not talk to either Nate or Adam. They didn't see me at all. What I did was find out what the hell was happening and check on my brother because I'm not about to let that skeevy soul stealing bitch take another of my family members."

Derek was quiet for long moments. Too long. Finally, though, he said, "I'm glad you told me before, and I'm glad you didn't go after Nate."

That waver in his voice was enough to tell her that hulking mountain move was preparation for kicking down doors on her behalf. She hadn't screwed this up. "I figured the only way to go after Nate is with more information and with you at my side." It hadn't sounded so mushy in her head. Aloud it was more than saying the L word. Heat scratched at her neck. She turned toward the front door, like a customer would make this less weird.

"Damn right, doll." Derek chuckled. "So what was Nate doing at the St. Jerome?"

He remembered where Josh was working. She smiled and turned back to him. The humor faded when she answered, "Other than trying to get my brother to rent a soul for free from him? He was handing an Anonymous Souls card to the construction site boss."

Derek dropped her hand. "For fucking real?"

He covered his mouth and started to pace. Callie was primed to commiserate in the WTFery, but the shop's door opened.

The woman who toddled in on stilettos picked the

wrong time to pop in. "I'm here," she announced like it meant something.

"That's nice," Callie muttered.

The woman opened her mouth again, but Derek spoke first. "Running a little late, Barbara."

Lovely. A return. Callie peeked at the time on her phone. She'd told Miguel and Savannah to send people in, and it looked like they were following through. Barbara's four-inch heels pushed her up an inch taller than Callie's five foot nothing, if you didn't count the hair. The renter's blonde mane was teased and spritzed to the point it had to be a fire hazard.

"This winter weather has me in the holiday spirit. I've been decorating and it got the best of me." Barbara's white button-up blouse and perfectly lined red lips didn't look like a woman who hadn't been carrying boxes from the storage room.

"You skip Thanksgiving in your house?" Derek was edging behind Barbara to block the door. He offered a half shrug to Callie. They needed the soul back, and apparently this one could be a runner.

"I just love the Christmas season, and we should keep our Lord in our hearts all year don't you think?"

Come the fuck on. This woman had a rented soul nestled between her tits and she was here preaching about loving the baby Jesus? Whatever this lady did with the rented soul was her business, but the incredulity here was razing Callie's already ragged nerves. "One should never skip a food holiday," Callie said like it was a joke.

The woman laughed. Derek's somber nod, though, was the correct response. He understood.

Callie walked over to the woman. The first flickers of fever tickled her skin. Callie grabbed the flask and the warmth faded. Callie didn't want to feel this lady's soul like she had Josh's. She didn't even know how to decide how much to push. Best to stick with the basics.

"How late returning is she?" Callie asked Derek.

The tiny woman drew herself up to her full height and then some. "I'm here to see the Soul Charmer. He's who I do business with."

Haughty tones would get this lady nowhere. "That's nice. He put me in charge right now. You do business with me."

"I will do no such thing." She pivoted on a wobbly heel toward the door.

Derek was waiting. His arms were folded in front of his chest. He looked right over the woman's head to maintain eye contact with Callie. He didn't even acknowledge the woman, which only further incensed her.

The woman began to sputter demands. Callie had no time for her. "Look, I can take the soul out of you either way. You might as well return your rented property, and get on with your Christmas decorating bullshit."

"Well…You can't blaspheme like that!"

"Look, *Barbara*, I've had a pretty bad day. I do not have the energy to pretend that you decorating for Christmas in November is interesting to me at all. Return the soul, and we can both be on our ways." Callie was exhausted and she let it show. After this she was going to need to pop some energy shots before heading downstairs. Snoozing before interrogations was probably frowned upon.

The woman sulked, but shuffled back toward Callie. A quick flip of the cap and a light connection of flask to sternum and the soul was safely extracted. Callie slipped the flask back in her pocket. Barbara turned to leave again.

"How much does she owe?" Callie asked Derek.

"Her bill is $375 last I checked," he said without any inflection. He could be intimidating as fuck when he wanted, and right now Callie loved it.

"Five hundred, please." She said please because some customer service habits simply couldn't be broken.

Barbara was already backing away, and tucking her purse securely beneath her arm. "He just told you the bill is $375."

"Before taxes and fees."

"The Soul Charmer doesn't charge taxes."

"Of course he does. He's an upstanding citizen and remits sales tax on all services as required by state law." The fact Callie managed not choke on her own laughter in this moment could only be attributed to the extreme stress she'd been under.

"He pays it out of the price. It's $375," Barbara reiterated.

Callie needed to be sure this woman wasn't going to come back for a bit. They needed time to sort things out. It might not be good business, but Callie was too worn to care. "Right, and the remaining balance of $125 is what we call the asshole fee."

Barbara turned to Derek and stepped toe-to-toe with him. The lady had some guts. "Talk sense into her."

"Do you have $400 on you?" Derek asked her with a conspiratorial current.

"Yes," she said.

They exchanged the cash, and he stopped blocking the exit. Barbara gripped the door handle. Over her shoulder she said, "I'll be sure your employer hears about this."

When she was gone, Callie said, "If she can find the Charmer to tell him, I'll deal with it."

"He likes extra cash," Derek said.

"Asshole fee goes to those who deal with them. That twenty five bucks is buying us beer later."

Derek kissed her forehead. "Celebratory beer."

"Perfect. Because whatever's going to happen downstairs needs to happen quickly. If I'm right about Nate being involved in this Anonymous Souls racket, I expect we don't have long before he makes a move."

The basement was colder at night. A wall of chemical stench concealed the musky scent she associated with the decrepit wooden stairs.

"How much bleach did you use down here?" She blinked away tears, and her eyes adjusted.

"Enough."

And then some.

The door where she'd found Beck and Miguel earlier had been replaced with plywood and was now closed. A muffled male voice rumbled behind the makeshift door. The last person held in this room had been an Anonymous Souls dealer, and he was gone. The last time this chance had arisen, the Charmer disappeared and blood had splattered the floors. Callie didn't know what safety steps Miguel or the Charmer had taken, but she wasn't going into that room without Derek at her side.

"We find out who's fronting the business, if she knows what Nate is up to, and if she drops the Soul Charmer's whereabouts great. And then we're done, yeah?" Callie whispered, needing the confirmation.

A single, heated grumble was all he offered, but it was agreement without words.

Lexi's head lolled to the side, but her eyes were open.

"Just tell me where you got the souls, and then you can rest." Beck's plea played as genuine.

The woman's eyes fixed on Callie, and then narrowed, but she didn't say anything.

"How long has she been like this?" Callie asked.

"Past twenty minutes or so. Whatever you did to

her was no joke." Beck didn't look at Callie. Whether that was to keep focus on their guest or to avoid letting Callie see his fear, she wasn't certain.

Lexi's lagging behavior and the drowsiness mimicked a concussion. Derek *had* asked if she's punched Lexi. Maybe she had. Callie moved further into the room until she stood next to Beck. He offered her the lone stool, but she declined. Magic simmered beneath her feet. It wasn't the creeping frost of soul renters or blaring heat of unprotected souls. This was new. It itched and tingled. She curled her toes inside her Chucks, and tried to focus on the ebbing sogginess from her snow steps earlier. The damp discomfort was expected, this pulling and scraping of her soles was definitively not.

Callie took a single step backward and the sensation ceased. This was more than memories of her time with Tess giving her bad vibes. This was some kind of warning.

With the biting at her heels soothed, she focused on the woman in front of her. Lexi's wild curls were limp as though they'd lost their body when she hit the van's floor. Callie didn't really want to touch this woman's soul. It wasn't about invading the woman's privacy. Hell, she'd knocked the woman out. It was the unknown. She couldn't escape knowledge. You couldn't throw the deuces and ditch out on what you saw in someone's soul. She might not see anything. She hadn't before. She'd ask the Soul Charmer if he was here, but once again she was left on her own. Trial by soul magic fire.

He'd told her the souls talked to him. He could *hear* them. Could she choose to only eavesdrop and not *know* the soul? Beck was watching her now and not bothering to hide his concern. She didn't have to peek over her shoulder to know Derek was directly behind her. He was watching, too, but had more patience.

Okay, Callie, you can triage this.

She prodded at Lexi's soul. It was almost like the beautiful ball of translucent light was bruised. Winding paths of grey and blue wove over the right side. She pushed a little on them, and Lexi groaned. So souls could become concussed. You learn something new everyday.

"Lexi?" Callie kept her voice gentle. "Do you know where you are?"

"What the fuck kind of question is that?" Beck said under his breath.

Callie ignored him. Lexi was quiet for a moment, and then said, "With Soul Charmer assholes."

"Good."

"We're not the assholes," Beck said.

Callie smiled. "I just wanted to make sure she was coherent, but I'm pretty sure she's going to think we're assholes. I knocked her out and you tied her to that chair."

He looked like he was going to apologize, and this simply wasn't the time or place. She waved him off.

Callie imagined pressing a cold compress to the soul. She didn't tell the guys because she was certain this was the closest to woo-woo magic shit that she'd ever gotten and she was not entirely comfortable with that. But Lexi's soul was bruised, and if they could stop it from whatever the celestial equivalent of swelling was, that had to be a good choice.

Lexi lifted her head. "What are you doing to me?"

"Helping you," she said with all the softness she could muster.

The scoff was scathing, but if Lexi had the energy to do that then she could probably answer questions.

"And now it's your turn. Care to tell us who you work for?" Callie's voice was high, but cut with the edge of a threat.

"You ordered a soul from them. Are you really that dumb?"

Oh, good. Callie was tending this woman's gateway to the afterlife and was getting name called in the process.

"We know you work for Anonymous Souls," Beck said. Could he hear Callie's teeth grind? "The question is, who specifically is your boss? We want a name."

"It's anonymous," Lexi snapped.

This woman was tired, and Callie could relate, but it was going to be hard to keep treating her metaphysical wounds if she was going to keep this up. They had to ease her into this, apparently.

Callie pivoted the questions. "How were you going to give me the soul?"

"What do you mean?"

"You had an aluminum jar. How were you going to get the soul out of it and into my body?"

"Standard way."

Callie rolled her eyes, and her pressure on Lexi's soul slipped. The other woman hissed a series of short breaths. Callie eased off. "How?"

Lexi attempted to shrug against her bonds. "Tool of the trade. I'm sure you have one, too."

Callie send a questioning look Beck's way.

"No flask," he said to Callie.

"A quill, honey!" Lexi squeaked. Callie reassessed her magical compress and realized she was probably giving a little too much sweetness to the soul, but it was working so she tried to stay steady.

"Where's the quill?" Callie asked Lexi.

The woman giggled.

Callie glanced to Beck.

"I didn't see a quill," he said.

Derek wasn't about to let them lose time. He stepped around Callie and gave Lexi a quick pat down. The brilliant blue quill had been tucked next to her calf inside her pant leg.

"Kind of inconvenient location," Callie said. "Like how do you pull that out all smooth on a street?"

"I've got a van," Lexi sneered.

Derek started to bring the quill back to the Soul Charmer team side of the room. The sensation of steel sliding over her skin ground on Callie's nerves again.

Metal and magic and malevolence assaulted her. A soul magic artifact. Hell. Another ancient item like this, a knife, had been used to steal and store souls before. Nate had put that into motion. That couldn't be a coincidence. She barely shook her head, but Derek saw it. He moved to stand behind Lexi. He was at a safe distance so the magic couldn't gnaw at her, and he could keep the Anonymous Souls dealer in check.

"How did you get the souls that were in the van?" Callie asked.

"I'm just a delivery driver." Rehearsed words from a foot soldier.

Callie pushed on the woman's soul again. She heard the scream but knowing there was a tool in the room that could allow almost anyone to steal a soul put Callie a bit on edge. "No, you're not. How did you get the souls?"

"Boss brought them in."

"When?" Derek asked.

"I don't know when he collects souls." Lexi's own soul seconded that statement.

"Fair enough. Has your van always been that stocked?"

"We get fresh stuff in all the time." Lexi was looking at Beck's shins like they had the answers.

Callie's tone was sharper this time. "That wasn't my question."

"There's some new shit out. Sure. Fine."

They could check the goods. Now that she could

feel the souls more clearly, she could probably identify the damaged ones. She'd have to go through them. Or maybe the Charmer could return and do that shit. A faint rasp hissed nearby, and it took Callie a moment to realize she was wheezing. Her hands were shaking. Holding onto this soul was draining.

"What's your boss's name?" Callie asked.

Lexi looked down like she was preparing to melt into the earth.

Callie chest ached. She took a shot. "Lexi, do you know a man named Nate?"

Lexi's head snapped up. Her shoulders banged against the back of the chair hard enough to scuff it back a centimeter with a hard honk. Her eyes were wide now and her nostrils flaring. Callie couldn't have gotten a more panicked response if she'd slammed a needle of ephedrine into the woman's vein.

"I don't want to talk about Nate." Lexi's words slurred together. Callie wasn't slamming pressure into the other woman's soul, though. This wasn't some sort of symptom of injury. This panic had nothing to do with Callie, Derek, Beck, or the Soul Charmer.

Callie doubled down. "So you know him?"

Sweat began to bead at Lexi's brow. "I'm not talking about him, and you shouldn't either."

"You know who our boss is, right?" Beck asked.

"The Soul Charmer won't accept your secrets," Derek added.

The men were so ominous that Callie shuddered.

Lexi, however, did not. What had Nate done to have this woman so terrified of him that she had zero fear of the Soul Charmer?

"Your magic man is gone, and Nate controls this city now. You shouldn't speak of him either," the captive dealer said.

Derek ambled to Lexi's side. Callie took steps away in equal measure. Now wasn't a time to get gutted by the weird ass magic of a damn quill.

Derek leaned close to Lexi, like he would be able to smell a lie. "Who says the Soul Charmer is gone?"

"V-V-Vega said your man is gone," she stammered.

Gone, but not dead.

Gone, but not captured.

Just gone. Well, what the fuck did that mean?

CHAPTER TWENTY-FOUR

A clean jingle drew Callie's thoughts from worrying over the Soul Charmer's whereabouts.

"Customer." Derek pointed a finger toward the ceiling.

Even if the shop owned a "Closed" sign, Callie couldn't have used it. No one could know the Soul Charmer had disappeared on them. If Vega and Lexi knew the Charmer was missing, who else knew? What did that mean for Callie, Derek, and the others? Had the Soul Charmer run off for a Vegas weekend? Unlikely. Wherever he was, Callie was convinced he wasn't dead.

If the Soul Charmer was alive, then he'd come back and force her into immolation lockdown if she didn't keep this damn business afloat.

"Let her sleep," Callie told Beck.

"But she hasn't told us…" Beck stopped, and then nodded.

"Watch her for now, please. We're going to go deal with that." Callie left the room, and Derek followed. He remained at the doorway until she was at the stairs. Once the interrogation room door was closed, he held the quill aloft. "What do you want me to do with this?"

Throwing it away was out of the question. "Is there somewhere safe we can store it until I can focus on it?"

"You sure you want to do that?"

"Want to? Hardly, but if Nate is giving his delivery drivers Cortean relics to let them yank souls, I want to understand them."

Derek closed his eyes tight as if readying for some unknown blow. "We could ask Henry to help."

His brother wasn't the boogeyman, but sometimes holding the sheets over your head really could make you feel better.

Callie understood. "With hiding it or with figuring it out?"

Derek met her gaze.

"Both. I can probably get him to store it in the church, but I think he's been reading more journals. I lent him the St. Petro one." There was an inherent apology in his voice.

"If he's studied it, that could help." Hopefully. "I was thinking we needed to read it again."

"He's read it. Probably has notes, too." Resignation rumbled with the memory of being second best, and Callie related to that, too.

She'd rather have Derek's thoughts, but his brother could help now. "Can you call him to get the quill, and then see if he can meet us later tonight at your place?"

Derek nodded, and then pulled a metal shelf away from the wall on his right. A small, metal safe was revealed. He flipped the dial to the right and left and right again. The door opened with ease, and he placed the quill inside. Once it was secure, he joined Callie at the stairs.

"I hate pulling him into this." Derek's soft words shook her.

His hand was on the bannister, and Callie rested hers atop his. "I don't want this for him either, but I think he's the right person to help."

"Because of the church's involvement?"

"Because he's your brother."

His hand was warm beneath hers. The muscle in Derek's jaw twitched, but he nodded slowly.

———

Two teenagers were inside the shop when Callie and Derek finally emerged from the basement.

"Can I help you?" she asked.

A tall guy shoved a slim brunette woman forward. "You tell her, Brin."

Brin elbowed him, but was also the kind of teenager who had the confidence to demand shit from adults. That was the kind of attitude safety earned you. Brin's parents would call the cops for her. Callie's mom was more the "if the cops show up here, I pretend I don't know you" style.

"How much does it cost to rent a soul for a night?" Brin asked.

Callie finally understood why the Charmer charged extra for overnight rentals. The collection was going to be a pain, and the work so close together made for busier days than required and fucking kids.

"How many do you need?" Callie replied.

"The price changes based on how many I want? Don't you have a menu or something?" *Oh, Brin.* Callie had asked the same thing the first time she'd visited the Soul Charmer's shop. Bartering for a borrowed soul wasn't black and white, though, and that meant no price lists.

The tall guy elbowed her again. "Buy more, save more."

"Business major," Brin said as way of excuse for the interruption.

Callie needed to move this along. "Do you need two souls or just one for you?"

"Two. We're going to a rave tonight, and it's going to be insane."

Callie tried to remember the last time she purposefully had a crazy night out. One without blood or souls or brandished weapons. She and Derek deserved a wild night with a matching hell-worthy hangover. She'd suggest it to him if they ever got out from under the boulder of obligations with the Soul Charmer.

For now, though, he was missing, and she needed to sell these college kids souls to have a debauched night. She almost wanted to double charge them for the reminder of how carefree her life could have been, but then she'd have to admit that her life never could have been as easy as theirs.

Brin didn't argue at the high price Callie threw out. The Charmer charged more for overnight rentals, and Callie decided the policy should also include a fee for the high probably of getting hammered and forgetting to show up to return the soul tomorrow.

Now was the part she really hadn't done, picking out the soul for each of these people. They were paying pure soul prices, which was good because that's all they really had in stock right now. She knew the purest one should be able to be safe with people who weren't planning to commit murder. Brin and the tall guy were going to get high, dance, and probably screw in the sand. It was a rave, not an occult ritual.

The back room was pristine again. The glass had been swept up, and the wooden picture frames were disposed of. The tile floor had been bleached until the blood was obliterated. Touching the Charmer's souls without him here sent a spike of dread to the depths of her belly nonetheless.

She'd have to do this sometime, but maybe it didn't have to be right now. Callie went to the back of the desk and found the drawer with spare soul containers. She pulled a trio of jars from the bin, and set them on the desk. Her flask had two souls from the well, and one from Barbara. She uncapped the flask, and whispered for the soft and sweet soul she'd pulled from the well to come forth. She lifted one of the waiting jars into her palm, and the glass quickly warmed to body temperature. The black of her flask pressed against the rich grey of the jar. The soul slipped out of one container and into the next like a flash of lightning on a cloudy night. She capped the jar, and repeated the process two more times.

Even Barbara's rented soul wasn't difficult. Given how many greedy, demanding souls had pulled on hers today alone, she wasn't sure she could have gone another couple minutes fighting the damn things. Her ribs ached and her stomach growled. If they could get these customers out the door, maybe they could sneak off for food.

When the Soul Charmer placed a soul in a host, he made extravagant motions. He waved his hands and he whispered gibberish that almost sounded like Latin. He anointed certain people like he was a priest. He might have this weird stranglehold relationship with the Cortean Church, but he wasn't holy. A direct line to purgatory was not the same as a direct line to God. Not that Callie was going to inform anyone of those facts. Callie did not play the put upon priest for the customers, but this time she tried to hold back her hostility. Brin and her boyfriend weren't determined to ruin anyone's lives. They'd been indoctrinated in fear of the afterlife, and wanted to make sure they weren't going to lose their tickets to Heaven with a single night of revelry. Callie wouldn't chide them for that.

She was gentle when she pressed the jars to each

of their chests. The words she offered were real ones, though she barely moved her lips. "Go on now. I'll see you tomorrow." She did not care that she spoke to these souls like they were toddlers. She'd taken them from purgatory, and she was going to do her best to keep them intact. Besides, maybe that would keep them from going off the rails and fighting the match.

Brin called the experience "transcendental" and Callie didn't even giggle. Derek was in her periphery, sentinel over the act. He smirked.

Derek took the teenagers' cash. "Be back here tomorrow by seven," he intoned.

Brin nodded solemnly, but the tall guy asked, "What if we need more time?"

"Then you should hand over more money now," Callie answered.

"Or we come to collect." Derek snarled. The tall guy shrunk an inch under the soul collector's unyielding gaze.

The two ravers walked out the door, and Derek dropped a heavy sigh in the room.

"Do I even want to know?" Callie asked even though she knew damn well she had no interest in whatever new bullshit was rolling their way.

"Savannah messaged. The first two people she went to say they'd already turned the souls in."

"People lie about that shit all the time." That's the whole reason they had people big enough to squish the renters show up to demand they come in.

"She believed them. Said they thought it was cool that the Soul Charmer's guys were now doing more pickups on site."

"Ask her what he looked like, how'd he do it?" Who the hell was taking these souls?

"No. I'm telling her to drag their asses in here."

"You want to question them yourself?" Where would they put them? Lexi needed to stay sequestered.

"I want to know if they're lying." His even tone didn't fool her. His gut—like hers—was certain they were telling the truth, and rankled at the realization that Anonymous Souls was likely snatching up the Charmer's souls. If Lexi and Vega knew the Soul Charmer was missing, others in their organization likely did, too. They weren't scared of the Soul Charmer now, and that was a big fucking problem.

Derek was tapping out a message on his phone back to Savannah when Callie's phone began to buzz. *Please don't be Josh.* She wasn't ready for more bad news on the Delgado side. They were all clawing out of a cold cavern, and bloody and broken hands couldn't make that climb again soon.

Well, it wasn't Josh. "Why is your brother calling me?"

Derek slipped his phone into his pocket. "Henry's calling you?"

Callie proffered her phone out between them. The screen asked for a decision to accept or decline. "It says Cortean Catholic Cathedral on the caller ID."

"I hadn't messaged him yet about the quill." Derek's brow drew tighter with each passing moment until he stared at the device in her palm like it was a blood-drenched dagger and not a mobile phone.

"We need to talk to him anyway." Callie tapped the "accept" button before the call could kick over to voicemail. She then tapped the speakerphone button because if Derek was wound any tighter something was going to get punched.

"Hello?" she said.

"Hello. Is this…" there was a long pause and a rustling of papers "…is this Miss Delgado?"

The voice was gruff, razed, and one hundred percent not Henry's. Derek was going to strain himself giving her an emphatic no with tight, fervent jerks of his head.

"May I ask who is calling?" Her customer service voice shot forward. Stupid nerves.

"This is Father Giles. I have an urgent matter I need to speak with her about."

The priest's voice was familiar, but it was his somber urgency that made her reply. "What can I do for you, Father Giles?"

"Oh. Miss Delgado. It's a complicated matter." In the background a door latched.

"I can keep up."

"It may be best we speak in person." His breath hit the phone line in uneven bursts.

A panicked priest was not something she was eager to take on. "Do you want to be seen at the Soul

Charmer's shop?"

Only the awkward cadence of his breathing filled the line.

"Didn't think so. I've got a bit on my plate, so just tell me what's going on." It's not like the cops were tapping the priest's line. The Church probably had some sort of secret, secure red phone to them.

Father Giles stammered for only a moment before regaining the composure of one of the highest-ranking clergy members in Gem City. "Your employer has not been to visit me in some time."

"He's a busy man." It would have bothered her to lie to a man of the cloth before, but something in his tone told her he'd understand the evasion.

"Well, he does have obligations at our cathedral. It is vital that someone with his skills attend…our private services."

Oh no. No. No. No. How could she not step in this? The soul well had been billowing when she'd visited. What happened if it was ignored? Could it spill over? What would that even mean? She was no theologian, and was still struggling to wrap her brain around the concept that she had snatched souls from purgatory to do some penance in other people's bodies with a celestial signoff. That was a huge load to take, and now she was supposed to think about what would happen if one didn't maintain the balance between there and here.

Now her voice shook, too. "What happens if he is unable to attend?"

"Souls only find salvation through penance and

prayer." The words weren't new. That phrase is what drove people to rent souls. It was a way around the penance part of the whole equation, a shortcut to Heaven. She doubted Father Giles was talking about confession with her.

"I don't think the Soul Charmer is available to assist in services at this time."

"I suspected as much. He has not returned my calls."

The muscle in Derek's temple was ticking. He glared at the phone like he intended to fight it, but stayed steady and warm at her side in the meantime. Callie needed to wrap this up before anyone else entered the room.

Father Giles's dry cough didn't dislodge anyone's discomfort. "Would you be able to assist me tonight?"

She opened her mouth to answer, but her voice failed her. How did she explain this to him? How could she tell him why it was a bad idea? Why she wasn't ready and why stepping away from the Soul Charmer's shop was dangerous for her? Why she didn't want to leave a hostage in the basement with only a single guard? She couldn't tell him any of those things. He hadn't contacted her as *her* priest. He'd called as a warden needing to prevent a riot.

"Miss Delgado, I would not ask this of you if it weren't vital."

Callie had spent her entire life attending the required catechism courses and getting her butt in the pew regularly. Zara had made it clear it was required.

The citizens of Gem City took strong stock in attending the Church. Callie hadn't attended services since she'd been fired from the retirement home. She no longer had to win the favor of society by looking respectable. The dual rituals of prayer and confession were exhausting. Now she had access to facts that dictated faith. She'd pulled away from the routine of showing her face at mass, but now believed. That was the mindfuck. She wasn't about to start coming to Derek's brother to shill her sins like the tally on her soul wasn't earned.

Only now she had a priest begging her to help him. That pleading tone from a man she'd only ever seen on newscasts before the Charmer led her down the winding stairs to the soul well. Father Giles was the hardened face of Cortean Catholicism in Gem City. He was stern and demanded devotion. Or at least he was on TV. Now, on the speakerphone, he was something else, someone else. He was a human, a believer, a man in need of help.

Callie's answer rushed from her mouth before she could overthink it. "I'll see what I can do."

"Bless you. I will be waiting in the sanctuary."

Of course he would. No pressure. Callie tapped the button to end the call, and then looked to Derek.

"You're going to go, aren't you?" he asked.

She hesitated. Her face pulled tight like it, too, couldn't decide how to feel. "I think I have to?"

His agreement was slow to come, but there was no question in his tone. "You don't have to do anything, but you should probably do this."

"What about what's happening here?" She inclined her head down, like Lexi and Beck were below their feet.

Caramel and kerosene clashed in Derek's throat to give her a "not your problem" sound.

"But customers…"

"But nothing, doll. They'll wait. The Charmer knows the demand is there. He's made people stand out here for an hour before."

She almost pointed out that he wasn't here, but those were words too dangerous to speak aloud. Even here. Even with only the two of them. "Okay."

"I'm going to call Henry, though."

"I can talk to him at the cathedral if you want."

"No," he snapped.

Callie flinched.

"Sorry." He meant it. "I don't want anyone but him to know about the quill. I don't think his bosses would be cool with him having that book we gave him, either."

"*We* gave him?" She sucked her lips in to keep from smiling.

"You got a problem with shared ownership of our fucked up life?"

"Not even a little." She skimmed the back of her fingers against his.

Derek wrapped his hand around hers and squeezed. "If we're dragging Henry into this, I want to limit how much hits him.”

“Agreed.” Callie didn’t need anyone else getting burned by Nate or the Soul Charmer or any other awful person waiting in the shadows.

“Plus, I’ve never gotten him to come into this place before. So that’ll be fun.”

Callie understood the pettiness of siblings. “You’re going to light extra incense, aren’t you?”

His grin was brilliant and warm and needed. “He’s going to reek of it for fucking days.”

“Call him, and I’ll go distract his boss with my mad nighthawk skills.”

“You almost sound excited.”

“I’m faking it.”

CHAPTER TWENTY-FIVE

Nighthawk skills? Who was she kidding? Callie's mark began itching far before she even arrived at the cathedral. She'd stayed at the Soul Charmer's shop long enough to let Derek phone his brother, and to convince him that it wasn't a terrible idea for her to drive herself to the church. Now, though, as she accelerated into an icy corner, her wrist was acting up and her stomach was making loud protests about its perpetually empty state. She finally had enough cash for decent food, and was too stressed to eat. That was some shit.

The cathedral sparkled at the center of the plaza. A shimmering layer of snow coated the grounds. The holy statues lining her path to the front steps wore the flakes like cloaks, and spotlights added to the ethereal brightness. The stone was too brilliant, too alive. The saints were watching her. Her feet moved faster. She hopped over a patch of ice, and then darted up the stairs.

Father Giles stood waiting next to the very last pew. His left hand was balanced on the back of the bench, fingertips fat against the wood.

He stepped forward and took her hand in his. "Praise be."

"In his name," she said automatically, but the ingrained words left dry wood on her tongue. She swallowed hard.

The priest didn't look like he did on television, but most people didn't. He also didn't look like the man she'd met before. He had carried himself with an air of nobility then with the kind of stance that said, "I miss the ways of 1800s Spain." Now he couldn't meet her eyes. His attention was snapping around the room. His hair was an unkempt mat, but his vestments were pressed to perfection.

"Come, come." He urged her forward, and she recoiled at his ripe odor. His mistook the move for hesitation, thankfully. "We cannot wait."

He hurried ahead, and she tried to wonder about priorities that put bathing behind ironing one's clothing. She didn't even own an iron.

The hawk mark on her wrist heated. Raised white drops poured into the black ink until the dark bird became something brilliant. She approached the gateway, and the mark grew brighter. The glow was a reminder to start pushing with her magic. She did not have time to be felled by metaphysical barriers. She and Father

Giles moved through the gateway and down the stairs efficiently. He didn't say anything about the relative ease in which she passed through the invisible partition, but simply nodded like he'd made a very good decision. Like he'd done anything that got her into this place. It wasn't his magic, and she was doing him a favor.

All that righteous anger evaporated the second she saw the soul well.

When she'd sneaked in before, the well had been full. The grey veil between worlds stretched across the top edges of the black and gold pool. It was no longer contained by the boundaries of the bricks. The grey barrier stretched out, up, and over the well. The layer separating here from purgatory heaved when she walked into the room. She knew there weren't bodies on the other side, but swore handprints were pressed against the taut material.

"You can see we need you to get to work." Father Giles gestured to the well. Helpful. Like she hadn't noticed the nebula shoving itself into their world.

She'd found a small cooler inside the Soul Charmer's desk. It had contained empty soul jars. She'd brought it. "How many do I need to remove?"

Father Giles was standing on the opposite side of the room from her—an entrance to purgatory roiling between them—and he still had the audacity to scoff at her. "You're the hawk."

Now was not a good time to call herself a baby hawk, but it was tempting. "Not *the* hawk, *a* hawk. A *new* hawk. I wasn't your first pick for a reason, Father."

The Church liked to preach about kindness and offering aid to those who needed it. Father Giles must have forgotten, because the next words out of his mouth were, "If you can't figure out what needs to be done, the consequences will be on your soul."

Her soul? Please. "I have no shame in wearing the scars I've earned." Sometimes she slapped on the ones for her family, too, because it was right. "But make no mistake that this well and your lack of knowledge about it does not make anything that happens all my fault. You chose to rely on the Soul Charmer. I'm here to help. Maybe you could be less of a dick about it."

"I—I—I—"

Yes, she'd just called a priest a dick. And while technically she'd done so in a church, it was *beneath* the church, which felt like less of a blasphemous way of thinking about it. "I'm here to help. I've got nine jars, and I'll do what I can."

Father Giles stopped his gaping. "Thank you, and I gather your mentor did not tell you much about this well."

Mentor? She might have laughed if her nerves hadn't been shot. "He made me promise to tend it, but didn't say much more."

"Yes. Part of our responsibility—your responsibility—is to maintain a balance between here and the other side of this well. These souls are brought here as part of an act of contrition."

"What if they just sit on a shelf and don't get rented?" That was too much trust to put in the Soul Charmer's abilities.

"Being in our world without a host is not a pleasant experience. It is considered to be a provoking part of the journey."

"So does the Charmer return the souls to you after a certain amount of time?"

"He can release them after a period, yes." Father Giles stiffened. "But now is not the time to worry over such things. This well is a problem. Get it back into its bounds before it burdens my church and the parishioners."

How it would jack up the cathedral crowd, Callie didn't know. Luckily, she also didn't have enough energy to care right now.

Callie carried her little, soft-sided cooler closer to the well. Who knew the perfect packaging for a lunch tote was also great for gathering souls. Versatility was key, she supposed. Her levity vaporized. Her own soul was suddenly too big. It was as though it had doubled and redoubled within her chest until she had so much soul in her body it was tightly caged and only her bones kept it from flashing out and escaping.

The well roared.

Voices upon voices upon voices called out. Some called to her, others simply screamed. Languages she didn't know and unintelligible keening assailed her. Fight or flight was riding her hard and the urge to drop the cooler and cut out grabbed her. Her fingers began to loosen on the handle when she heard a lone voice amid the cacophony.

"I'm ready, please," it called.

The soft words among the hungry many caught her attention. This wasn't about the magic or about escaping for a night of sin for these souls. This was about redemption. What kind of asshole would she be if she let this go on? Father Giles didn't want to share the particulars about what happened if this well was ignored, but Callie could imagine souls who weren't ready escaping. She could picture them bypassing the whole atonement bit and sneaking around the law. As much as she was a fan of flipping the bird to the rules, she wouldn't want more people at risk. She didn't know if those souls would sneak off to be reborn or latch themselves onto unsuspecting people or simply disappear, but none of those options were acceptable.

Callie knelt next to the well. The floor was cold, and despite the denim she wore the stone bit into her knees. She unzipped the cooler and removed the jars. She lined them on the ground next to her. The well heaved and jerked toward her. Her own ward snapped up to block it. The well surged up the invisible shield in front of her, and poured over top. She blocked that, too.

"Climbing on me without consent has never ended well in this world, and isn't going to end well for you, either," she said. Father Giles shifted uncomfortably, but she wasn't talking to him. If she'd had a knife on her, she probably would have brandished it, too, to make a point.

The swelling edges of the veil receded enough to let her focus. She uncapped the first jar, calling to the polite soul who promised it was ready. It stretched forward. The shining strands pierced the gelatinous barrier, and slipped into the jar. A second soul wrapped itself around the trailing threads. It knotted itself into the other soul. The other souls bashed against the border, begging for release.

"Do you want him to come with you?" she asked the first soul. It didn't seem to be bothered by the second soul hitchhiking. Could one find family in purgatory? Seemed like that'd be counter productive but hey she wasn't the man in charge.

The first soul tugged the second one along with him, and all Callie got was a plea. Good enough for her. "You'll have to unbind yourselves in the jar, though," she said as she capped them inside with a twist of the lid.

Souls gathered in clusters before her. A dozen charged on her like this was a football game and they were determined to break her defenses with teamwork. They slammed hard against the veil closest to her face. Her protection wobbled and heat poured through. Fire ripped across her cheekbones. She closed her eyes and slapped her hands against her cheeks. Snuffing oxygen wasn't going to dampen these flames. She gritted her teeth, and opened her eyes. The souls on the other side were rallying. A great ball of light was forming before her, just on other side of the charcoal net. She held a hand out toward it. Flakes of black ash and sticky red clung to her body. She ignored it. Her face would heal. Souls that would pull this? They might not.

Purgatory wasn't a team sport.

She shoved her hand forward and past the wall

she'd erected to ward the worst of the souls' effects on her, and punched her fist straight into the other side of the veil. She bit the inside of her cheek. They would not hear her scream. Electricity sloshing with the power of ocean waves surged up her forearm. It was dark and frigid. It was feverish. Her hand locked like all the muscles had hyperextended. She turned her arm and forced her hand to cup the soul collation crafting the ball. She snapped her fingers shut on them. An explosion flared behind the tinted wall. A mini supernova flaring orange and yellow and then cooling to an echo of white. She released her grip, and bladed her body away from the veil until her hand was free.

Skin was a memory. Her fingers were only bone now, burned clean of muscles and tendons. Bits of flesh still clung to the back of her hand. She slammed her magic out around her body, until she was wrapped in a soul ward cocoon. She took a deep breath, and the muscles began to reappear. Two more breaths later and light brown skin started to grow in patches along her fingers. Finally, after five long seconds, her hand was back to the same status as moments earlier, down to the chipped blue nail polish.

Father Giles prayers filled the room. He kept to the classic Spanish, and called only on the Lord to protect them. Callie didn't mind that he was including her in the request. She would get the rest of the required souls out of the well, and then get the fuck away from anything that could literally melt her face off if she screwed up.

The process was easier after that. The souls rushed

forward alone, and she began to pick whichever ones battered the veil the hardest. Taking out the trouble-makers might buy her more time. She'd prefer to let the Charmer be the next person to visit this well, but if not, she didn't want to be in this place every other day. As she siphoned off the souls, the energy of the room settled into something less frenetic. Her organs no longer screamed from the sharp shove of her own soul. The well's contents slowly slipped back into the boundaries. She stuffed two souls to a jar twice.

She zipped the cooler lid closed again, this time with the eleven souls stacked safely in their jars. She stood, and looked to Father Giles for the first time in twenty minutes. He had pressed himself against the far wall, but clearly had been watching her the whole time.

"Your hawk is quite bright," he said.

Was that a compliment? "Sure."

"I haven't seen that happen before."

Sure enough, the hawk on the inside of her wrist was casting damn near disco ball radiance. "I'm sure it's nothing." Another lie to a man of God.

"Never doubt a sign. You've done a good deed here today. Thank you, Miss Delgado." She appreciated he didn't bring up the whole slipping a hand into the after-life and squashing some asshole souls part.

"It needed to be done. Hopefully, the Soul Charm-er will be available to you again shortly." Would it be worth it to say those words upstairs with a rosary in hand?

Father Giles only nodded.

CHAPTER TWENTY-SIX

Callie entered the Soul Charmer's store and the attentions of four men snapped to her. Father Henry fidgeted at the edge of the front room, a slick, styled man was pacing a tiny circuit its center, and Miguel stood near the counter with a death grip on an older man's arm. All except for Father Henry spoke immediately. The volley of demands might have been worse than the gang of souls trying to barrel through the veil at her. Or maybe she was fucking tired.

She didn't stop to listen to their pleas. She walked straight to Father Henry, and took his hand. She didn't stop moving. She plowed directly to the back curtain, towing Henry behind. She held up her other hand, and hollered, "I'll be back in a minute."

Holding her breath as she moved through the protected hallway was habit. Callie exhaled once she was back into the newly pristine office space. The Charmer's ward over the door was in tatters. She should put up a protection of her own while she was in here. The tarry sensation the Charmer had crafted might have seemed like a jerk move, but there were real threats. She got that now. Only she wasn't certain how to make a ward that didn't require her standing there and focusing. If her boss ever returned, she'd ask.

"Have you been waiting out front for long?" she asked Father Henry.

"Not at all. I've already spoken with Derek. He went downstairs for a minute." His voice hitched on 'downstairs.' How much did he know about what happened in this basement?

"How long ago was that?"

Color dappled his cheeks. "Ten minutes."

The radiator hummed and the fan whirred, but no harsh noises rose from the floorboards. Whatever was happening downstairs, at least it wasn't a fight. "I can run down and check on him."

"I got the impression he wanted us to talk, actually." The priest had been trained to read the room. Did that mean he could tell how badly she didn't want to go down another set of stairs to another set of problems?

She, however, could read Derek. Henry might be his brother, but that didn't mean he understood how she and Derek worked. They were a team these days, and while he couldn't venture into the cathedral's well with her, he certainly could be part of this. Father Henry might have taken vows of honesty, but she'd made a promise to Derek. That counted more to her.

"I'm going to go take care of the problems up front first," she didn't bother saying they were going to wait for Derek either way. "You can hang out back here."

"I'm not sure…" Father Henry was already trying to touch as little of this store as he could. If he could have stood on his tiptoes without anyone noticing, Callie thought he would have.

She set the cooler containing the souls from the well on the nearby desk.

"There's a stool behind the desk, if you want it. Make sure not to touch anything."

She didn't wait to hear him stammer through another request. She pushed back through the curtain and to the guests at the front of the house.

The men began shouting when she appeared again. Hell. Did she need to bring the priest back out here to remind them of their manners? She pointed at Miguel. "You. Start."

The other men grumbled, but let Miguel talk. "Charlie here is overdue by a full week," he said.

The man he'd brought in had six inches on Miguel, and the extra layer of donut around his belly probably gave him a full forty pounds on the soul collector. Callie wondered what moves had been used to get this man into the shop.

"I don't owe you nothing," Charlie said.

Callie looked closer. The man's eyes were milky, the film of white deadening the iris. With signs like that he couldn't be new to the soul rental game. "Of course not. We've just met. Do you owe the Soul Charmer, though?"

"You ain't the Soul Charmer, lady." He spoke to her breasts.

A heavy band of tension clapped against Callie's belly.

The other man in the room unbuttoned his suit jacket. "I'm here waiting for the Soul Charmer. When is he going to be here?"

Another thick band snapped against her stomach. Dread bit into her like some industrial strength rubber. She glared at each man in turn. "He put me in charge today, so if you owe him money, you pay me. If you want a soul, you pay me."

Miguel dropped his grip on Charlie. He was back near one of the incense tables in half a breath. If he moved any farther away, he'd be wrapped in a wall tapestry. At least someone could read a room.

Suit guy stepped up to the counter. "Why would I pay you if you can't even give me a soul?"

The cables crushing her abdomen frayed and snapped. The edges igniting darkness and power and *action* in her blood. Rosewater filled her lungs. Iron, her mouth. She stared pointedly at the businessman's chest. He squirmed. She stepped closer, and he mirrored her steps in the opposite direction. "You'll pay me because I decide what souls go in you. You'll do business with me because if you keep looking at me like you're in fucking charge of me, I'll borrow your goddamn soul and send it on with any person who looks like they could commit a mortal sin. You'll give me some fucking respect or I'll make sure you spend the rest of your life on your knees in a pew working out a never-ending debt of prayer and penance to scrub the fucker clean."

If Suit-and-Tie could have sucked his head into his neck like a turtle, he would have. After several failed attempts, he whispered a "sorry."

It said a lot about the type of people who rented souls that the man didn't leave. She'd literally threatened him with eternal damnation—not that she would actually do that—and he'd found a chair near the wall and sat. He even had choirboy posture.

Callie turned her attention back to Charlie. His deep brown skin had sallowed in the last few seconds. She asked, "You were saying?"

"I'm supposed to give this soul back." It wasn't a question, but his voice lilted at the end. His confidence had puddled somewhere in the floor. Maybe that's why the carpet was squishy.

"How much does he owe?" she asked Miguel.

He gave her a figure, and Charlie confirmed he had it. She stretched out to his soul, the one hidden behind the borrowed one. It was shredded. She wasn't surprised, but sad. He wasn't going to be able to function well without another soul holding him together. His arms didn't bear the signature track marks she associated with the men and women who went the tweaker route to cope with what was missing after abusing soul rental. It wasn't the definitive reason they used, but part of the damn cycle. For the first time, Callie was morally obligated to offer this man another rented soul if only to keep him from crashing hard.

"Do you want to swap out for another?"

"That's what the Charmer does," he muttered.

"If you've got the cash, that's still what the Charmer does. I'm just doing the hard part."

They brokered the deal, and before Callie knew it she'd taken a soul from this man, put a new one in, and was up a grand. All while the other man waited patiently for his turn. Miguel stood guard.

The businessman wanted a week's rental for a casino trip. If Zara had still been working her game, he would have been the perfect mark. He had the cash, and he was determined to do wrong. That was the best kind of person to steal from. Callie wasn't in the con game, but in this moment she could understand the appeal. She didn't need Suit-and-Tie's money to feed herself, but she didn't hate the idea of there being consequences for his pride and gluttony. She overcharged him for the "quality" soul he demanded. She wasn't putting anything immaculate in that man.

When the businessman was gone, Miguel said, "You want me to stay up here and keep watch for you?"

She might have scared him too with her rant earlier, but there was no ambiguity in his voice.

"That'd be great. I'm going to go check on Derek." And Father Henry.

***

The Shepherd brothers were together in the office.

Derek whistled when she walked in. "I'm pretty sure I heard those guys pee themselves from here in, Callie."

She angled up on her tiptoes and kissed his cheek. "Someone had to put the fear of God into them."

"Pretty sure that's Henry's job," Derek said.

Father Henry laughed. "It's more about saving mortal souls than necessarily scaring them into obedience, but what you told that man wasn't exactly wrong."

"I thought he'd leave, honestly," Callie admitted.

"Be careful or the Soul Charmer might be proud of your work."

Callie moved around the guys to the desk, and tugged the still sealed cooler closer. She'd used the Charmer's wares for the customers. The shield doors on the cabinet were still open. She started placing the souls she'd obtained on their own shelf.

"You going to mark them?" Derek asked.

She shuffled the souls onto a center shelf. "No, I know which ones are mine."

"Mine?" Father Henry's incredulity was probably warranted, but she understood Derek's urge to slug him.

Callie ignored him. "Do you have information for us, Father Henry?"

"Some, and call me Henry. I left the collar at home." He was still clad in all black, but sure enough he was off duty in as much as a priest could be.

"I showed him the quill," Derek said.

Callie stiffened, and Derek moved closer to place his hand in the middle of her back.

"And?" she prompted.

"It's clearly one of Petro's artifacts," Henry answered.

Callie hadn't gotten a good chance to read the book. Clearly Henry had, though. Derek supplied more context, "Like the knife."

"A quill and a knife that can collect souls? Those are rather random objects."

"Not really. St. Petro was a monk who tended the original soul well in Seville. He was tasked with devising a way to protect the Cortean conquistadors as they journeyed to explore the new world."

Callie folded her arms across her chest like it would get her distance from this weird-ass history lesson. "That knife was not a conquistador's knife."

"No, it was a monk's knife," Henry explained. He was leaning closer to them with each word. It was clear he really loved this shit. "St. Petro imbued a number of items within the monastery with the power to help protect the explorers. If we trust his journal—and it sounds like we should—those tools would allow the transfers of souls."

"Why'd they need to borrow souls while on a mission of expansion?" Good question, Derek.

"Expansion is a bloody thing. The leaders found peace in doing necessary, but horrific things in the name of extending the Cortean empire. They had not found the well here yet, but as you know that's how

Gem City became this continent's seat for the Cortean Catholic Church."

Callie was not about to remind this priest—her boyfriend's brother—that normal people had no clue that the soul well is why the church was here. She vaguely remembered hearing the stories about this being the place the conquistadors found salvation, but she'd thought it had merely been the place they'd been when they got tired of walking.

"How many of these artifacts are there?" At least Derek was ready to get them back on the practical side of the conversation.

"Tough to say." Henry sounded excited by not having a solid fact.

Lack of facts was not helpful now. The consequences of Nate and his crew having access to tools to snatch souls were too great to wing it. "We need to know how many people could be stealing people's souls, Henry. How many could show up at the cathedral and steal from the well."

Derek's hand began to rub her back in small circles before she'd even finished speaking.

The priest bristled. "The artifacts wouldn't get you into the well. We've never let Nate in. You know that."

Sure, he'd told her that before. She also barely knew him, and was pretty sure Derek had also promised to punch Henry in the nose after that meeting. She was beginning to understand the urge.

"What do you mean the artifacts won't get you inside? They can pull and push souls from a host, can't they?"

"From a host, yes. Not from the well." His words came at the pace doled out to two-year-olds.

If he wanted to be that way, she'd prod until she got something useful. "Why not?"

"I'm not certain," he admitted. His patronization stopped immediately, too. "The journal doesn't explain the mechanics of why one person is gifted with the flight and others are not."

"Flight?" She wasn't a goddamn pilot.

"You." Was it a priest thing to be cryptic? Weren't they supposed to explain things to people? Her local priest growing up had been big on interpreting every-thing for them.

"Excuse me?"

He grabbed her hand and pulled it forward until her wrist was exposed. The nighthawk had changed. The black outline remained, but some of the white that had pooled into the mark when she visited the well hadn't left. White cut across the throat and ran brilliant near the ends of the wings.

"This," he said, "is the mark of the nighthawk. Only those who bear this mark can enter the well. Only those who have the ability of flight, who can ferry souls from one realm to another, may bear this symbol."

"The only people in Gem City and in this state with the nighthawk are you and the Soul Charmer. Only you and he can touch the well. Even if someone with the artifacts could connive a way to get past the require-ments to enter the location, those tools would not be able to cross the veil. If you believe St. Petro, and I do," Henry posted his hand on the desk. His breathing was slow and steady. A man of faith in action.

"We believe you," Derek said. His expression was open, and not one he'd worn in this room before. The brothers had a tenuous relationship, and this help could be a bridge for them if Callie and Derek could manage to keep the Charmer's issues from burning it down.

"So if Nate was able to put together at least a van full of souls, he acquired them without the soul well," Callie said.

Whether that made things better wasn't clear. Access to the well would have damning consequences for the people of Gem City, but if Nate was harvesting souls from people that was a problem, too. If he was slinging the tainted ones from the Soul Charmer's shelf of filth, the situation wasn't prettier.

"Did the journal provide instructions? Like would it have shown someone how to use the artifacts?" If they had any chance of stopping him, Callie needed to know how much Nate had learned about the mechanics of soul magic.

"Of course not. It's a monk's text. This is about the nature of the Lord's work and the tools crafted for the task, but it was not his place to share the inner workings of gifts bestowed by God. The ability of flight is a miracle and one cannot explain *how* when it comes to wonders." Henry wasn't trying to be a dick. This was a normal Cortean response.

There were mechanics to this, though. There were rules and restrictions and dangers. Callie attempted to find solace in the fact there was not actually a guide-book for this shit, because it would have made the Soul Charmer's 'let's set you on fire' teaching style even more painful.

"We have one of his tools," Derek spoke only for Callie. "We'll find out what else he has, and put this to a stop."

If only it could be so easy.

Callie turned to fully face Father Henry. "How would Nate have even gotten this hands on one of these artifacts, much less several?"

"I wish I could tell you. The Church has housed some of the artifacts, but I'm not privy to everything in our cathedral." It was a prime gig to work there, but Father Henry was the youngest by far.

"I can't see Father Giles handing any Cortean rel-ics over to anyone," Callie said, forgetting the others didn't know she'd met with him more than once.

"No, he wouldn't. Not if they weren't affiliated with the Church." Henry's words came slow, but were solid. "Though Nate does have connections to be in more private areas of the cathedral."

"How private?" Derek asked. His hand stopped moving.

Father Henry's answer was plain. "If he arrives with the Ford family, he has the same access they do."

"Which is?" his brother nudged.

"Everything. The Ford family is the largest patron to our church, and they are paramount in upholding the tenets of the faith.”

Callie and Derek shared a look. Henry folded his arms and unfolded them twice. “What?”

“You really don’t know who they are?” Callie asked.

“He doesn’t,” Derek answered her, and then to his brother he said, “The Ford family are mobsters, Henry. I know you can’t spill the details of what people confess to, but you aren’t much of a liar either. They can’t be paragons of the fucking faith if they aren’t spending hours in that box unloading their goddamn souls. Soul renters can’t be your *perfect* parishioners. So they must have told you something.”

It was good Henry was already balanced on the desk, because his knees wobbled. His fingers pressed harder against the wood until the tips of each one turned white.

“They only confess to the bishops.” His voice hitched and the office tiles only amplified it. The truth of the situation bounced from every surface.

Derek didn’t make a move to comfort his brother, but offered careful words. “This isn’t on you.”

“He’s right, and thank you. Knowing what is coming could help us protect people from him.” Callie couldn’t say more without putting the priest in an even more precarious situation.

Nate had stolen religious relics from the Cortean Church. Someone had stolen souls from the Soul Charmer. It wasn’t a leap to guess the two were related. The hard part was what would come next.

Fixing this shouldn't be her problem, but it was quickly becoming apparent that dealing with the Soul Charmer's shit storms was her specialty.

CHAPTER TWENTY-SEVEN

Callie left Beck and Miguel to cover the shop. She needed food and sleep, and maybe not even in that order. She and Derek picked up drive-thru tacos around the corner from the Soul Charmer's, and had devoured them in the few minutes it took to get to Derek's place.

They should have immediately crashed, but Callie plopped down onto his modern-but-surprisingly-comfy couch instead. "It feels good to sit."

Derek only nodded.

She slid off her shoes. He sat at the center of the couch. She turned so her back was against the arm of the sofa, and pulled her feet up onto the couch. He didn't even flinch when she wedged her toes under his leg.

"Today was a fucking day, doll."

Callie had buzzed from one staggering situation to another, but she wasn't the only person in the thick of it.

"Anything extra happen at the shop?" In the basement?

"Extra?" He slid a hand behind her calf and held her loosely. "Beck and I were able to get more out of Lexi."

Regret reverberated in a hollow pipe within him. Callie folded her arms atop her knees. He had more to say, and she'd long learned that comfort can come too soon when you need to get the bad shit out.

"What did she give you?" Callie asked.

"She knew of three warehouses that could be key points. She'd picked up souls there, which could be nothing or everything."

They needed this lead. Callie tugged her feet back toward her, readying to get up. Derek's hand held steady on her leg. "Beck and I both sent people to look into it. We'll hear back if any of the locations has actual viability," he said.

She stilled for a breath, and then relaxed into his touch again. "That sounds almost like a plan. You know I love plans."

He chuckled, and moved a smidge closer to her in the process. "That you do. She still wouldn't use Nate's name of course. Whatever demo he did for them, it was the kind of act that melted any steel in someone's spine."

Callie yawned, and didn't bother covering the fatigue. She didn't have to with him. "I'll admit Nate can make a threat legit, but if he's got the backing of the Ford family? I can imagine even his spindly ass could be imposing."

"I hear threatening jacking someone's soul and forcing eternal damnation is scary as fuck." His tone was serious, but his grey eyes danced with light.

"You keep that up and I'll throw you against a wall," she made the joke, but it soured on her tongue. What she'd done to Savannah and Lexi shouldn't be joked about.

Derek laughed loud and boisterous. "You going to put me up against a wall?"

Callie pressed her fingers against her lips. "Do you want me to?"

He turned, and knocked her knees wide as he did. Her whole body flushed. He tilted his head down to gaze at her, and when he lifted his eyes to meet hers there was nothing but hunger. "Seemed like you were good with me keeping you on that counter."

The air between them was thick and heady, and Callie gasped it in. Low in her belly began to clench. His hands were searing as they slid along her jeans. He pushed her legs wider, and quickly filled the space. He let his full weight land on her. It was crushing and possessive, and she loved the reminder that he could be powerful when she needed it.

She speared her fingers into his hair, and pulled him closer. Their lips met in a feverish hunger. He sucked her lower lip into his mouth. Their kiss grew deeper, and Callie wrapped a leg around his back. She couldn't hold him there, but she'd try. She grappled with the hem of his shirt, edging it up, but was unwilling to break the kiss to give him the freedom to toss it overhead. Her own shirt rode up, too, and electricity snapped between their bare skin. It was the promising prickle of expectations. Her body needed something good. Her soul needed it, too.

He gave her a small nudge, and pushed himself back to pull off the shirt. "Just a sec, doll."

Callie wasn't interested in waiting. Not tonight. If today had taught her anything it was how volatile the world could be. How quickly circumstances could change. She was going to feast on love and sex and Derek, and she wasn't about to wait for an invitation for more. She placed her hands on his shoulders. His muscles hardened, and it only made her wetness increase. His chagrin put her over the edge. She pulled a pinch of her magic forward, and throttled Derek to the other side of the couch. The sofa shifted closer to the wall as his back hit the other arm. Callie hadn't throw *him*, though. She'd thrown herself, too. She straddled his waist, and ran her nails down his bare chest.

"Oh," Derek said.

"Oh," she repeated and then leaned in to get more of the kiss she needed. His mouth was already swollen. Hers was too. She bit his lower lip, and then licked it. His groan was one of both pain and request. His hand cupped her nape, his hold firm. Her spine shot signals to every part of her body until all her nerve endings were primed for his touch. Her nipples tightened against the heat of his chest. She leaned into him, needing to be closer. To get more. More of him. The hardness in his jeans had similar ideas. He rocked his hips beneath hers in a steady rhythm that was slowly short-circuiting her brain. Only Derek could find the places to shut off her mind. His touch was freedom, and she craved more. Derek pulled her mouth to his again, and devoured. His free hand found her hip and yanked her down sharply against him. She whined, and he did it again.

He arced up until his lips grazed her earlobe. "You good with me pushing right now?"

She loved that he asked. That he wouldn't reverse their roles again without permission. Callie hadn't ever seen herself in leadership roles. The problem solver? Sure. Today, though, she'd had to give people instructions, she'd had to make decisions for other people, she'd had to protect people. It was goddamn exhausting.

"Put me where you need," she whispered. "Take over."

He didn't hesitate. His hands slung under her ass, and he stood in a swift motion that both underscored their size differential and just how fucking strong the man was. He headed toward the bedroom, but paused across from the bathroom. He sat her back onto the floor.

He kneeled before her and reached for the button on her jeans. "Pants."

Her jeans and panties and his jeans and boxers were kicked to the side. Derek's mouth once again collided with hers. Her shoulders bumped the wall behind her. His fingers slid between her legs, the move more exploratory than teasing. She arced toward the touch. The gravel of his groan grazed her breasts. She bit back a small cry, and reached to offer a similar touch. But he locked his hands on her hips and spun her to face away from him. His chest was heat and promise at her back. He nudged her forward until the cool drywall was pressed against her cheek. Tiny, tender kisses warmed her shoulder. He trailed them up the side of her neck. Each contact edged her closer to oblivion. She needed him. These teasing strokes were not enough.

His voice was hoarse in her hear. "I love you, and I've got you."

And he did.

Callie and Derek made it into the bedroom thirty minutes later. Languid limbs were usually reserved for people who could fork over two hundred bucks for a stone massage, but Derek had brought Callie to that level of relaxation.

The ceiling fan churned silently overhead. "I needed that," she said.

"Me, too. I need this, though, too." He pulled her closer until her cheek was pressed against his chest. The musk of sex and sweat clung to him. He smelled like hers.

"We should do more of both."

Derek was quiet long enough, she'd thought he'd

fallen asleep. "We should get out from the Soul Charmer."

She agreed. They'd made that plan, but Charmer's status had changed since then. "Do you think he's coming back?"

He pressed her more firmly to his side. "I wish I knew, doll."

"How long do we wait?" Could they wait?

"For him to return or for us to leave?" Derek asked.

"Both maybe?" Only could she leave now?

Reality crashed into the room like the Kool-Aid Man.

"If he doesn't come back," an eerie tang tainted her tone, "I don't think we can leave."

His breath hitched. "I suppose if he's gone there's no reason we have to leave." The words were cautious, and that made Callie uneasy.

She needed to tell him about the well. Her nighthawk vows involved secrecy, but they also probably hadn't allowed for her to punch a fist into purgatory and bust the afterlife equivalent of skulls. "Someone has to tend to the soul well. You heard your brother. It's me and the Soul Charmer who can do it."

Derek sucked in a breath big enough to move Callie's head on his chest. She continued before he could shoot the idea down. "You weren't there today. The thing was overflowing, and there were some souls we would not want escaping doing their best to take over. Father Giles was not particularly helpful, but, Derek, my gut says if someone doesn't keep that thing stable souls that should not be in this world will get here."

"What does that mean?" he asked quietly.

The phrase 'hell on earth' wasn't appropriate for bedroom talk. "If we want to protect our people here, we have to stay until the Soul Charmer comes back."

"A temporary stay. That can work. I just don't want to see him forcing you into more of this kind of bullshit. You shouldn't be fighting battles over stolen souls."

"And what should I be doing?" Callie kissed his chest.

"Whatever the fuck you want, doll. Whatever the fuck you want."

CHAPTER TWENTY-EIGHT

Morning came too early. Derek made coffee, and then he and Callie drove to her place so she could shower and change clothes. The desert had this stillness when the sun was still low. The golden rays danced on every surface, and brought the adobe homes they passed back to the rich clay color of its earlier life. The packed snow on the streets glistened, but the sky was clear. If it weren't for the thirty-degree temperature, it might have been lovely out.

"Did you check who needs souls picked up today?" Callie hadn't.

Derek kept his eyes on the road. "Nah. We can get an update at the shop, and figure out what's next. I know you wanted us to get more souls on the shelves…"

She wasn't the boss, but he hadn't meant it that way. Right?

"I want to make sure Nate doesn't steal them. Once he grabs them, those souls could be lost to us." She toggled the air vent to point over her shoulder.

"I know." He gripped the steering wheel tighter, and his left knee bounced a rat-a-tat.

"But?"

"We should start hearing back from the scouts soon. I want to stay close in case we need to move on the missing souls." He wanted to stay close to her.

Relationships were weird. Part of her felt she should have been bothered by his need to hover right now. The other part said this was how their relationship worked. He showed her he loved her with actions. If he busted someone's face, it was more an act of devotion than one of protection. Would he admit he needed her close for him?

"You hear from Josh this morning?" He was also great about diverting attention away from the awkward moments.

"He messaged. Zara's making progress and Aunt Lily is driving her crazy."

"Any other Nate sightings?"

"Not that he mentioned, but I told him to call if he saw anything."

They parked around the back of the shop. The interior was quiet. Miguel texted to tell them he'd tapped in to watch Lexi in the basement, and promised they'd given her food and water. Beck was seated behind the Soul Charmer's desk, feet kicked up.

"I'm guessing the boss isn't back?" Derek knocked Beck's feet off the oak desk. His shoes clopped against the floor.

Beck didn't miss a beat. "Callie's our temporary Soul Charmer, though, right?"

Ugh. "Don't ever call me that again."

"Soul Charmer 2.0? Soul Charmette? Soul Sister?"

"Beck if you don't stop, I'm going to let Derek punch you." Not that he actually needed her permission.

Beck snickered. "You two are an uptight power couple. Is that a thing?"

Derek snaked his arm around Callie's waist and tugged her close. "Jealous?"

Callie elbowed him away. "We're the kind of couple that can break your bones and steal your soul, and one hundred percent do not need your commentary."

"You really are no fun."

Callie shrugged him off and went to review the contents of the cabinets. All the souls that should be on the shelf as of yesterday were still there. It's not that she'd expected any of the Charmer's crew to pilfer them, but she needed to know the souls she'd saved from the well were safe. This mother hen deal had to wear off eventually, right?

"Your guys hear anything?" Derek asked Beck.

"Yeah, the two warehouses nearest the center of town were busts. One of my guys broke in and it was empty. Property rolls still show it belonging to the late Ford, and it looks like no one has moved to make changes."

"And the other?" Derek began to pace in front of the desk. He had very few tells when they were at the Charmer's, but it was like his feet had to move when his brain was turning over something big.

Beck scrolled the screen on his phone for a moment. "The other place was in use by Ford's dad. They did not break in there."

"So that leaves the one south of town?"

"Right. I've got one of my guys and one of yours sitting on it. They're supposed to ping me if they see anyone coming or going." Beck sat his phone on the desk. Task complete.

Derek wasn't done though. He paused in front of the desk. "How long have they been watching it?"

Beck straightened his spine. "Since seven this morning."

"Not bad." It was high praise from Derek.

Beck nodded slowly and the two fell back into relative quiet.

The silence bit at Callie. Her mom seemed to be okay for now, but they still had problems. Like the soul dealer held hostage in the basement. "How's Lexi doing?"

The way Beck and Derek looked at one another made Callie's stomach drop.

"She's fine," Beck said, too quickly.

"What aren't you telling me?" Callie looked to

Derek, then Beck, and then back to Derek. Someone was going to tell her what had gone wrong.

"She *is* fine," Derek said. "She's been in and out, though. Usually the people downstairs don't sleep. We got the other info out of her, but there might be more."

"Boss usually has us take them off site." Shame slathered Beck's face.

"He's not here," Callie snapped. "Keep her comfortable."

Derek's lips thinned.

"Comfortable, but secure," she amended. "Once we've dealt with the Anonymous Souls group, we'll find a safe way to let her go."

Derek didn't argue, but Beck said, "You sure that's a good idea? The Charmer wouldn't sign off on that."

"Thought you said I was Soul Charmer 2.0."

He was quiet for a long minute. Callie prepared for the possibility this was going to get awkward. Finally, Beck said, "I knew you liked that one."

The sharp ting of the front bell rang throughout the office. Callie peeked at the time on her phone. "Who needs a bonus soul this early in the day?"

"Sometimes it's part of running errands, Callie." Beck laughed at his own joke. No one else did.

She looked to Derek. "Come up there with me?"

If this were the business guy back early or another person who wanted to throw their weight around, then she'd rather Derek's presence quell any potential trouble. No need to go supernatural Kung-Fu fighter again.

A man and a woman waited for them. Both in navy blue uniforms and badges reading Gem City Police Department. Lovely. Just lovely. At least they weren't the same police officers who had visited last time. That had to be a good thing, right?

"Sir, ma'am, we are here to speak with the proprietor of this establishment," the woman said. Her badge read Sinclair.

"He isn't available at this time. If you'd like me to take your card, though, I can pass it along." Did she sound overeager? Too helpful? Could you be too helpful to the cops? What was the right balance between civic duty and up-in-your-shit to please the people?

"We're here to see the Charmer," the male officer said. The familiarity in his voice was unmistakable. He'd met the Soul Charmer before. Callie kept her distance from him. Now most certainly was not the time to kick-start her magic.

Derek loomed behind her like an emboldened bear. "She already told you, he's not here."

"Maybe you can assist us," Sinclair said. She'd come here for something, and determination like that stuck in her teeth. "We believe a recent crime victim visited this establishment last night."

"Oh?" What if Suit-and-Tie was dead? What if her magic was too much? Was Lexi dying in the basement from wounds to her soul? Was it the guy from her apartment? Wasn't there some cop rule about proximity and guilt?

The policewoman continued like Callie wasn't

having an ethical crisis. "Would you mind looking at a photo?"

Like she could say no.

The four-by-six image the officer pulled from her pocket was greys and silvers, but still in full color. Callie covered her mouth to hold back the cry kicking in her throat. In the picture, a jaw hung slack from a bruised face. Unseeing eyes stared out from the frame. They might have been green when the man was alive, but now their color was diluted. The image was sharp, but everything about this man had blurred. The metal coroner's table beneath the head shone brightest in the picture. Callie tried to focus on it, because staring at a dead body had not been on her agenda for the day, the week, or the year.

"I haven't seen him before," she said, her fingers still hovering near her mouth.

"What about you?" The officer held the photo out to Derek.

"No. He's not a customer," he said.

"And you'd know if he was?" the male cop asked.

Derek was still fixed on the photograph. Callie understood. The horror jarring her brain had needed a way to place it context. There simply wasn't one.

"I've worked here for a long time. I know most of the customers. That isn't one, and he wasn't here last night." Derek's voice was that even calm that came from years of being the person who controlled the level of tension in the room.

"You know we heard this place might have something to do with the murder of Mr. Ford's son."

Were they supposed to say something to that? It wasn't a question, but ignoring it might draw even more interest. They could not cope with more interest from Gem City PD.

"Not sure where you heard that," Callie said, doing her best to look tiny and helpless. "We rent souls to those seeking to stay in our Lord's good graces, and that's all."

"You know criminals use your services. It'll be outlawed before you know it." The male cop was in a snit.

"If that's the case, then we'll deal with it then. The Soul Charmer always complies with the law." Fuck. She was starting to sound like him. If Beck was eavesdropping, she'd never hear the end of it.

"If that's the case, why don't you let us see the logbooks from last night? Prove our suicide vic wasn't in here?" the cop huffed.

Suicide? A bad match could do that. She'd seen the attempt herself, but how would they know if it was because of the soul?

Derek dropped the nice guy act. He angled closer to Callie, and she could almost smell the sickly sweet disdain dripping from his pores. "You know damn well the Soul Charmer doesn't keep a logbook."

"He had to try," the policewoman said. "If you or your boss hear anything, please give us a call." She dropped her business card on the counter, and then the two officers exited the shop.

Callie exhaled and leaned backward into Derek.

He didn't budge.

"Do you think it was a bad match?" Her words were soft.

His harsh grunt was a maybe.

Her shoulders ached, and her toes cramped. She stretched until her fingers were far above her, and her Chucks slurped off the floor. When she released the move, she was no less tense. So much for staying off the edge.

"Did you actually recognize the guy? I didn't."

"No."

Callie turned around. A harsh line cut between Derek's eyebrows. His mouth was drawn in a tight bow.

"Nate did this," he said as though it were fact.

His rage was hers. It glowed in his eyes, and that same spark kindled her own. "Yes. He did. Whether he snatched this soul from someone else or shoved one of the sullied souls from the back room into that guy, this is Nate's fault."

"We're going to find him." Derek nodded to himself. "Are you ready to recollect the souls when we do?"

"Stopping Nate comes first. Souls are second. We need a plan, though, because if he's got them stored like he had in the van, I'm going to have some difficulty."

"How bad?"

"Full-body flame," she said honestly. When he flinched, she added, "But I have a better idea of how it works now. I just need more time to test. I can try it with the souls here first before we go there."

"Practice as much as you need, doll. He isn't going to know what's coming, so let's make sure to bring the new tricks."

Agreed. She was not willing to look at the face of another dead guy because of Nate and shitty attempts at soul magic.

Beck poked his head past the velvet curtain. "We clear for you two to come back here?"

Derek didn't move until Callie agreed. She led the way and he followed closely behind her.

The image of the postmortem photo continued to bat at Callie's brain. That man might have died as a result of soul magic. Callie thought of Lexi then, and her lolling head and limp limbs. Had she damaged the woman permanently? The Soul Charmer had thrown his magic at Callie from day one, and it hadn't knocked her out. He'd turned her into a human soul detector out the gate, and now she was sucking souls from other planes. Other than the overall ick factor and the mountain of guilt that continued to grow at her back, she wasn't ill. But not everyone could take the magic like she could. She wrapped a hand around her wrist, and could almost believe the wings beneath were fluttering.

"Is everything okay downstairs?" she asked when they were back in the relative sanctuary of the back workspace.

"Why wouldn't it be?" Beck asked.

"Just answer her." Derek loomed over Beck. When

they stood this close the differences widened. Derek's height, his broad shoulders, and his glare offering the plausibility of potential murder were juxtaposed against Beck's rangy frame and whatever-the-fuck attitude.

Callie rested a hand on Derek's arm. The cops clearly put him on edge, and she could relate.

"The woman's sleeping. Miguel is reading a book. No big news from the basement contingent," Beck said without looking at Callie.

Derek shrugged like it was an apology. Beck nodded. Whatever worked.

"So what news do you have?" Callie didn't want his take on the Gem City PD visit.

"I heard from the man I've got in front of the warehouse. A couple guys just showed up."

"Nate?" Derek prompted.

"No, but he said they were toting oversized backpacks and were definitely not in school."

Those backpacks could hold anything: groceries, drugs, souls.

"They still inside or did they drop and dash?" Derek asked.

"Still inside as of five minutes ago," Beck said. "I didn't want to interrupt."

Callie inhaled sharply, and Beck didn't continue that thread.

"When do you want to do this?" Derek asked.

"They could move tomorrow for all we know." She couldn't have that. She couldn't miss this shot to block those souls from finding hosts. What if Josh had taken one? Or Zara? She wasn't going to lose someone she loved, and she wasn't about to be the reason someone else fell into that heartache, either.

She squeezed Derek's arm, and hoped to absorb some of his stoic determination. She continued, "I think I need to test a few tricks now, and we plan to go tonight."

Derek rapped his knuckles against the desk. "We can make that work. We keep the guys scouting the place. We need all the entrances and our best guess on a head count."

"I can help with that," Beck offered. He picked his phone up from the desk, unlocked it, and began tapping out messages.

"Is that second room downstairs manageable for me to free a few souls to see how I do with control?" she asked Derek. He might not have first-hand experience with the magic, but he understood the Charmer's setup better than anyone.

"It's probably safer up here. That room would work if we didn't have someone in the other room." He didn't point out that if it went wrong the soul might find the soul dealer or she might burn something important. Other than herself.

"I can work with that." She began pulling the souls she'd collected from the well from the shelves. The labels on their jars were bare, but as she picked up each container a glimmer of memory fluttered before her.

The familiarity was new, but nice.

Callie phone vibrated. She set the next jar onto the desk, and then pulled the mobile from her pocket. The number was unknown. "Would the hospital call with an unlisted number?"

She wasn't certain whom she had been asking, but Derek answered. "Probably not, but answer it on speaker."

Nothing good came from unlisted phone numbers calling her. Collections used that. Her debts were paid up right now, so no one would have to hear about the medical bill she was seven months late on or the disconnection threat on the electric bill. She swallowed her concern, and accepted the call.

"Hello?"

"Callie girl. What cha wearing?" Even without the disgusting commentary she would have recognized Nate's sleaze-slathered voice.

"Fuck off."

"Aw, now now. Is that any way to treat the man who spared your mommy's life? I could take it back."

Callie's hand began to shake. Derek slid his beneath hers. The act both kept the phone steady and rooted Callie into the moment, here with her lover. "Why are you calling me, Nate?"

"Well, it would have been nice to get a thank you," he sneered.

"Pretty sure the bonus gifts I sent along with your soul covered that."

His breath hissed on the line as though his mouth covered the whole of the receiver. "That was payment."

Her patience was waning and taking her worry with it. "Did you really call to gloat?"

"I called with a proposition for you, Callie girl."

She didn't need to hear whatever he was about to say. "I'll pass."

"No you won't."

"We're done. I returned your soul. I gave you what you asked for. The deal is done. Move on."

"I am moving forward. I'm finding the soul business is easy to break into these days. No wonder the Soul Charmer never leaves his work. Everyone's looking for a quick soul these days, and the bank on it is fucking nice."

Callie was not about to snap at that jab about the Soul Charmer. Nate might know he was missing. Whatever. She was not on this call to talk to him. "There's only one Soul Charmer in Gem City," she said. Her thumb already hovering over the end button.

"Or none." He waited for a long moment before giving her anything more. "Funny thing, I liked the souls you brought me. It's time for round two."

"If you want to rent souls from the Soul Charmer, you know exactly how that works."

"You know that's not what I mean."

"We're done."

"Wonder how dear Henry here feels about that? Henry, did you want to let Callie know how you feel about her disinterest in bringing me souls?" Wood scraped against something harder in the background. Two heavy, wet smacks rang across the line followed by a long, low groan.

"Looks like the priest has taken a vow of silence, too. If you're not going to help me, I get to find out what it takes to break a man of God. I win either way, but I thought you'd want the chance to save your priest buddy."

"Nate…" she ground his name between her teeth. If only it would pulverize him.

"Are you not fucking that brick wall asshole anymore? This is his brother. Did you know that? Enforcer for the Soul Charmer and his brother is spending his days trying to save souls. Wonder how their mom feels. How many fingernails do you think it'll take before Henry tells me? I'm putting my money on three, but cards are really my game."

Had Nate been this demented before? He'd been scary in a grabby way, in the kind of unnerving way where you were certain he saw you as an object to undress and use. Her gut had always put Ford as the one who would stab and slice. Nate's gleeful tone, though, crawled beneath Callie's skin until she thought her muscles would all lock.

"Torturing a priest. Really? I know rising to Heaven was off the table for you, but you planning to bypass purgatory and just burn for millennia?"

"I've got souls now, bitch. I can kill and maim to my heart's delight and the Big Man still has to let me in with open arms."

The fuck he did.

"Why a priest?" Would avoiding Henry's name make a difference at this point?

"Other than he's your boyfriend's brother? He could let me have access to souls. I know it. He refused, and now you're going to have to do."

Another wet smack rang from Nate's end.

"What do you want?" Desperation leaked into her words.

"Souls. You're going to bring me a dozen souls today, and I'll let you have the padre back."

"That's a lot of souls…"

"Bullshit. You've got them, and you're going to keep bringing me souls every week or I can pay another visit to your brother at work or maybe put a hit on that giant asshole you like to screw. Deliver for me, or I'll cut away what you love. You hear me, Callie girl?"

She fucking heard him. This couldn't be happening, but she heard every syllable sliding from his forked tongue.

"Yeah." If rage could be packed into four little letters, her reply would have combusted.

"I'll text you an address. I expect my souls by six tonight or I find out how much pain a priest can take before he curses his maker."

The call died, and so did a piece of Callie.

CHAPTER TWENTY-NINE

Every bit of guilt gristle Callie had packed to her ribs in the last fifteen years sloughed from the bone and turned on her organs until spikes skewered her insides.

"We can't wait to go to the warehouse." Her voice was shaking, but even she didn't know if it was from fury or fear. Her hands fluttered. Should she put the souls away? Should she find the car keys and haul ass over there now? They couldn't let Nate have Henry. Whatever it took, she was getting him back.

Derek wrapped his hands around hers, and he brought them to his chest. The heavy battering ram heartbeat beneath focused her. It was his brother this time, and yet he was here comforting her. She pressed herself closer and let him wrap his arms around her. He squeezed tighter than he ever had before, and she didn't make a noise. The hitch in his breathing made it clear he needed this, and if that meant she skipped a little oxygen, so be it. She nuzzled closer and kissed the cotton covering his heart.

Steel scraped over steel when he spoke. "Killing that fucker is priority number one."

Callie escaped his grasp, but left her hand on his chest. "Saving Henry is the top priority."

He huffed.

"If Nate dies in the process, I'm not stopping you. But speaking from experience, you want to put Henry first here." Being the voice of reason was weird. Having experience in this kind of shit was weirder.

"So," Beck dragged the word out until they cared he was in the room. "Nate's definitely behind Anonymous Souls. Figures."

"We'll shut that shit down today." Derek's eyes narrowed.

The hate was for the man who held his brother captive, but Beck still dropped his gaze. "If Nate wants souls, luring you two out of here makes this place prime pickings. Now, I know you have to save that priest—not saying you shouldn't—but can we have a plan?"

"There's not time for a plan. We need to get over there now." Strategy would have been fucking nice, but that shit didn't matter when family was on the line. Derek was family, and apparently that meant Henry was, too.

"We can't go in until we know what we're walking into." Molasses could have poured faster than Derek's admission.

"Fine," Callie said. "What do we need to figure out, because if we wait until the pickup time he'll be ready for us and might move the warehouse?"

Her phone buzzed, and she showed the guys the display with the cross streets for the drop-off.

"Ten minutes from the warehouse," Beck said.

Derek's breathing was steadier now. "If he knew about Henry, he's been watching us. He probably still has a lookout on the shop."

"How do we get rid of eyes on this place?" Beck asked. "It ain't easy to get here without being seen."

Getting rid of people was do-able. "We give them business," Callie said.

"You can't give them souls," Beck said.

"Cash comes first for Nate. He'll do whatever it takes to get a buck in his pocket. We need to draw his guy away from here."

Beck cocked his head to the side. "You want to bribe them, but not with souls?"

Derek followed her, though. He knew Callie better than most anyone these days. "No, she wants to keep them so busy they don't have time to watch us."

"Exactly. Do you have enough people on the streets who we could have order soul delivery from Anonymous Souls? If we pick drop sites that are far from downtown and the warehouse, we should be able to draw everyone away."

"My woman's brain is fucking perfect." Derek's

gloating was fleeting.

Beck nodded. "We can make sure enough people use burners to make it happen."

"How much time do you need to get it done?"

Beck was already typing like a madman. "I'll have them all over town in thirty minutes."

Callie tugged Derek toward the corner of the room. "As soon as his guys say they've got Anonymous's dealers en route, I want to go to the warehouse. If we have all the souls, we have Nate by the balls, which means we can get Henry."

"We should take his dealer from the basement as leverage," he said.

"He does hostages, we don't." Bringing people in for questioning was bad enough. She wasn't going to trade the woman. She wasn't going to be that person.

"Fine, then barter with her if it makes you feel better. That woman is our best way to get inside the building and force Nate's hand."

"Nate doesn't value her."

"How do you know that?"

Because if he said half the shit he'd said to Callie to that woman, she wasn't going to be running to him for safety. "Gut feeling."

The muscle at Derek's temple twitched. "She knows the building, Callie. She can get us inside."

She was loath to bring more people into this clusterfuck, but he had a point. Still… "I don't know about trusting her with your brother's life."

"You haven't seen her recently, Callie. She's not in a state to do damage." He's lucky she loved him, because that hard slap of words wasn't welcome. She'd freaked when Zara was taken, too, though. This was what family did to us.

Callie headed downstairs to see Lexi. If Derek was right and she wouldn't risk Henry's life, this might be okay. She pushed open the interrogation room door to find the chillest ambiance that room had ever held. Miguel had one leg folded with his ankle over his knee. He had a tattered copy of *One Hundred Years of Solitude* open in his right hand. He lifted his head to acknowledge them, but then went back to reading.

The soul dealer didn't stir at first. Callie squatted near the woman until their faces were level. "Lexi?" she said softly.

Her only response was a groggy denial. This woman better not be hemorrhaging somewhere. Callie reached forward to lift one of Lexi's eyelids. She wanted to see pupil response, but got Lexi reeling back instead. "What the fuck you doing?"

"Making sure you're not dying."

The other woman's eyes were wide now, and her pupils were a little dilated due to the dimness of the room, but exactly as expected.

"How do you feel?" Callie asked.

Lexi sucked her teeth. "Like I've been tied to a chair for too long."

She had set herself up for that one. "Want to change that?"

The Anonymous Souls worker narrowed her eyes. Callie watched the woman's hands, though. She expected them to be fiddling the with zip ties. Hers would have been. Instead the skin had shifted sallow and plumped, and she began to understand Derek's assessment. Lexi was weakened, and did need real medical attention. Callie pushed quickly with her magic, and found the other woman's soul humming along just fine.

If nothing else, she hadn't broken this person.

"You're not going to kill me?" The wariness in Lexi's tone, the confidence that this ordeal was going to end everything for her reminded Callie of how different she was than the Soul Charmer. He didn't see anything but enemies and tools when he looked around a room, and delighted in doing so. Callie had to use this woman, but she wasn't going to enjoy it.

"If we wanted you dead, you'd be dead," Derek intoned from somewhere behind her.

"Let's make a deal, Lexi."

"What kind of deal? I'm keeping my soul." Her words rushed together.

Callie didn't bother telling the woman that if someone with the skill wanted her soul, it was going either way. That wasn't useful. "I don't want your soul. I want your help."

Lexi was agreeable, but then she'd been bound to a chair and offered an out. Callie promised that if the dealer could get them inside the warehouse without a problem, they'd let her go. While the suggestion she should get out of the soul delivery business was obvious, Callie said it anyway.

Miguel took care of releasing Lexi and keeping an eye on her. Derek and Callie returned to the tiled office upstairs.

"Souls are ordered," Beck said. "My guys already saw two cars out on the street from here pull away."

"Not bad. Thanks." Callie was impressed he could mobilize people so quickly. She wondered how long the collector had worked here. She'd been doing soul pickups for weeks. Had he been doing it for years? It hadn't even occurred to her that the job would require contacts. She wasn't out there to make friends. She'd picked up souls to keep the Charmer off her back.

"Doll." Derek touched her back.

He had contacts. She should have realized he had made this whole thing so much easier. She wouldn't let him lose his brother. Wouldn't let Nate hurt Henry. This needed to stop now, or everyone they loved was at risk.

Callie leaned close to Derek.

He pressed a heavy folded knife into her hand. "I want you to carry this."

"It's massive." The knife weighed more than the purse she carried sometimes, and there was a reason she rarely took it with her.

"It's effective." He closed her fingers around it. "You used one like this before?"

"Did you really just ask me if I've ever used a pocket knife?"

"This is a defense weapon, doll. Sure, it works for cutting boxes, but that little hole there?" He took the knife back, and pointed to the hole at the edge of blade. "That's your quick release option. Slip your thumb into it, and lift."

He demonstrated and the sharp, shiny blade *zing*-ed out of the metal sheath. He depressed the back of the knife, and then folded the blade back into hiding.

"I don't know about this." The blade was almost four inches long. The knife was bigger than her hand.

"I can't do this without knowing you have a weapon." His brow drew tight.

"We've never needed me armed like this before."

"You want me to save Henry. I do, too, but I can't do that if you aren't ready to cut that bastard Nate."

"I didn't say I wasn't willing to cut him…"

"This is not a joke, Callie. I can't lose either of you." There was a tenuous relationship between anger and fear. Derek rarely let the latter rise to the surface. His anger was proof of his fear. Now, though, he was dropping the ire for her. The harsh lines on his forehead smoothed, and his lips pursed, and hurt raged a widow's song in his stormy eyes.

She took the knife, and hoped it would be enough.

CHAPTER THIRTY

It had been three minutes since they'd seen a person outside. Derek drove slowly past the dull, grey buildings on the south side. The massive warehouses were quintuple the size of any of the big buildings in Gem City proper, and carried the cold veneer of the new. Smashed metal in red, yellow, and blue rioted like wildflowers behind a chain-link fence, but no people were outside the adjoining chop shop.

The wind whistled and even inside the protection of the car it echoed in Callie's bones.

She turned to Lexi, whose silence had been appropriate. "You sure this is the one?"

The warehouse in front of them proclaimed it stored corrugated cardboard. Not a chief export from Gem City. The windows that weren't boarded had cardboard behind the glass. Bits of silver industrial tape peeked at the corners.

"Yeah. There's a door around to the left. That's where I went in to pick up last time." Nerves jangled in Lexi's throat.

"No cameras?" Derek asked.

"I have no clue. I just came here to pick up souls before heading out for delivery," the soul dealer said.

Callie searched the eaves of the building, but couldn't find any of the signature black bubbles to indicate cameras in use. "Do you see any?" she asked Derek.

"How long has Anonymous Souls been using this place?" he asked instead.

"I started three weeks ago."

"And they were using this place then?" Callie asked.

The woman nodded.

"So how do they stop anyone from just walking in?" This looked too easy, and anything that looked like it wasn't going to be a problem was a goddamn trick. Callie could practically hear Nate's sniveling snicker already.

"No one seemed worried to me. Maybe because it's in the middle of fucking shit town out here. There's a guy inside the door. That's all I know."

It didn't matter if this was a ploy to get them inside. Options were thin. They could wait and meet Nate when he expected it and fight over shoveling souls for him, or they could bust into this place and rescue Henry—and hopefully all the souls in Nate's possession in the process.

Derek killed the engine, and they exited the car. He gave Lexi a small shove forward, and she led them around the left side of the building. The door was riddled with rust and frayed edges of metal, but the brass doorknob was shiny and new. As was the matching deadbolt above it. At least Lexi hadn't lied about this place being in use. Maybe they could luck out and there was a lone door guy inside. They could crash in, grab Henry and the souls, and book it.

The large folding knife Derek had foisted on her protruded from her pocket. The end bit at her hipbone with every other step. She wouldn't forget the weapon was there, which was perhaps the point.

Lexi's left foot dragged in the gravel more than her right, but she made it to the door. She slapped her open palm flat against the door. Callie's hand went to her hip and the blade.

Lexi edged closer to the door. "They can't hear when I knock otherwise," she said in a tone reserved for murder plots and confessions.

Callie relaxed, but the tendons in Derek's neck were bulging and tight. She might not be ready for this fight, but he was starving for it.

The door opened a few inches, and a man Callie didn't recognize peered out at them. He wasn't much taller than Callie. His thick moustache twitched when he saw Derek. "Who are they?"

Lexi stepped more fully into his line of sight. "New drivers. Vega asked me to help."

Vega sure as fuck better not be on the other side of that door. Callie's heart pounded until her ribs rang in response. Seconds stretched into eons. Derek was practically pulsing with malevolence. He'd never been anything but calm and calculating in emergencies, but his energy scraped against hers. The temptation to push her magic toward him to help maintain the cover of new hires was quashed quickly. He deserved to feel the way he did. He also knew a whole lot more about situations like this than she did. Conserving energy and waiting for the chance to strike was what *she* needed to be worrying about.

"Vega just left." The door guy opened the door completely, and stepped to the side. "He dropped off a batch of fresh souls in the back."

"Thanks," Lexi chirped, and swung her loose curls over one shoulder. The door guy's eyes stayed on her even as Derek and Callie followed the woman past the threshold.

The door clunked closed behind them, and the doorman dropped back into a folding metal chair. He resumed playing a game on his phone. They'd passed. Holy shit. They were inside, and no one was running at them with guns. Callie let out a little breath, and the edge of panic riding her heartbeat ebbed. They walked down a bare corridor, echoing footsteps announcing their approach.

Pictures lined the left wall. Familiar ones. None of the images were framed, but the photographs had been taped to the wall like this was a detective's office on a TV crime show and not a warehouse in the industrial park. Callie squinted at one of the images. Benton. One of the soul rental clients, one of *her* clients, was on this wall. Fuck. These were the images from the Soul Charmer's store. Nate had made his team steal the pictures of clients, too? As if she needed more proof this man was out to get the Charmer.

"Souls are off to the right," Lexi said.

She might have been maintaining their cover or letting Callie know which way trouble would come from. Callie wasn't certain how much this woman was on their side for the moment. The warehouse opened wide at the turn, but it wasn't empty. Industrial pallet racking lined one wall. Two-ounce tins littered the shelves. Callie stepped closer, and the off-key buzz of a dental drill hit her. Her ankles wobbled, and her footing faltered.

She paused to steady herself. Derek held at her side, too, and she appreciated not being left alone. The thick wet smack of meat against meat filled the air. Each slap was followed by a harsh *oof*. Lexi continued forward without them.

"What the fuck you doing here?"

Terror punched down Callie's throat and sunk its talons into her stomach. Nate was here.

Lexi was already on the verge of hyperventilating when she said, "Picking up souls, Mr. Nate. Sorry."

Nate was hidden by the wall on the right, but Lexi was only fifteen feet ahead. Tears tracked the beautiful woman's face. Whatever move Nate made, Lexi's eyes widened and she darted toward Callie.

Ca-click.

Pow.

The single gunshot rang in Callie's ears.

Lexi stumbled forward to face plant on the painted concrete. Blood poured from the hole in the middle of her back. The stunning curls covered the woman's face. Her fingers twitched.

Callie's magic flared. There was no calm collection of energy this time. Another person who didn't deserve to die lay shot damn near at her feet, and Callie was fucking done. She was done hiding. Nate needed to know he couldn't do this. He needed her too much to shoot her anyway. Probably. Derek had oozed volatility before. Maybe owning rage was power. Callie walked forward and did her damnedest to project nothing but menace.

Nate held a black pistol at his side. His finger was still in the trigger guard. The bomber jacket he'd worn before was thrown in a heap a few feet away, but the lanky asshole was wearing a basic white tee and trying damn hard to convince people he was a gangster from a bygone era. He was a thug and a psychopath and she was fucking done with him.

"Only an idiot would kill his own people." She was seething and needed to see him unsettled.

"She wasn't fucking mine if she brought you here, but it doesn't matter." Nate snapped his fingers, and three men in the corner looked up. "Take care of the big one. Callie girl and I need to have a conversation."

The trio of men also dressed like they'd recently

discovered vintage clothing broke away from their huddle to charge at Derek. What they left behind was a battered Henry. Callie ignored the gut-punch visual as much as she could, but her heart wept. He was bound to a chair in almost the same fashion they'd secured Lexi, but unlike their hostage Henry wasn't healthy. His right eye was swollen shut, and his entire face was mottled in blacks and purples. His shirt was torn open, and blood smeared his skin. Nate's men bypassed her and jumped at her boyfriend.

Derek's muffled, "I got this," kept her on track.

She tore her gaze from the injured priest. Nate's lips pulled back in a rictus grin, revealing yellowing teeth.

"You going to shoot me, too, Nate?" The pure taunt bought her time to push her magic shield a little farther out.

He dropped the magazine from the gun, and cleared the chamber. "You saying you want my hands on that little body, Callie girl?" He tossed the gun and ejected magazine onto his jacket. "Because that can be arranged."

Pallets behind her rattled, but she couldn't risk looking away from Nate. Derek had to have this. There wasn't another option. The mob boss pulled a small glass pipe from his pocket and pressed it to his lips.

Callie's soul magic shield shook, and a flash of fire streaked before her. "Who taught you to store souls? This place is a fucking mess."

The dig hit bone. "I wasn't given shit. The Soul

Charmer—" he sang the name like it was a mythical children's character "—tapped you with magic. I had to work for it. I had to learn. You didn't have to gather souls or figure out how to get them in and out of people. You had tools and a teacher."

Callie took three more steps toward him. Pressure built on all sides. Her head throbbed, and her limbs bloated. She was the closed can of beer tossed into a bonfire. "Who said you were meant to touch souls?"

His fingers fluttered against the small pipe. He hadn't repacked the one-hitter, but he puffed on the pipe again. The drilling whine ground against her pelvis. Every step was wrong, painful, but she couldn't stop. If she could grasp his soul, she could stop him. She only needed to get close enough.

"You don't get to decide that shit, girl. You're going to work for me or you ain't going to work at all."

The fuck she was. "Working is overrated."

Nate shoved his pipe into his front pocket, and then barreled at her. Her shield had held back the flames, but it wasn't meant to block a 190 lb. man from tackling her. Callie's shoulders smacked the floor first, but it was the back of her skull that offered a solid crack against the concrete. The barrier she'd erected to hold back the sizzling energy of the souls shuttered and vanished. Nate followed her to the ground, his knee wedged between her legs. Wrongness fused with her bone marrow until her very insides were crawling. She slammed a knee in to Nate's side, but it didn't so much as knock the wind out of him. Searing heat ate at her toes, her fingers.

Nate's hands clamped around Callie's throat. "I'm going to take your fucking soul next."

He dropped his weight onto her neck, and she bucked hard. He jostled, but didn't budge. He brought his face close to hers, and gnashed his teeth together. Heat licked up her arms and legs. Nate squirmed and squeezed her throat. Callie coughed and began to claw at his hands. Flames danced in her periphery. Her skin, alight.

"What the fuck?" Nate's grip loosened as the fire roared up Callie's neck and engulfed his hands.

He pushed back. Sticky gobs of burning flesh clung to his palms. Whether it was hers or his wasn't clear. The fire usually didn't sting, but now agony roared in her bones. The drill bit grinding from the inside out now dipped in acid. She stared at his sternum with every bit the ownership Nate used when ogling her breasts. The souls she reached screamed and begged. One after another. How many souls had he inhaled? She couldn't find his soul, but the five she found were not interested in helping the man holding them hostage. They were tainted and their keening cries pleaded for escape. She wrapped her mind around them, and kicked hard. Nate flew back from her. Black and grey ash clung to the outside of his white shirt, red pooled from beneath it.

Callie staggered to her feet. Orange and golden flames flickered in her vision. The fire was hers. It was these souls. It was everyone fucking done with Nate stealing their lives and their hope. It was power and pain and promises. It was hers.

Nate took another hit from the pipe, the fucking artifact of St. Petro. How many souls had he pushed into the glass for his personal use? He held the pipe tight in his left hand. Callie tried to grab the new soul, too, but her magic shuttered as he held the artifact out in front of him. "It'd be better if I was inside you, but I'll take your soul as my own little pet. Dead or alive, you're getting dirty, Callie girl."

He thrust the pipe toward her, and began whispering words Callie couldn't follow.

Two big hands slammed into Callie's ribs. "Go," Derek yelled.

She flew to the right, not needing the verbal encouragement when the physical took over. She spun to see him fall where she'd been standing. Another man thrust a knife where Callie's heart had been moments earlier. Derek ducked beneath it, and blasted a rock-hard fist into the man's solar plexus. The thug doubled over, and Derek landed another hard blow to his face. Callie didn't need a medical degree to diagnose the shattered orbital socket. The attacker didn't get back up.

Henry groaned loud enough to pull Callie's attention.

"You get him. I've got Nate," Derek shouted.

If anyone could, it'd be him. Callie rushed to Henry without hesitation. She plucked the knife from her pocket. Her skin was melting, but the bone hooked into the tiny hole without much fuss. She cut the bonds, and reached to help Henry up. He eschewed the offer. Horror coating his face that had nothing to do with his body being tenderized and everything to do with see-ing Callie *en fuego*.

Derek was on his back. Nate stepped forward, and dropped a heavy foot onto her lover's chest. Derek coughed and grappled for Nate's leg. His grip slid. Blood coated the leg of Nate's pants. Whose blood was it? Nate moved the pipe closer to Derek. The artifact's vibration resonated in her ears.

No. Nate could take from her, but he could not take from Derek. She called the flames to her palm, and the magic pooled there. She threw the heat at Nate with the speed and stealth of a knuckleball.

A sharp scream.

A sickening pop.

Falling glass.

The pipe was gone, and Nate's cry reached for Heaven. Only Hell could answer.

Power surged throughout the warehouse. The flo-rescent bulbs overhead shattered. Flecks of glass and filament floated down. The walls bowed out. Boards flew away from the windows. Power ignited the air. It bit at Callie's soul. Pushed and primed.

The soul magic sonic boom quieted quickly. Glass continued to fall. Nate sputtered like a two-year-old priming a tantrum. Derek posted his arm to the side and levered himself up from the concrete. Nate dodged toward Callie and his jacket.

From beneath the empty firearm and the coat Nate pulled a palm-sized revolver. Even in the shadows the barrel shone with intent. He cocked the hammer, and

Derek stilled.

Callie was done with this man taking from her. She was done with his threats and done with being afraid.

He lifted the gun.

The pocket knife was still in her hand. Open and ready. She lunged forward and buried the blade deep in Nate's armpit. The weapon and the arm dropped loosely to his side. Nate bellowed. *Everything's connected, fucker*. Blood seeped onto her exposed muscle. Callie backed away and threw magic around herself again. Her skin began to rebuild. She hoped the flames could disinfect the asshole's blood from her hand.

"Derek?" she asked.

Her boyfriend glowered. He bent over Nate's body. The other man was squirming to grab the knife from his side.

"I'll get that for you," Derek ground out. He plucked the knife from Nate's armpit. Blood oozed with Nate's heartbeat.

Derek flipped the knife in his hand, and then plunged it into Nate's carotid. He left the blade in long enough to meet Nate's panicked gaze.

"I won't let you hurt her again," Derek said, and then yanked the knife back out.

Nate's death was swifter than the deserved, but he would never find a way out of Hell if she had anything to say about it.

Callie pulled the rogue souls from the corners of the room, from the flimsy containers, and from the pallets, and pushed them all at Nate's bleeding body. She shoved the dark ones in him. The tainted and corrupt. Every filthy soul he'd slapped in a tin can and planned to shill to unsuspecting citizens found a new home inside the mobster. His chest glowed a fierce red.

"Doll?" Derek ambled to her side.

She pushed more magic and more souls into Nate until his back bowed and his torso stretched. Callie released the magic she'd clung to for protection, too, and thrust it at Nate's convulsing form. Blue flames ignited his clothing, his skin underneath puckered immediately. A moment later this corpse was pure pyre, and the cries of freedom from the burning souls rose bright behind the flames.

CHAPTER THIRTY-ONE

Callie's apartment had the good medical supplies. Her skin had regrown, but Henry continued to peer at her with his one eye like he expected to see something magnificent happen. She was all out of tricks. Derek lumbered to the couch with his brother's arm over his shoulders. He deposited the priest on the sofa, and then turned back to Callie.

"I'll need a minute to find the right supplies," she called out.

She bent to retrieve the hydrogen peroxide and first aid kit from beneath the bathroom sink. When she rose, Derek was behind her. She squeaked, and then lightly smacked his arm. "I told you I'd be out in a second. I'm not prepared for surprises right now."

He skimmed his fingertips over her temple, and brushed a loose strand of hair back behind her ear. "I needed to confirm you're whole."

She sat the supplies on the edge of the sink. "That flame doesn't really touch me. Everything comes back. You know that."

His hands skimmed her upper arms, and then her shoulders. Like he was rediscovering her. "That's not what I meant." His touch was gentle when he ran his hand over her collarbone. "He bruised your neck. How sore are you?"

So the skin grew back with the bruises? That was a flaw in this magic shit. She pulled his hand away from her chest, and lifted it to her mouth. She pressed a tender kiss to his knuckles. "I'll be fine. I'm whole. The souls are safely moving on to another place. We got your brother back. Those are the things that matter."

"You matter." A storm churned those grey eyes.

"We're together. That's what I need. You're bleeding, too, you know." She thought it was Nate's blood smudged at his nose and in a stripe across his thigh, but both had grown since they'd left the warehouse.

"I'm fine." He didn't budge. "I needed to know he couldn't come after you again."

"What do you mean?"

"I know the goal wasn't to kill him, and after what happened at Ford's we weren't going to do that shit anymore. No one even asked me to do this—"

Oh. Derek didn't hang onto guilt the way Callie did. He didn't squirrel it away for lonely nights and handles of vodka. That was a Delgado way of dealing with life, and while he was hers, he wasn't a Delgado. He wouldn't let it fester, which was great, but this guilt wasn't even warranted.

"He deserved to die," Callie said plainly.

Derek was quiet for a moment. "You're okay with what I did? For real?"

"What we did. You weren't the one who lit his ass on fire."

Derek's smile widened a little more with each passing second, like his brain was catching up with the moment. "So we're good?"

"We're wounded, but yes, you're still stuck with me." She found more comfort in those words than she expected. The consistency was nice. Her family was supposed to be that rock for her. They were supposed to come running when shit got bad. Lord knew she did. Derek was better for her, though. He was solid and steady and was purely motivated by protecting her in those dark moments.

"I'm a lucky bastard. You know that, doll?"

"Careful now. The Charmer would take credit for that shit if he could."

"One more reason I don't mind him being missing."

"Paychecks would be good."

"Beck handles all that shit for the Charmer. I'll make sure he cuts the cash for us."

"Great, but can we first tend to your brother? Or did you forget what he went through?" A playful tone could only get her so far. The truth was they'd pulled another innocent person into their mess.

"I didn't forget, but I doubt he will either. He knows you saved him, and he understood the risks in helping us."

"*We* saved him," she corrected. "Now let me get the rest of this shit together. You go pull some frozen peas from the freezer for his face."

"You have to ice your neck, too."

She made a shooing motion, and he cleared out of the bathroom. Callie re-gathered the first-aid gear, and studiously avoided the mirror. Tending to the cuts and bruises wasn't as bad as she'd feared. Henry had been worked over, and the bruising was extensive. He could swallow, though, so she gave him some anti-inflammatories and a quality painkiller. She and Derek convinced him to stretch out on the couch and packed frozen vegetables over all the worst bruises.

"I can't apologize enough," Callie said as he snuggled a package of vegetable medley against his ribs.

"You stopped someone perverting our faith. That man was an affront to God. It was not his place to torture souls, and there is no question in my mind that is what he was doing." Even with a busted lip and a puffed face Father Henry brought the serious talk.

"Yeah, well, we couldn't let him hurt you." She paused and realized her words. "Hurt you more, I guess. We thought we'd get there before all this."

"We all have trials." He closed his good eye.

"Rest. I'll come back for the ice packs in twenty minutes."

"Thanks, and Callie? I'm glad he has you."

"Me, too."

The Soul Charmer's shop was welcoming for Callie these days. It'd been two weeks since she and Derek had extinguished Nate and his Anonymous Souls gig. The drivers disappeared and the number was now disconnected. Callie had tried calling a few times, but it was never reinstated.

Miguel had left the day after Nate's death determined to find Vega and get more answers. He'd sent customers back to the shop for their returns, but otherwise had remained mostly radio silent. Beck, however had his feet up on the Charmer's desk again when she walked in.

"Don't you have work to do?" she asked.

"Not until you pick a new boss lady name."

"I don't need a boss lady name. Just go to work."

There had been no word from the Soul Charmer, but also no news of his death. Callie wasn't sure what to make of it, but Father Giles had called her to the well twice already. Until the other soul magician returned, she was stuck.

"How about queen of hearts?"

"That doesn't even make sense." Callie didn't have time for his ridiculousness, but she didn't totally hate it.

"All your new jars have hearts on them."

She'd shifted the Soul Charmer's fraction notations to a five heart system. Each new soul she brought in she'd draw five hearts in chalk on the jar. After each rental, she'd erase half a heart. When it was empty, it was time to put them in the do not rent pile.

"That measures how many times they've been rented. They're still souls."

"I'll come up with something you like."

Derek entered the room. "That's my job."

Callie hid her smile. She picked up Beck's flask and tossed it at him. "Bring me back something nice."

He groused, but took the tool and headed out of the room.

"You're settling in," Derek said.

She shrugged. "This is it for now. How are things outside?"

They'd had some increased foot traffic in the alleyway, which Derek was convinced was a result of Anonymous Souls crew poking around for jobs. "It's quiet for now."

The front bell rang the warning before Beck blasted back past the curtain. Callie needed to figure out how to make a barrier like the Charmer had if this continued.

"Someone left this for you." He held a cream parchment. It was folded in half. The paper shook in his hand.

"Is it addressed to Soul Charmer 2.0, because then I know it was from you."

He didn't laugh.

She accepted the sheet. The front of the card had her name in blocky letters. The ink bled out from each line. She opened the page, and would have stumbled backward if Derek hadn't propped her up.

"We aren't done." Her words were hollow. Sand coating her tongue would have been more comfortable that the liquid dread filling her mouth.

The same block letters carried the interior message:

APPRENTICE, FIND ME OR WE BOTH DIE.

Lower on the page drips ran down from the signature.

The script in the rich red of blood was legible:

Soul Charmer.

ACKNOWLEDGEMENTS

Charmer Crew, y'all are the best. A huge thank you to everyone who has read, reviewed, and handed a copy of a Soul Charmer book to a friend. It's a joy to get to share Callie's journey with you. These books are packed with all the things I love, which means you have excellent tastes. #BookTwins.

I have to give extra love to Amanda Bonilla and Megan Frampton for giving good advice and replying to my texts. Additional thanks to Amanda Bouchet, Melissa Marr, Rachel Vincent, Cathlin Shahriary, and Joanna Hoskinson for being great friends and creative sounding boards. You should all come to Texas.

Thank you to Patricia Schmitt for the beautiful cover art.

Finally, thank you to my family for both the support and enduring my plotting rambles.

ABOUT THE AUTHOR

Chelsea Mueller writes gritty contemporary fantasy. She founded the speculative fiction website **Vampire Book Club** and blogs about TV and romance novels for numerous websites. She loves bad cover songs, dramatic movies, and TV vampires. Chelsea lives in Texas, and has been known to say y'all.

For the latest updates, join her email list at ChelseaMueller.net or follow **@ChelseaVBC** on Twitter and Instagram.

www.ingramcontent.com/pod-product-compliance
Lightning Source LLC
Chambersburg PA
CBHW051602100726
47898CB00001B/193